Feather Island

Tad Callant

Feather Island

Library of Congress Control Number: 2012944809

ISBN 978-0-945980-39-1

Prologue

During those years when our backyards connected, our lives were so intertwined that even his socks were my socks. My top bunk was his for the asking. My music rattled his bedroom walls. He knew everything that was in my top drawer. We shared each other's secrets. He knew about my teddy bear. I knew he occasionally wet his bed. His mom and my mom schemed against us together. We schemed against our younger brothers.

Our souls were filled with the joy of living in a kid's paradise. We were alive, so alive, running side by side, laughing, daring, taunting, fighting, forgiving. We were an unchallenged team, always knowing what the other would do. There were so many promises solemnly made in whispers and ritual. So many rich memories only we would ever know.

We shared the smells of seaweed and the touch of the bumpy skin of starfish as we explored below the wharves at low tide. We smelled the sweet freshly-cut grass on the school ball field before a game, and felt the wet beach sand between our toes as we walked home barefoot. We both understood that lonesome feeling at the pond after the last swim in October. And we burst with excitement with the first fresh ice in December. In April our bicycles were held together with tape and any bolts and nuts we could scrounge.

I've heard it said that being a teenager means teetering on disaster while diving into the thrill of discovery. Our adventures on that small island were many and rich. Oh, so many. But none were as spectacular or as devastating as that spring when we both turned fourteen.

Does he still remember after all these years? His baseball glove still sits in my old trunk next to our skateboard, next to my old teddy.

Does he still remember that spring when we grew up so fast, so very fast?

CHAPTER ONE

THAT SUNDAY IN EARLY JUNE

It should have been called Axe Head Island. It was shaped like an axe head, one and one-half miles long from beach to bluff, and almost one mile wide from ocean to bay. Pine trees grew abundantly along its surface. The ocean winds had eroded the bluff into a crag-filled cliff. Axe Head Island would have been a very appropriate name. It was called Feather Island. No one seemed to know why. It didn't matter.

As three early tourists observed the island from the top deck of the small ferry, they estimated that the southern end rose to a height of about one hundred eighty-five to two hundred feet. Tad and Lance, who had been shopping across the bay in Lassiter, listened and each said quietly, "One hundred ninety-three."

A large house commanded the view at the top of the bluff. Smaller cottages descended the bay side of the bluff until they formed a closely packed colony at the northern end. The ferry wharves, the ancient government wharf, small shops, and a large marina congregated around the edge of the inner bay and gave way to a large well-kept beach along the northern colony.

The two young teenagers knew well that the ocean side and the center of the island were overgrown in a tangled forest of pines and spruce, with homes spotted here and there. They also knew there was little that was spectacular about Feather Island. It was simply a place to get away from it all for about two thousand summer cattle, and home for about four hundred year--round residents.

As the ferry approached the wharf, a young deckhand threw a looped rope around a piling. A cheer went up from the two island boys, who on occasion jeered and taunted the futile efforts of the amateur seamen. As the rope tightened, the ferry gave a lurch, and settled in close to the wharf. A stern rope was secured. The deckhand slid the gate open and pulled the gangplank into place.

"Better brace yourselves," Tad told the tourists who were anxious to get off. They looked first at the dark-haired boy with the piercing blue eyes, and then at the slightly taller blond-haired boy behind him who nodded. The waves from the wake of the ferry as it had made its U-turn, hit the boat broadside, causing them to bump each other.

The boys smiled and moved quickly across the gangplank. "What do you want to do?" Tad asked Lance.

"I have to get home with Mom's stuff from uptown. Dad was in a lot of pain when I left, so I have to check on him. I'll come over after supper if I can."

"Okay, I have homework I have to finish anyway."

Climbing the rise from the wharf they turned left. The Dusty Gull Café sat on the right just at the curve between Finney's Grocery Store and the post office. The Department of Public Safety, known as the fire barn, sat diagonally across the street at the edge of the beach, just up from the car ferry wharf. The black public safety van, known for years as the jeep, pulled in alongside two older pumpers and a tanker still glistening and wet in front of the station. A large newer engine sat alongside the modest building.

"You got any raffle tickets on you?" Tad asked.

"Didn't think I'd need them."

"Neither did I." Tad fished through the pockets of his jeans to make sure. Lance did the same. "I'll get the lieutenant when I go for my papers in the morning."

"Yeah." Lance's thoughts were already at home. As they walked up Main Street Tad was determined to keep up with Lance. His legs had suddenly become longer than Tad's. Lance seemed to be walking with a bounce which irritated Tad. Lots of things about Lance irritated Tad lately. Little things. His face had changed. It really had. It had become leaner, longer, and different somehow. More grown up. It had also become sadder. He was quieter now. The fact was that Tad hated it when Lance got in one of his quiet moods, but he understood him better than anyone else. Lance's father had been sick since November.

Lance said he didn't know what was wrong with him, but Tad had overheard his mother talking on the phone. He knew it probably was cancer. It had been difficult to watch the rugged fireman waste away in pain between trips to the hospital over the winter.

Tad wished his own father would come home. This construction job had lasted longer than the others had. Tad had seen his father only once since Christmas. He had called every Friday night, but it wasn't the same. Tad had asked him two days ago the same old question and received the same old answer. He would be home when the job was done and it was a big job. Maybe by the end of June. Last month it had been maybe by the end of May. Tad had a lot of unasked questions. His father was well. Lance's father was sick, but Lance's father was here.

The boys turned right up Maple Street. Tad could see his nine-year-old brother Mickey sitting cross-legged on top of their old Chevy in the front yard on the left halfway up the street. Mickey held his head in his hands with his elbows resting on his knees. Tad jabbed Lance and pointed. Lance didn't even grin. He just nodded. All thoughts of tormenting Mickey vanished as Lance bounced closer to the house.

"Don't plan on going anywhere after supper, Tad," Mickey stated as they came closer. He hadn't moved an inch, even though his glasses were twisted on his face. "You have homework to do."

"Eat worms," Tad said. "See you, Lance."

"Yeah, see you later." Lance continued through Tad's backyard to his back porch.

By the time Tad was through his front door, his mother was saying, "Did you have a good time? You have homework. Don't plan on going out after supper."

***

The fog, which had been drifting in and out of the bay all evening finally succeeded in conquering the bay. The eleven-thirty boat from Lassiter docked at Feather Island. Instead of tying only the stern line, which was the normal procedure, the deckhand tied the bow line also. Seeing this, the Public Safety Department lieutenant stepped out of the jeep and walked along the wharf.

No passengers were waiting for the return trip. Under the usually harsh old mercury vapor lights, the wharf took on a pleasant dreamy look in the fog. The plank was shoved out and one passenger got off.

The lieutenant noticed he was a stranger, quite old, with a beard and long gray scraggly hair. His clothes were well worn and he wore a large knapsack on his back. There were so many strangers coming and going as summer approached, it was impossible to keep track of them all. However, it was the job of the Public Safety Department to attempt to do so. From the boxes being unloaded the lieutenant made a quick judgment that this gentleman was headed for the old artist colony on the southeast side of the bluff. There had been lots of activity going on up there during past summers. Not all of it was acceptable.

Just as the deckhand came down the ramp, the taxi pulled onto the wharf and turned around. The old man got in and handed a note to the driver. Hal, the driver, loaded his boxes and the taxi pulled out. The lieutenant turned to the deckhand and asked, "Ever seen that old guy before?"

"Never. He's a strange one. He stayed up on the top deck in the bow all the way over. Must like fog, but he didn't even shiver when we let the horn blast. This fog really came in fast. Clear as a bell over in Lassiter."

"I see you've tied up for the night," the lieutenant said. "Have a place to go?"

The deckhand laughed. "Don't we always?"

From the deck, the captain of the boat shouted, "Hey, Lieutenant, can we catch a ride up to Millie's?"

"You guys know that's against regulations. Besides, I don't see why I should be contributing to the moral degradation of the community."

"You'd only be helping two sailors lost in the fog," the captain explained, laughing.

"In that case, I guess it's my duty to serve you. We can't ignore those who are lost and are seeking their way."

Shoving the plank back onto the boat and pulling the gate shut, the captain jumped down. The three men walked to the jeep and headed up the bluff. Most of the cottages with their neat, freshly painted white picket fences and new flowers were dark. Millie's was brightly lit. The lieutenant could see two women through the windows. Soft music flowed over their fence. The men got out, and the old panel truck continued up the steep part of the bluff in the direction the taxi had taken.

As he rounded the curve in front of the old Richards place, the lieutenant saw muted headlights coming toward him. He stopped and turned on his red-and-blue lights. Hal spotted him and slowed down. His ever-present cigar came out of the window. "It's none of my business, Lieutenant, but we've got a weird one this time."

"Where'd you take him?"

"Really weird. I mean, he gets in the taxi and I ask him where he's goin', and he hands me this letter. Don't say a word, but just hands me this letter. It's from some Portland real estate agent, telling him that the deal for the house has gone through, and he can have it for the months of June and July."

"Which house?"

"That's what I'm tryin' to tell you. It was the Wood's place on the ocean side. You know. The one that Riggs woman bought. About halfway up the bluff above the pond."

"The old Madison place?"

"The very one. I dropped him off top of the driveway. I couldn't get down there in this fog even if I wanted to, what with all them roots. And the most important thing...maybe I'm just sensitive, but I tried to make conversation, and he don't say one word. Not one word. I tried the Red Sox and then even the Yankees, and then the weather, but not one word. When he gets out, he waits for me to unload his boxes, just hands me a few bucks and heads off down the path. I hollered to him to ask if he wants his change, but he didn't even turn around. Left his boxes right in front of me. Then he just disappeared. I mean, my headlights was shinin' on the fog, you know, and there he was, and all of a sudden there he wasn't. Really weird."

"You'll be seeing spooks next, Hal."

"I think I just did, or the closest I care to come to it. Like I said, it's none of my business. I keep these things to myself. None of my business."

As the taxi pulled away, the lieutenant jotted down on his pad, "Old Madison cottage—one occupant." He'd write it in the log when he got back to the station. One more trip around the island and he would call it a night. The thought of Hal being so desperate for conversation that he actually offered to return change caused him to suddenly laugh out loud.

He looked over at the large old Richards place and shut off his flashing lights. If any place invited spooks, this was the place sitting on the southwestern edge of the bluff. No lights ever shone in its windows even though its newest owner, a doctor, occupied it. The lieutenant started the jeep and remembered the night a few years ago when they discovered old man Richards had died. The town of Lassiter then took the house for unpaid taxes. None of his relatives wanted anything to do with him or his property. The town never did anything with the place, either.

Old rumors spread among the islanders. Some remembered the huge house when Richards was a state senator. Stories of large drunken parties in the magnificent gardens attended by Maine's elite mixed with stories of secret passageways down into the cliff. Stories of smuggling booze back in prohibition mixed with stories of treasure and pirates.

Just two years ago, he had a call here when the house was empty. Kids had decided to solve the mystery of the passageways once and for all. One night they broke into the place. As they told it, the dare turned out to be frightening, complete with the dirt and ancient furniture. No one had kept the place up. One boy dared the others to find the passageways, but the kids stayed in the cellar. He went on alone with a flashlight. He came back with stories of an old rock stairwell that led to the base of a cliff and a large cave. But he couldn't find a way out of the cave. Couldn't find the passageway again when he was encouraged to do so by the captain. He said it was all just a joke.

Now a doctor had bought it and no one else had been inside. This doctor was a strange duck. Said he wanted his privacy while he worked on a project. Lived in that big place all by himself. The lieutenant turned off of Upper Island Avenue onto Central Avenue near the ocean side. Lots of stories in such a small place as Feather Island, he thought. Lots of stories he and the captain decided they should just keep to themselves. The rest went into the log.

CHAPTER TWO

MONDAY

By morning, the fog was thicker. Tad Callant rode his bike toward the wharf to pick up his morning papers. Seeing the Bay Queen tied up he knew there were no papers. He also knew his mother would be getting calls soon from a few irate customers who still didn't understand fog or the ferry company. He was glad that it was only early June. In July when it happened, the calls were fantastic. His mother took the phone off the hook.

Turning around, he headed up past the fog-shrouded fire station. The lieutenant hollered, "Boats running yet, Tad?"

"That you, Lieutenant? Are you kidding? I can barely see you." Tad remembered that the lieutenant needed his super sales pitch for the TV raffle. He pulled his bike in front of the small brick fire barn and said, "How'd you like to win a new large screen plasma color TV with surround sound, Lieutenant?"

"I hope I do. We could use a new one around here. I bought some tickets from the Bridges girl yesterday."

"Becky?" wailed Tad, his voice breaking slightly. "This island's getting too small when they allow girls to sell raffle tickets. I think we've just about run out of people. They should've had the raffle in a couple of months when the summer cattle's here."

"They'll have another one, Tad. Never run out of raffles. Why is it so important to you? You're a super salesman. A few girls shouldn't upset you."

"A few girls! All the girls in the eighth grade have tickets this year. Last year they didn't even care about selling anything. It was all because they raised the prize to twenty dollars for the one who sells the most tickets. I need that money. Lance Deiter and I are going to get licenses this year. We've got thirty traps ready to go."

"With competition like you two, all the other lobstermen on the island will have to go out of business."

"Ha, ha," Tad said, sarcastically. "A kid's got to start somewhere."

"True. True." The lieutenant thought a moment. "Maybe we can help each other, Tad. I don't promise anything, but I just happen to know that a new fellow came to the island late last night. Maybe he'd like a new TV. But one thing, Tad, I don't know anything about him. As a matter of fact, I'd like your opinion. I wouldn't advise going there alone. We've worked this type of thing out before."

"Sure, where is he?"

"The old Madison place."

"Lance and I can go up after school. Now, you say you want to know about him. I can remember stuff a lot better if I'm not weighed down with raffle tickets, Lieutenant."

"Oh, that's the way it is, is it? I do you a favor and you hold me up for another ticket."

"I was thinking about two, actually," said Tad, his soft face breaking into a wide smile.

The lieutenant dug deep into his pockets and came up with two dollars. Tad handed him the tickets and a pencil. The lieutenant filled out the stubs and gave them back to him. Tad gestured for the pencil the lieutenant had stuck in his pocket. They both laughed.

"We'll let you know. Thanks. See you later."

Going up Main Street, Tad wondered whether he should go to Lance's house as he usually did after his paper route. Maybe he should go home since he was early. He decided to go to Lance's anyway and turned up A Street. On the dirt road, Tad felt the fog was getting even thicker. Maybe school would be called off as they did last year when the teachers couldn't get down from uptown. Then they could go to the old Madison place early.

Riding through Lance's front yard he leaned his bicycle against the small back porch and ran up the steps into the kitchen. Mrs. Deiter was at the stove making French toast.

"I figured you'd be here early today, Tad. Lance is still asleep."

"Want me to wake him up?"

"Might just as well, but be quiet going through the living room. Mr. Deiter had a bad night."

"How is he? I mean . . ."

"He goes for another treatment tomorrow, Tad. Maybe we'll know more then."

Tad watched Mrs. Deiter and thought she looked a lot older. There were dark circles under her eyes and she seemed very tired. She looked at him and smiled. "You better go wake up Lance."

"What? Oh, yes ma'am," Tad said. Turning and walking through the living room he saw Mr. Deiter asleep on the couch. Tad thought he looked dead. Walking closer, he stood until he saw that he was breathing. Very quietly he went up the stairs.

Turning down the unfinished hallway he opened and closed Lance's door quietly so he didn't wake up Jackie or Lance's two older pain-in-the-ass sisters. Grabbing the shade, he let it snap up. The noise made Lance turn over. His long blond hair fell over one eye. "Hi," he said, his voice muffled by his pillow.

"Hi."

"You early?"

"Yeah, fog. Bay Queen's tied up here."

"School?"

"Probably. Old man Nelson'll be there and the aides."

"Yeah," Lance said, shutting his eyes. "At least next year in high school we'll get a day off when the boats don't run."

"They'll probably get radar this summer, finally. Breakfast's almost ready," Tad said.

"What're we having?"

"French toast. You getting up?"

"Yeah, I guess. Dad had a lot of pain last night. I didn't sleep too well."

"He's sleeping now," Tad told him.

Lance nodded, sat up, and let the blankets fall away. His chest shone much whiter than his neck and face.

"We've got to get out in the sun more. You've already started to get a tan on your face."

"Pond'll be good soon." Lance swung his feet over the side of the bed. "Throw me my pants."

"That reminds me. I tried to sell the lieutenant some tickets this morning, but Becky already got him yesterday."

"Figures."

"Anyway, he told me about a guy who came down on the boat last night. Nobody knows about him yet. He's in the old Madison place just above the pond. If we keep our mouths shut we can get him after school."

"Great." Lance slid on a red T-shirt from his drawer. "Why would anyone want to rent that place? Nobody's been in it for a couple of years."

"Donny was in it last fall."

Lance hesitated and grabbed a sock. "Yeah, but he told too many people and the cops got him. But what I mean is nobody's been living there since that lady from Portland bought it. She stayed there only one summer and that was two years ago. Nobody ever goes up there, not even the kids now. Did the lieutenant say any more about him?"

"No, not really. He said he'd like to know more about him himself. I told him if we learned anything we'd let him know. Of course, it cost him two tickets."

Lance's face lit up into a broad smile. "I gotta piss."

* * *

By three o'clock, the fog was as thick as it had been in the morning. Tad and Lance played hide-and-seek with each other as they slowly pumped their old dirt bikes up the gradual slope of School Street.

"We need forty speeds," puffed Lance.

"I'll settle for a three-speed."

"Fat chance of either."

"If we make enough money with the traps, maybe we can get new bikes."

"We can't even afford licenses yet."

"Too bad we had school today. We could've been out selling."

"Who'd have thought they'd send the teachers down on the fireboat? The last I heard, the town wasn't going to do that anymore."

Tad grunted. "That's what my Mom said, too, but she was smiling about it."

"Want to stop by the pond?"

"Okay. We can leave our bikes there and cut through the woods up to his place."

At the corner of School Street and Central Avenue, the boys got off and pushed up a steep grade. At the top they got on again, rode about a hundred yards, then pulled off into a patch of furry sumac bushes. A narrow path was quite overgrown. They placed their bikes at the foot of the familiar sandy hill which served as a natural dam for the pond.

Over the top and running down the other side, their footprints became the first of the season to join those of the gulls. At the sight of the boys, the gulls rose up from the middle of the pond and settled near the far end about a hundred yards out.

"It's warm!" yelled Lance, bending down at the edge.

Tad felt the water and agreed. "Anything would be warm today in this fog. Want to try it?"

"We'd freeze our balls off when we got out. Let's wait until the sun's out. Maybe tomorrow."

"Okay," Tad answered, skimming a stone toward the gulls. "I want to meet this new guy anyway."

"Yeah."

Tad raced up the hill toward the woods. Lance followed close behind, running harder to keep up with Tad. Lance knew he should be able to outrun him now, but Tad always seemed to find more energy somewhere. Lance couldn't figure it out.

Near the edge of the woods the path disappeared. The boys ran through budding reeds and sumac. The wind had little mercy on the ocean side of island. Once in the woods, the boys were forced to slow down as they traveled through the tangled brush and fallen pines. Avoiding the widow makers that could fall at any time, they climbed and crawled before finally coming to the edge of a clearing.

Tad asked, "How do I look?"

"Weird as ever," smirked Lance.

"You know what I mean," Tad said brushing back his unruly dark hair.

"You're okay. How about me?" He brushed his dark blond hair down straight over his forehead.

"Good idea, covering your face. You may not look like a super salesman, but you won't scare him anyway. I guess I'll have to make do with what I have. Let's go."

The old Madison place was indeed old. It was one of the oldest houses on the island and had passed through many hands, many ideas, and many changes. The result was a large, oddly shaped, dark red house with ancient rhododendron branches climbing above the front door and finally peeking into the third floor windows. At present, they were already in blossom and strikingly beautiful.

Before knocking, Tad paused. Peering through the oval window in the front door, he let his eyes get used to the dark living room. He could make out an old upright piano, several large wooden rockers, and a leather couch placed before a huge fireplace. Small antique mugs covered the mantel. The room, although comfortable, looked deserted. Tad knocked loudly.

There was no answer. He knocked again. Lance pushed in close and also looked through the window. "It doesn't look like anyone's been here for a long time. In fact it doesn't look like they even planned for anyone to be here. I mean, they would have dusted at least."

"Would you? Try the door. If he came in last night, something might have happened to him."

"Locked."

"Side door?" Tad called out as he ran to the left side of the house. Opening the ripped screen door, he grabbed the doorknob.

"This one's locked, too. And I can see the refrigerator. It's open and empty. I don't think he's here."

"It figures," Lance stated with a sigh. Surveying the backyard beyond the house, he said, "Let's look out there."

They walked down to where a large glassed-in porch rose above them, spreading across the rear of the house. An old carriage house was on their left in old bushes, and next to it, a rundown cottage all covered with bushes and vines. Carefully pushing through a section of blackberry brambles, they finally came to a stone wall with a gate. The gate was open. The boys stood at the edge of the cliff where the waves were crashing more than one hundred feet below.

"Do you see him?" Lance asked.

Tad got on his stomach and searched for openings in the fog below. "No, but the fog makes it hard. You don't think he fell, do you?" he yelled.

"The gate was open."

"Dumb place for a gate." Tad got up and grabbed the old iron. It was rusted badly. They both tried to swing it shut, but it wouldn't budge. "That's dangerous," Tad fumed.

"Nobody comes here, hardly."

"Donny did."

"Yeah, but he got caught inside." Lance pointed toward the house. "Funny."

"That he got caught?"

"No, that third-floor window is open a little."

"Maybe it got stuck like the gate."

"Maybe. Let's get out of here. This place is gruesome."

"I like it," Tad insisted. "It's a great place. I wish I lived here. My family could use the room."

"Mine too, but it's only got summer water. All these places up here do."

"Even in the summer it would be great," Tad sighed. "Maybe we should check out that window. I'll bet the view of Goat Island is great from up there. Especially at night. You could really see the Goat Island light."

"No way. We better get out of here."

"Not yet. Let's check out that little cottage in the bramble patch, anyway," Tad suggested.

"That place? That used to be servant's quarters I'll bet."

"So pretend you're a servant. Come on. We won't hurt anything." Tad waded cautiously through the brambles once more.

Not bothering to knock, Tad opened the small door. The cottage looked very old and barren. The boys entered a tiny kitchen with a large wood burning stove and an old rusty sink. The musty odor, low mildew-stained ceilings, and the narrow room made the boys curious.

"This would make a great place to make out," Lance commented.

"A lot you know about it."

"A lot I don't tell you, you mean."

"Yeah, right, like I don't know everything you do." Tad opened another narrow door and entered a bedroom. An old metal double bed frame took up the center of the room. Walking toward the window at the rear of the room he said, "It sure is dark in here." He snapped up the ancient shade which ripped as it hit the top. Turning back toward Lance, he froze.

Lance was staring at an old man with long white hair and a beard who had come out from behind the door.

As the boys stood gently trembling, unsure of what to do, the old man took out a small pad of paper and a pen and began to write. Tad and Lance looked at each other wondering whether to run or not. The tall old man handed the paper to Tad.

The note read: "Don't be afraid. I am deaf-mute. Rented large house. Locked myself out. Looking for tools. You frightened me."

Tad smiled. "Can you read lips?"

The man nodded.

"We heard you were here and came to sell you a ticket for a TV raffle. When we couldn't find you, we decided to explore this old cottage."

The man smiled and wrote: "Will buy ticket. Money is in house. Can you help me?"

"We'll try," Tad said, passing the notes to Lance.

"I know a way in," Lance said. "Donny told me." He headed for the door and hesitated as he crossed in front of the man. When he got outside he realized he was sweating. Tad and the old man followed. Tad's mouth was still open with wonder and surprise. Why did Donny tell him? Why did Lance listen to him? Why didn't Lance tell me?

Below the large sun porch was a locked entryway. On either side of the door was a nine foot tall latticework wall. Lance counted up from the bottom of the left side of the door. Smiling, he pulled gently and moved a piece of lattice aside. Then he reached inside and unlocked the door.

As Tad and the old man entered, they saw that they were in a storage area under the porch. Logs for the fireplace and more lattice sections were stored there. There was another solid-looking door built into the large rock foundation itself.

"Okay, big shot, you got us in here under the porch, but how are you going to get into the cellar?" Tad wondered why his best friend knew about this in the first place.

Lance stepped over to the door and studied it. Tad was sure he was stumped, but Lance ran his hand down the stone foundation near the left side of the door and pulled a chunk of stone loose. Placing his hand through the opening, he found the long wooden bar inside that held the door shut. Pushing it gently, it slipped out of place and fell to the ground. Lance opened the door. The old man went in and up the stairs.

"Do you know any other brilliant tricks you didn't tell me about?" Tad asked, angrily.

"I couldn't tell you, Tad. Donny swore me to secrecy before he got caught. When he got caught, I decided to keep my mouth shut. He had been here quite a few times and he wanted me to join him. He wanted to start a club and make this his hideout. When he showed me the pot that he had, I said no way, and I never came in with him. Honest! But I did keep my promise. I never gave him away. The problem was that he bragged about it to everyone else, and you know what happened."

"The problem was the pot, and that he came in here in the first place." Tad started up the stairs.

"Let's stay down here."

"He seems okay."

"You don't know that. You don't know anything about him."

"It's all right," Tad insisted. "I just know it is. Besides, there're two of us. But I'll go alone if you want. I want to sell this ticket."

"Let's make it quick. And don't tell anyone I broke in here, even if I did have permission. My mom would be pretty shaken up about this and she doesn't need it right now."

"I'm shaken up about this, Lance, but I won't tell. Come on."

Tad continued up the stairs into the kitchen. The foghorn on Goat Island blasted loudly and seemed to echo Lance's feelings. Tad followed the old man into a dining room with a large, heavy, oval, mahogany table beneath an old Tiffany lamp. Chairs with cane seats surrounded it. A mahogany buffet filled one wall and a large built-in hutch cabinet filled another. In the corner of the room was a small fireplace. Tad figured it must have backed up to the huge fireplace in the living room. Two glistening cherry wood columns separated the two rooms. The back wall contained narrow glass doors to the sun porch.

The old man came to the table from the living room and handed Tad a note: "How much is ticket?"

"One dollar."

The man handed Tad a dollar and began to write rapidly. "I am artist on assignment. Under pressure of time. Please cooperate with me. Tell no one I am here. Cannot afford to be disturbed."

"Assignment?" Lance asked. "Artists don't have assignments."

"Wealthy man wants paintings of sea in a month for new home," was written on the note Lance handed to Tad.

"We won't tell anyone. May we see some of your work?"

Without moving his lips Lance warned, "Taad."

The man beckoned them into the living room and up the stairs. Once more Lance hung back, but finally followed. On the second floor the boys saw very little except very dark woodwork in a dark hallway, and doors to four or five rooms. All the doors were shut except the one for the bathroom straight ahead.

The old man continued up the next flight to the third floor. The top of the rhododendron bush was framed by a window above the staircase.

In spite of the fog, the large top floor was very bright. The wooden narrow-slatted walls were painted a pale yellow. Very short doors led under the eaves to storage areas. The room had five large windows above the sun porch that looked out over the ocean. A portable easel, stool, a variety of paints, bottles, knives, and brushes were placed near the windows. A canvas was on the easel, but it was blank. Tad noted large opened boxes, and tried to figure out what would go in them.

The view from the windows excited the boys. The fog was lifting and they knew it was a perfect place to paint.

The man handed Tad another note: "Just getting set up. Started to go to store to order groceries, but locked myself out. I need privacy and you can help."

"How?"

"Bring list to grocery store each week and you can see finished paintings."

"We'll take your list today," Lance said. "But you buy another ticket." The man laughed and nodded.

"What is your name? Mine is Tad Callant and this is Lance Deiter."

"Periander Sage. How many tickets do you have left?" he wrote.

"Twenty."

They started down the stairs. At the bottom the man began to write again: "If you bring grocery list today, and I'm not disturbed except by grocery man I'll buy five more. Agreed?" He passed the note and the grocery list to Tad.

"Agreed, but we have to turn in the ticket stubs next Monday. Is Friday okay for us to collect?"

The man smiled and nodded. Tad noticed that his teeth were remarkably good for an old man. That bothered him a little. Finally, he realized that they were probably false. As he walked out the front door he turned and said, "Make sure you take your key with you." The man smiled once more, took it from his pocket, and waved. The boys headed for the road and for their bikes at the pond.

At the grocery store, they explained to Mr. Finney, the tall thin owner, who the list was for and where he was living. Henry Thompson, the old island handyman, joined Finney. If these two men didn't know someone on the island, they made it their business to find out. The boys found it very difficult to keep their word to the old man and professed ignorance. The two men pressed them for details of their visit, which Tad kept as simple as he could.

"We were out selling tickets and this old man asked us to bring down the grocery list. He said he would buy another ticket if we did. He's old and he's busy painting. He says he wants to be left alone," Tad finally said in exasperation.

Mr. Finney handed the list to Billy at the register and told him to fill it. The boys walked to the back of the store to go through the magazines. Finney and Henry walked into the back room.

"At least this guy Sage makes sense," Henry said, holding his brightly striped wide suspenders away from his red plaid shirt. "Not that I particularly like artists, mind you. I could tell you some stories."

"You have, Henry," said Finney pulling a large roast from the freezer.

"I've lived on this hunk of rock fifty-seven years and I know everything that ever happened here."

"I know, Henry. The rock talks to you."

"At least this Sage guy sounds like he'll keep to himself and not bother anyone."

"You mean, at least we know what he's doing, don't you, Henry?"

"What do you mean?"

"The old Richards place."

"Oh, that Banville fella! Lord only knows what he's up to."

Tad and Lance turned from the magazines to listen to the conversation in the back room. The old Richards place was a magnet for every island boy's attention. They moved closer, each carrying a magazine, and avoiding Billy's eyes.

Finney's raspy voice went to a whisper. "That's what I've been wondering ever since this morning. Banville called down his order. I asked how he was planning to pay for it. He says to charge it. So I reminded him that his bill is getting a little high. He says to send the food and he'd pay me for the whole shootin' match.

"So instead of sending Billy, I go up myself first thing. Instead of putting the groceries at the gate, as usual, I go to the door. I must have made four trips from the truck. He comes to the door and asks what I want. I mean, here I am surrounded by boxes and bags of stuff, and he wants to know what I want." Finney's voice turned falsetto and became a little louder. He was getting a little emotional. The boys moved across the aisle and sat as close to the back room doorway as they could, still looking through magazines.

"So, I told him a check is what I want. So he gives me one. It covers his older bill and the groceries I brought him."

"Wait...wait a minute," Henry interrupted. "What's these four trips to the truck and surrounded by boxes? How much can one fella eat? How often does he order groceries?"

"Not often, Henry. When he needs them."

"Stop tryin' to be evasive with me, Finney. You never were a good liar. What's going on?"

"Okay, okay," Finney said, "this whole thing's getting on my nerves. I've got to tell someone and it might as well be you, Henry, but you may regret it." He lit a cigarette. Tad looked through the glass in the meat counter to the back room and saw Finney's hands shaking as he held a cleaver.

"It all started when this guy Banville came to the island in February. The first week he comes in and tells me who he is, and that he wants food sent to the house. He gives me his first order and it was a big one. I mention something about him having a large family. You know, just making conversation. He says he has no family, except for grandchildren that love the island. He wants to be prepared.

"So we filled his first order and I had Billy leave it at the gate, just like he tells me. I figure dogs'll get into it, and I mention it to him when he comes in. He says he's working on a project and can't afford to be bothered. Well, I was curious, but an order is an order, especially one this size. None of my business what he's doing anyway. But then he calls the next week and asks for the same type of order. Now, I figure it's enough for four or five people for a week, but I don't say anything about it. Good money and none of my business as I said.

"Then the next week he sends down for another order the same size, and I begin to get suspicious. I mean this guy isn't fat, so where is all the food going? When I deliver, I bring it to the door and I asked him whether he's planning to have the same size order every week."

"That's a reasonable question," Henry said. "You have to plan." Tad and Lance looked at each other and nodded.

"That's what I tell him, but he sees I'm curious and he invites me inside. Something's funny, I says to myself. I mean, he looked real angry, and yet he was smooth. He jokes about being a heavy eater. We go into the kitchen and it's as clean as a whistle. I mean, first I think there might be a half a dozen others living there, but nobody else is there, and the place is neat as a pin. I noticed that the kitchen table has only two chairs.

"I guess he read my mind about the size of the order, because then he says if I know what's good for me I'll just mind my own business. I tell him that his order is my business and I need to bring extra food from the mainland if he's planning to do this every week. He tells me not to tell anyone about the large orders. I begin to ask why, but he keeps going. He says why he orders this much food is his business. His family is his business. His grandchildren are his business. They love the island, but need their privacy. He tells me if I keep my mouth shut he would give me a little more each month when he pays his bill. I say it would just foul up my bookkeeping. He says to forget about the bookkeeping since it would be in cash anyways.

"Then he says that if he hears one thing about it, I'll be real sorry. You can imagine how I feel about him talking to me this way, so I tell him he can take his business elsewhere. He says I might want to wait until the next morning before making that decision. So I leave pretty well pissed off. The next morning I have money in the mail. Cash."

"How much money?" Henry asked.

"Never you mind, how much. Enough so I know he means business. So I decide then and there I'll just keep selling groceries to him. I mean, it isn't as if he's breaking the law or anything. I figure the guy is simply sick in the head. The weeks go by and the extra cash comes regular every week, but lately his bill is getting higher and higher.

"So this morning he pays me in full, and as I'm about to leave he says that he'll only need orders like this for another month or so. After that the payments will stop. He asks me if that will bother me. Well, I ain't greedy, Henry. You know that. I mean, I may raise the prices a little on tuna fish, toilet paper, and peanut butter when the summer cattle's here, but I'm a fair man. You know that, too. But the extra cash has come in very handy. I say to him it's been great and I'll miss it, but that it's okay and I understand.

"He asks how business is and doesn't wait for an answer. He says it might bother me if the payments stop. I might want to tell somebody about the large orders. He then says, he wouldn't want to put me out of business.

"I ask him if that is a threat. He says he's ill and very tired, and doesn't want to make threats. Then he walks over to a drawer and pulls out a small case. He opens it and takes out one of those hypodermic needles; holds it up, looks at it, and puts it back in the case. Then he puts the case in his pocket. Doesn't say a word about it. I can tell you, Henry that needle scared hell out of me. I mean, I can't watch every stranger that comes into the store and wonder whether he's poisoning my oranges. What if I go to bed and someone calls me up and calls me the murderer of their children? And maybe it wouldn't even be a stranger. Maybe he has other islanders working for him. I was scared shitless, Henry, and he knew it. I said I would keep my mouth shut forever. But damn it, now I'm mad." His voice rose again.

"Shhh," Henry said, waving his hand. "Maybe he didn't mean a thing by it. Maybe it's just your imagination. Maybe he's diabetic and he remembered he had to take his insulin."

"Maybe, but I don't want any of this to get out, Henry. I know I can trust you. In all these months, I ain't seen another soul at that house, but the food keeps disappearing. I have no business asking this, Henry, but I need your help, and it needs to be done quiet. I want to know more about this guy."

Tad and Lance both inhaled deeply. Tad stared into Lance's deep brown eyes, wondering whether it was time to leave or not. From the front of the store they could hear Billy greeting Susan Brown, so they crept back to the magazine rack. Lance grabbed a new skateboarding magazine. Tad took his favorite off-road truck magazine.

They heard Henry whisper, "I know just the man for this. He's a rich young writer, interested in the old Richards place among others. Maybe more than a writer. He has a vision for this island he told me. Got guts! Knew he was my kind of man the first minute I met him. He was down here over the weekend looking for a summer place. May want to invest a chunk of money in this rock."

"Afternoon, Tad, Lance."

"Afternoon, Ms. Brown."

"Hello, Susan," Finney called from behind the meat counter. "What can I get for you? Have a nice pork roast today."

Tad and Lance headed for the door.

"You guys going to deliver this stuff to that artist?" Billy asked as they went by.

"We can't," Lance said. "We have no way to carry it."

"But if the guy is deaf, how will he know I'm there?"

"Just leave it by the front door and put a sign in the front door window. I guess we'll bring you the money. I really don't know yet."

"Okay," said Billy, as the boys opened the front door.

Once outside Lance started to speak, but Tad motioned him down the street.

"They wouldn't hear us," Lance said.

"Maybe not, but then Mr. Thompson and Mr. Finney didn't know we were listening either. No one can know. No one. What do you think we should do?"

"I'm not sure. I want to spend tonight with Dad, with him going to the hospital again tomorrow. You know."

"Yeah. Do you want to go up by the old Richards place now before supper and look around?"

"I don't think so. Who's this writer Mr. Thompson mentioned?"

"Who knows? How about tomorrow after school?"

"Dad'll be in the hospital by then. I'll need something to take my mind off him. That'll be a good way I guess, but not too close."

"Not too close," Tad promised.

CHAPTER THREE

TUESDAY

The blaring fire horn broke the stillness of the early hours just before dawn. Volunteers all over the island dressed rapidly, and ran or drove to the fire station, or to the old town barn. The tanker, pumpers, and ladder truck in the fire station were soon covered with adrenaline-filled men including some older teenagers. Three other men began the wearisome process of trying to start the ancient ladder truck in the tarpaper-covered town barn.

"Where is it, Cap?" yelled one of the volunteers.

"We don't know. The lieutenant's out in the jeep seeing if he can find it. We just got a call from a screaming woman saying her house was on fire, but she didn't say where or who she was. Couldn't make out who it was, she was coughing so bad. The lieutenant went up Central and is going to cut over Cross Street to Island Ave. Wally, take your truck and go up Island and come down Central to School from the bluff. Take this portable with you. You're unit two."

"Right, Cap," said the young plumber, pulling out quickly.

A moment later everyone in the station heard, "Unit one to base."

"Base."

"Cap, I can't find a thing here. I'm going to head up to the bluff."

"Negative, unit one. Unit two has that. Take B Street."

"Ten-four on B Street."

"Unit two to base. Cap, it's Finney's house, fully involved."

"Ten-four. Copy unit one?"

"Affirmative, copy direct. Responding."

"Feather-C-One responding," said the captain.

Sirens screamed as the two pumpers roared up the steep Island Avenue hill. Tad and Lance reached the station on their bicycles just as the others left. "Where is it?" Tad yelled to old Murray, who was now covering the radio and the phone.

"Finney's house," Murray yelled, "but you boys keep back. You hear me? And mind the ladder truck. It'll be comin' up behind you soon."

"If they ever get it started," Lance yelled to Tad, grinning.

The boys headed up Island Avenue with sudden strange feelings in their stomachs. Several cars rapidly passed them. Soon the ladder truck coughed slowly by as Dale gently persuaded the relic to go where he directed it. The former driver, Dave, as old as the truck itself, sat next to Dale, passing down the tradition of the truck's idiosyncrasies and praying they didn't end up in the bay.

As the boys reached the steep section between Cross and Water Streets, they could see cars pulling off to the left side of the road. Men ran up Water Street toward the burning building which lit up the sky. Others were laying hoses and attaching them to the hydrant, pumpers, and the tanker. The engine was already screaming on the other side of the house. Ladders were aiming for the roof with a few problems due to the ferocity of the heat and flames. The boys left their bikes against a fence near the street, and ran the rest of the way. The scene, when they approached, was one of futility.

Several hoses were already pouring water on the old two-story house as the engine and pumpers whined with power, but a wall of fire consumed the early morning sky. Its heat burned Tad's face and he wondered how the men who were close to the house could stand it. He couldn't believe it when he saw men cutting holes in the roof.

"Watch it, boys!" a voice yelled behind them. Sparks from an electric wire spit next to them as Danny, from the power company, pulled it in. The boys moved to the left of the house where a small crowd was quietly roasting.

"Did they get out?" someone asked.

"Don't know," another man answered.

"Wally got her out," said an older man, "but I ain't seen Finney."

"How'd it start?"

"Old house. Probably wirin'."

"Where is she?" Tad asked.

"Jeep. Called the fireboat. Don't think she'll make it, though."

The boys ran over to the jeep. One of the younger volunteers was manning the radio. "Hey, Pete," Tad asked, "how is she?"

"Shhh," Pete whispered, turning to Tad. "Charcoal."

"Why aren't you down at the wharf waiting for the fireboat?" Lance asked quietly.

"Orders are to wait to see if they find Finney. Cap and the lieutenant are inside searching."

"Inside there?" Lance shouted.

"I told you to be quiet," Pete snapped. "They should be out soon."

Suddenly the horns on the engine and tankers blared, followed shortly by a loud crash. The roof had fallen in. Orders were shouted into the radio and loudspeakers. The boys relaxed a little as they recognized the captain's voice over the crackling of the flames. Soon a soot-covered man, with a black face, foul dripping nose, and smelling of wet charcoal, came over to the jeep.

"Shove over, Pete," he said. The boys finally recognized him as the lieutenant. "Cap says to take her down to the wharf. How is she?"

"Oxygen's on and she's breathing, but that's all," Pete whispered. "You find him?"

"Yeah, let's go. Watch it, guys."

The boys watched the jeep as it went down the road and turned down the hill to the wharf. They stared at each other as the meaning of the man's statement penetrated. A wall of the house fell, followed quickly by another.

Tad felt bone tired and more than a little sick. With the jeep gone, he realized how bad the smell had been inside it. "I don't want to stay here anymore. Let's go home. Moms'll be worried."

"Yeah. I'll have to tell Dad all about this. He really misses it. Why, I don't know."

"Lance."

"Ummm?"

"Do you think it was an accident?"

"Who knows? They find the cause most of the time."

"If it wasn't . . . well that means that Banville might've done it."

"Tad, don't even think that way. We don't know that."

Coasting down the hill, they could see the fireboat just pulling in.

"Tad."

"What?"

"Tad, I didn't see Mr. Thompson at the fire. Did you?"

Tad stopped. "No, I didn't. He must've been there. He just lives a little way up around the corner. Maybe we just missed him."

Lance turned his bike around and began the difficult climb back up the hill. "I've got to find out. Are you coming?"

"We're going to be a wreck in school tomorrow."

"You mean today. It's almost five o'clock."

"Oh, no, I've got to get up soon and do my paper route. Let's get this over with fast. Leave the bikes here."

Running toward the house, they saw part of one corner wall and the chimney still standing. The flames were still taunting the firemen who were continuing to pour water on it. People were beginning to leave. Henry Thompson was not among them.

Tad walked over to one of the blackened fireman who was drinking coffee next to the engine. "Mr. Davis, have you seen Mr. Thompson?"

"Henry? Yes, let's see. He was over behind the house the last I saw him, but that was right after we got here. I've been a little busy."

The boys breathed a sigh of relief, thanked the man, and headed back for their bikes.

Henry's body was found below the trees behind the house when the sun came up.

Later in the day, the island went into mourning. Mrs. Finney hadn't made it. Mr. Finney had been found behind the front door. His body had prevented the firemen from getting to him immediately. Henry Thompson apparently, upon hearing news of the death of his old friend, had wandered off and died of a heart attack. No one remembered telling him about Finney, but everyone knew that was what happened.

The chimney in the house and the last wall had been pushed down during the morning by the big island loader. It had been determined that the fire was probably due to old wiring.

* * *

As school let out Tuesday afternoon, Tad and Lance walked slowly up Main Street. It had been a difficult day for them. The news of the three deaths struck the whole community very hard. The Finneys had been well liked, and Henry had been an island institution.

"Do you want to go up near the old Richards place? You said it would take your mind off of your father."

"I thought it would, but it won't. Nothing can. He's probably just getting to the hospital now. Besides, something else is bothering me and I just can't shake it."

"What's that?"

"Well, like here we are talking about going to the old Richards place to see Dr. Banville, just like we were when we came out of Finney's yesterday afternoon. The only difference is that yesterday Mr. Finney and Mr. Thompson were alive and today they're dead."

"Yeah, and Mrs. Finney, too."

"But you don't see what I mean. All the people who knew about Banville are dead except us, but nobody knew about us. Remember when you asked me this morning if I thought it was an accident?"

A shiver went down Tad's back. "Then you don't think it was wiring or a heart attack like we heard in school?"

"I don't know. It looks like an accident, and they say it was probably wiring. Fire marshal will probably figure it out. It looks like a heart attack, but what if…what if it was supposed to look that way?"

Tad stopped and stared at him. He turned away and shook his head. He began to tremble. "I can't handle that, Lance. Don't even think that way. Maybe we should tell somebody. I don't know what to do. I just want to hide."

"Now you're scaring me. You always know what to do. Who would we tell anyway? Tell them what? They'd think we were a couple of wise-ass kids making a real sick joke. We don't have any proof. It's no good, Tad."

Lance kicked a stone to the side of the road. "The other thing I was wondering is if Banville or someone did kill Mr. Finney, how would they know he talked? I can't figure out how they would know about Mr. Thompson. They couldn't know about him."

"Maybe it was just a coincidence. Maybe it really was a heart attack. Unless…unless they had an electronic bug in Finney's store. That's the only way. They might have heard them talking."

"You see too much TV."

"You sound like your mother. But what if they did?" Tad persisted. "Look, the only other person in the store when they were talking was Billy. I don't think he could hear them because he was way up front. We had to get real close."

"Maybe Mr. Finney told Billy. Maybe he mentioned it to someone and it got back to Banville."

"Maybe. Let's go talk to him."

"Talk carefully, Tad. If he doesn't know, but if he knows that we know, maybe then Banville will know, and then we're in trouble. Maybe Billy's next even and then we would be."

"Okay, okay. I'll be careful. Is the store even open?"

"Mom said this morning that Mr. Finney's nephew from uptown would probably keep it open, like when Mr. and Mrs. Finney went on vacation, because a lot of people depend on it."

Fifteen minutes later the two boys entered Finney's store, a little out of breath. Three women were in the rear of the store talking with Martin Finney near the meat counter. Twenty-two year old Billy was slumped on a stool near the register reading a comic book.

"Hi," Tad said.

Billy waved and continued reading.

"Billy?"

"Umm?" Billy mumbled, biting into an apple.

"Billy, when's the funeral?"

"Thursday."

"Will the store be open?"

Billy looked up and stared at Tad for a moment. He looked like he had been crying. Something touched Tad's heart, even though Billy was hardly one of Tad's favorite people.

"Of course not. What kind of dumb kid question is that? We'll be closed all day. The only reason we're open today is because Marty felt obligated to the island people."

"I didn't mean anything disrespectful," Tad said. "I liked the Finneys and Mr. Thompson, too."

"I'm sorry, Tad. I didn't mean to bite your head off. It's just that people have been asking dumb questions all day to make conversation, and it's hard for me to talk about it. They were good people, and that's a horrible way to die."

"We know," Lance said. "We saw Mrs. Finney in the jeep."

"I can't think of anybody who didn't like Mr. Finney. Can you, Billy?"

"Some people argued with him, but they were his friends. Everyone liked him. He was a good, fair man."

"We just wanted to know when the funeral is," Tad said.

"Thursday at three o'clock."

"See you later."

The boys walked out of the store.

"Why didn't you ask him?"

Tad turned on him angrily. "Ask him? Ask him what? Billy, are you a spy for Banville? Billy, did you, by any slight chance, happen to murder your boss? Didn't you see his eyes, Lance?"

"Yeah, what are we going to do now?"

"It must have been an electronic bug. There's no other way."

"Or a coincidence."

"We've got to find out."

"How?"

"On Thursday, when the store is closed, we can go in and look for the bug."

"You are out of your mind, Tad Callant. Breaking and entering? And you talk about me and the Madison place. Besides, how would we get in?"

"That's your department. You're good at getting in places that are all locked up."

Lance became angry, started to say something, saw pain in Tad's eyes, and said, "You're still sore at me for not telling you about the Madison place."

"I guess, a little, but not really. I shouldn't have said that. Forget it. I'm sorry."

"I had to keep a secret. You aren't worth anything if you can't keep a secret."

"Yeah, some secrets to some people. Maybe I don't think Donny's worth a secret."

"Probably right. You really want to go in there?" Lance asked.

"I don't know. We've got a couple of days to think about it."

As the boys entered the Callant yard, Mickey hollered to them from inside the driver's seat of the old Chevy. "You're staying here tonight, Lance."

"How would you know?" Tad sneered.

"I know a lot of things," Mickey snarled back, his glasses sitting near the end of his nose.

"How do you know?" Lance threatened, coming to the side of the car.

"I heard my mom talking to your mom. She's still on the phone, I think. You're staying here and Jackie's staying at your grandmother's, and your sisters are staying uptown at your aunt's."

"How did you get all that from listening to your mother?"

"I listen good," Mickey said.

"Don't even bother," Tad said, pulling Lance by the arm toward the house. "He's nine. He may not be too swift, but he's nosy and always knows the latest gossip, just like my mom."

"Just for that, he can't take my bed."

As they entered the house they heard, "Oh, no trouble at all, Sylvia. You know that. Don't even think about it. He can have Mickey's bed, as usual."

Tad and Lance smiled at each other and sat down at the kitchen table.

"The boys just came in. Lance, it's your mother."

Rotund Marge Callant motioned Tad into the living room as Lance took the phone. "Lance is going to stay with us tonight, Tad. His father is going through some treatments now. The doctors have told Lance's mother that it will be a while before they know anything, so she's going to stay uptown tonight."

"Is Mr. Deiter going to die, Mom?" Tad whispered.

Marge placed her hand on the back of her son's neck and looked him in the eyes. Then she looked away. When she looked back she rubbed his neck. Tears were in her eyes. "We honestly don't know, Tad. He is a very sick man. Sometimes the treatments work for awhile and sometimes they seem to make him worse. Maybe they can operate soon. Don't say anything about this to Lance. I suspect he has enough on his mind right now."

"You can say that again."

"Is something else wrong?"

"Oh no . . . I mean . . . well, with his father so sick and the funeral coming up Thursday."

"Yes, I see what you mean. Perhaps you boys shouldn't go to the funeral. We'll just have to wait and see."

"Yeah."

"Yes," his mother corrected. Lance entered the living room.

"Yes," Tad said.

"Now, Lance, before we forget, you boys had better go over to your house and get your sleeping bag and some clothes. If I'm going to let you have Mickey's bed, I'll have to give him his favorite new blanket to use on the couch, or there will be no living with him. If you need anything washed, bring that over, too."

The boys walked back into the kitchen, took an apple from the bowl on the table, and went out. They looked for Mickey near the car, but he was nowhere to be found. Cutting through the backyard they saw him sitting on Lance's back steps.

"What are you doing here?" Tad asked.

"Just waiting for you," Mickey said, eating an apple. "Bet you wonder how I got the apple, too." He smiled, showing two huge front teeth with apple pieces stuck to them.

"We don't even care. Besides, we know something that you don't know. Lance is going to have your bed tonight and your blankets, too."

"Not my green one! Mom said he would have his sleeping bag and I would have my blanket!"

"We knew you were in the kitchen, so after you left we talked her into letting Lance have all your blankets, including the new green one. Mom said okay."

"She didn't say that! She better not've. I'm gonna go check!"

Mickey ran off. Tad and Lance smiled at each other. They both stuck apple pieces to their teeth and laughed out loud. "I'll get my stuff. My sleeping bag's in the trunk under the stairs."

"I know. I'll get that," Tad said moving toward the cellar door.

Within ten minutes they were back at Tad's house and out the front door again. Mrs. Callant called after them, "Back at five."

Mickey hollered from his perch, "You lied. I got my blanket, so there."

Lance grimaced and said, "Why do we each have to have a nine-year-old brother? I hate nine-year-old brothers. So what now? I'm your guest. Entertain me."

"Some guest. We've only got a half-hour. Let's go down to the station and tell them about Mr. Sage."

As they entered the fire station, a very exhausted fire captain was on the phone. "We'll check it out, Mrs. Tucker. Thank you." He hung up the phone and turned to the radio. "Base to unit one."

"One."

"Tom, Mrs. Tucker just called. She just came back from the dump. Apparently, there's a group of kids over there playing with the hose again. Check it out."

Tad and Lance broke up laughing, and then tried very hard to look concerned as the captain turned to face them. "Hi."

"Hi, Cap," Tad said. "The lieutenant asked us to tell him yesterday about the new man in the Madison place. We didn't get a chance, so we thought we'd tell him now."

"The lieutenant is out on a call."

"We heard," Lance snickered, desperately trying to control himself.

Tad continued. "Well, the man's name is a little different. It's Periander Sage, but he seems okay. He's just an old man who says he has to paint a lot of ocean pictures for some rich guy who's building a house somewhere. The pictures have to be done when the house is done, so he just wants peace and quiet."

"We haven't had much of that today."

"It wouldn't bother him. He's deaf and dumb."

"Well then, I would say he at least has quiet when he wants it, doesn't he?"

"I didn't mean—"

"Neither did I, Tad. I'm sorry. I shouldn't even be thinking like that. I'm very, very tired. It's been a long horrible day."

"Don't you get any relief?"

"Yes, in a couple of hours."

"Mr. Sage asked us to bring his grocery order to Mr. Finney. Mr. Thompson was at the store, too. That was the last time we saw them alive," Lance explained sadly. Tad's look warned him to stop.

Tad jumped right in, "Did Mr. Thompson really die of a heart attack?"

"That's right, unfortunately."

"But how do you know?" Tad asked. "I mean, did anyone see him die?"

"No, not to my knowledge, but Dr. Banville examined him and signed the death certificate. He said it was a heart attack."

"DOCTOR Banville!" both boys exclaimed.

"He's a doctor?" Lance asked.

"Yes, he doesn't practice now, but he's licensed in Maine. We call him in for special emergencies."

"You mean the new man who lives in the old Richards place?"

"The very same. Do you know him?"

"No, not really. We were thinking about asking him for a job to clean up his yard," Tad lied. "But we didn't know he was a doctor."

"But that doesn't make sense," Lance added. "I mean, he's not too old, and he's single, or at least the whole island thinks he is, and a doctor. It doesn't make sense that he would come here and just sit around all day."

"How do you know he just sits around all day?" the captain asked suspiciously.

"We don't, really," said Tad, "but what else is there for him to do? I mean, look at his yard."

"You may have a point," laughed the captain. "I don't know much about him myself. I understand he was pretty sick and is recuperating here. Nothing to do is probably just what he needs, so don't you kids go bothering him."

"How was he sick?" Lance asked, nervously.

"I don't know. I really don't. Besides, you know how rumors are on the island."

"Yeah, if we don't understand something, we make up something so we can understand it. It doesn't matter if it's true or not."

"That is, without a doubt, the most honest explanation I have ever heard an islander make. That is exactly what happens."

"Have you bought a ticket for the TV raffle, Captain?" Lance asked.

"I guess I could use another one. By the way, you guys haven't been playing with that hose over at the dump have you? A four inch hose can be very dangerous. We'll be happier when and if they open the recycling center. That's for sure."

"Not us," Tad said. Under his breath he muttered, "Not anymore."

CHAPTER FOUR

WEDNESDAY

"Well, you goin' in?"

"Yeah, you?"

"You first."

With a splash that made Tad's skin quiver, Lance dove into the pond, completing the island ritual of "first in the pond". The gulls burst into the air above and pushed out over the cliffs to the sea. Lance came up shouting, "It's beautiful!"

"Cold?" Tad shivered.

"No, it's great. Come on in."

Tad reached down and gently splashed water on his arms and rubbed them. Water suddenly exploded toward him. Relentless in his attack, Lance soaked Tad thoroughly. Tad found himself below four feet of water with the cold attacking him and the thought of them being the first ones in warming him. He came up for air.

"No, it's great, he says! It's freezing!" he coughed.

"Yeah, isn't it?" Careful to stay out of Tad's way, Lance laughed.

"At least it's clean. Not like last September."

Remembering the green algae-covered edges of the pond, both boys dove down again. Their nude bodies slid skillfully through the cool clear water.

"We still really need a place to dive from," Tad said as they came up for air again.

"We'd have to get out about twelve or fourteen feet to get deep enough. Maybe a raft. Let me check." Lance dropped straight down with his hands over his head. His hands disappeared below the surface. He soon bobbed back into view. "It must be about ten feet here and freezing even more. Ten feet would be okay."

"Good. We should be able to get boards from—"

"You have a cramp? What's the matter?"

"There's a canoe over there."

"Where?" Lance whispered.

"In those reeds. See? Just the stern. We can use it to dive from now."

"I still don't see it."

"Follow me." Tad swam to the right side of the pond about fifty feet from the dam. Lance caught up with him and quickly passed him. Both boys arrived together at the side of an old canvas canoe.

"It's Judy's," Lance said quietly.

"I know. I wonder how it could have gotten here."

"There're sneakers in it."

"Maybe there are footprints," Tad said standing. He walked up to the bow of the canoe, which was on shore. Looking down at the mud he said, "There are footprints. I hope she's okay." He wandered up a path. Lance followed very slowly.

About thirty feet from the pond they stopped. Someone was crying ahead behind some bushes. The boys stopped and listened. Tad started up the path again.

"Wait," Lance warned in a loud whisper.

"What?"

"We can't go in there."

"Maybe she's hurt."

"We're naked."

Tad looked down at himself, suddenly realizing the implications of going any further.

"Let's go back very, very quietly," Lance whispered.

The crying stopped.

"Come on!" Lance whispered desperately, walking backwards, then running.

"Tad!" Judy exclaimed.

Tad looked into Judy's tear-stained face. He wanted to go to her to find out why she was here and crying. He wanted to tell her he was sorry about her father; but his body was spinning around. He raced down the path, watching Lance dive back into the pond. He quickly followed, surprised once more at the coldness of the water.

As he poked his head out he saw Judy standing near her canoe, wearing a red plaid shirt and jeans, and looking very confused. Her long blond hair glistened in the sun. Her blue eyes were as light as Tad's were dark. Lance swam up beside him. For a moment no one knew what to say.

"Are you okay?" Tad asked finally.

"Yes, are you?"

"We're okay," Tad answered. "A little embarrassed at being bare-assed, but okay."

"Why...why are you here?" asked Lance.

"The clearing back there is one of my favorite places. I come here when I want to be alone. I really didn't expect anyone to be swimming for the next few weeks."

"First in," Lance explained. "We're sorry about your father, Judy."

"Thank you. How is your father, Lance?"

"Mom called this morning and said things look very good this time. I'm staying at Tad's for awhile."

"I'm glad for you. How about your father, Tad?"

"He's still in Michigan. The job should finish in about a month, and then he'll be home for a few weeks."

"That will be nice."

"Yeah, I hope so." Tad hesitated, trying to make up his mind whether to ask Judy a question he had been wondering about or not. Finally he said, "Judy, I know it's none of my business, but did your father have heart trouble?"

"Yes. Why do you ask?"

"He always seemed pretty healthy to me."

"I guess he did, but he was supposed to take it easy, and to exercise properly, and to lose weight, and to stop drinking, and he didn't do any of those things. The fire, with the Finneys being in there and all, must have been just too much for him to handle. They were very close."

Knowing he was really pushing his luck, Tad said, "Do you know some guy who's a writer and who is interested in the old Richards place?"

"Yes, Carl Linderman. I met him Saturday when I saw him sitting at the end of our driveway. He was drawing pictures of the island. I drove him around and showed him the sights, such as they are. Daddy got awful mad when he saw him with me in our old truck, but Carl, ah, Mr. Linderman asked for his help and Daddy bought him a drink. When he came home, he told us how Mr. Linderman was going to write about the island, and maybe invest some money here. He wanted to know all about it. Well, you know Daddy. He was willing to tell him everything. But how do you know Carl?"

"We don't," Lance offered.

"I don't understand."

"Judy, can you get in touch with him?" Tad asked.

"He's coming to the funeral tomorrow. He called me just a little while ago. It's awful nice of him. He didn't have to do that."

"Did your father tell you Monday that he wanted to talk to him?"

"How did you know? I didn't know how to contact him. Daddy was really upset. Mr. Finney calmed him down as we walked to the truck. I was driving him home and I told him that Mr. Linderman would probably call him. And this morning he did."

"You were at Finney's when he asked you for Carl Linderman's number?"

"Yes, outside. I had just driven up. What is this all about?" She sat down on the bow of the canoe and pushed her feet into the mud. Tad swam up and hung on to the stern. Lance stayed where he was, shivering.

"Judy," Tad said, "we were in the store a little while before you must've driven up. Mr. Finney and your father were talking about the old Richards place. Your father said they should tell it all to the writer. Who is he, anyway? I mean is he a newspaper reporter?"

"I don't know, but I like him. I like him a lot." Tad glanced at Lance, who smiled in a cold grimace. "I wonder if he wanted to tell him about the time we broke into that place. Timmy went down into the cliff or he says he did. Nobody really believed him. But we all got caught and my father was with the Public Safety guys. I think he turned us in. I really caught it that time, but we didn't have to go to court."

"I doubt that's what it was about," said Tad. "Now you have to promise that what I'm going to tell you is kept a secret. We can't prove anything yet and it could be very dangerous." Tad related what they had overheard and finished with, "There may be nothing to it, but we're both a little scared. Since Dr. Banville signed your dad's death certificate, we wondered about your father's heart. We really don't know what to think. Maybe we could meet this Carl Linderman and talk to him about it."

"I don't know what to think. This is awful. It's horrible. I think we should go to the police. Are you sure it's true? Maybe Carl shouldn't know about it. I just can't believe anyone would do such a thing. Have you told anyone else?"

"No, we're being very careful," Tad said.

"We could be killed if it got out and it was true," Lance said. "Besides if we told anyone else the word would spread like crazy."

"The islanders would tear the old Richards place apart and Banville with it. Then they'd burn it and Banville too, whether he's guilty or not," said Tad.

"I doubt they'd go that far, Tad, but they would be angry, and several might overreact without thinking. In fact, if anyone sees me here with you both like you are, rumors of another kind might start. I better go. Lance's lips are turning blue."

"My whole body's turning blue," Lance shivered.

Both boys searched the shoreline for watching eyes. As Judy started to push out the canoe, Tad stood up in knee-deep water and pulled at the stern. Judy climbed in and paddled out near Lance. Before pointing the bow toward the stream that led to the lower pond she looked directly at Tad in front of her and said, "You guys have got to get more sun."

Tad grinned, "Maybe you can join us next time."

"I really don't think that would be a good idea. In fact, I would appreciate it if I never hear about this. Okay?"

"Don't worry," Tad said. "I don't want my Mom to hear about it either or Lance's mom."

"I'll speak to Carl tomorrow. He may want to talk with you."

As Judy paddled off, the boys swam back to the beach and began drying off with their clothes. Lance said in disbelief, "Do you realize that you just stood naked in front of a high school senior who is also a girl?"

"Yeah, but she had seen me already up the path, so what difference does it make?"

"Maybe none, except for that boner. I don't know how you could have the guts to do that. I couldn't."

"No big deal. You're just jealous, like always."

"I'm too damn cold to get hard. Why aren't you?"

"She's really beautiful, isn't she?"

"For cryin' out loud, Tad, she's a senior. She isn't going to give a shit about you."

"Yeah, maybe. Where do you suppose she keeps her canoe?"

"Somewhere in the lower pond or the stream, I guess. I haven't been down there except partway with you when we went to the tower those times."

"Nobody goes down there much. It's pretty swampy. I hope she knows what she's doing."

"I hope you do," Lance insisted. "Let's go home."

As the boys walked back to their bikes Periander Sage slowly made his way along the wooded edge of the pond heading toward the lower pond.

CHAPTER FIVE

THURSDAY

To accommodate the large funeral, school closed at two o'clock. As the boys entered Tad's house, Sylvia Deiter said, "Oh, I'm so glad you came right home."

"Mom!" Lance yelled. "How's Dad? Is he home? Are you home for good?" He hugged her.

"Slow down, Lance. Dad is doing fine, but he's going to stay at the hospital a few more days. He's very tired. I'm home now, but I will be going uptown every day for awhile. The girls will stay uptown for the weekend, and you and your brother will come home. For this afternoon, though, we want you and Tad to stay with the kids while we're at the funeral."

"Oh, Mom," Lance whined, "we had something to do."

"Like going swimming again?" Marge Callant asked, entering the room.

"Swimming?" Tad said, his eyes roaming the ceiling.

"Don't play dumb with me, Tad Callant. I guess I know what wet hair, blue lips, and damp clothes mean by now. I didn't say anything yesterday, but today is different. You can't go swimming."

"We were first in."

The dimples in Tad's grin melted Marge's heart, but she held fast. "And probably first to get pneumonia. Now you boys have to be responsible, and that's that. We'll be back as soon as we can. Donsie's changing. Mickey will probably be home soon, and Brian is out back with Jackie."

"We have to take care of Jackie, too?" sighed Lance.

"He's your brother, Lance, and I don't think we're asking too much. We have to leave for the funeral now. It shouldn't be too long."

As their mothers left, both boys invaded the refrigerator. "What should we do?" Lance asked.

Tad whispered, "I don't know yet. I'd still like to figure out some way to get into Finney's store."

"But we haven't even checked it out, and with the kids along it will be impossible."

"Maybe not. All we need is a little time."

"Here we go again. Tad, I don't know about this."

"Look, I'm not going to do anything stupid."

"It always worries me when you say that, too."

"What's for snack?" asked five-year-old Brian, slamming the screen door. "I think oranges."

"Oranges," Tad said, pointing toward the refrigerator. "Right again."

Jackie slammed the screen door. "Hi, Lance. What's for snack?"

"Oranges," said all three boys.

Brian brought out an orange and handed it to his brother. "Unzip this, please, Tad. Mom said you were going to take care of us."

Tad peeled the orange for his brother and, seeing his eight-year-old sister, he said, "You want one, too?"

"No, I don't want to get all sticky. What are you going to make us do this afternoon?"

"What do you want to do?"

"Watch TV."

"Mom said we have to go outside," Tad lied.

"How about hide-and-seek?" Brian offered.

"Yecchh," Donsie answered.

"Here comes Mickey. Let's ask him."

After five minutes of negotiations, the six children were out the front door, ready to play hide-and-seek.

"Let's make this game a little different," Tad said. "Everybody is at the funeral, so let's play down front."

"Where down front?" asked Mickey.

"Around the stores, but away from the fire barn and wharves. Stay on this side of Main Street and Island Ave. Better stay on the other side of Maple behind Adam's, Peter's, Jean's, and the town barn. Don't come back here."

"Can we go up to Allen's?" Jackie asked.

"You better not," Tad said. "Their dog'll bark and give away your hiding place."

"Or chew you up," Brian said.

"And don't do anything dumb or get into trouble," Lance said, looking at Tad.

"Where's goals?" Donsie asked, almost into the spirit of the game.

"Front of the café, the bottom step," Tad said, then shouted, "Not it!" and started the game.

"Not it!" flew around the circle, bouncing off minds and mouths.

"Donsie's it!" yelled the boys, racing down Maple Street.

"Count to one hundred really slow," Jackie yelled over his shoulder.

The five boys stayed together as far as the post office. "You guys hide somewhere around here. We'll go up a bit more." The two nine-year-olds took off, determined to never be found.

As Tad and Lance reached the corner of Island Avenue they realized Brian was still with them. "Brian, you were supposed to stay back there with Mickey."

"I'm going with you, Tad."

"You can't."

"I'm going to," Brian insisted.

Lance started to laugh. "Mighty Tad strikes out again."

Tad said sternly, "Come on, then. You'll have to keep up."

Brian was all smiles as his short legs raced to keep up.

On the far side of Finney's was a large pile of empty cardboard boxes. Tad found one large enough for Brian and helped him in. "You stay here. We'll hide right nearby."

At the rear of the store, Lance said, "Where'll we hide?"

"We're not going to hide, you jerk. Let's take a look at this door," he whispered.

The door was locked. He moved to the window. "I think I can get this open. You keep a lookout."

As Lance moved to the edge of the building Tad opened the window and slipped onto a shelf in the back room. The far wall, next to the inner door to the store, was covered with stacks of unopened cardboard boxes. Shelves along the back wall near the window, and on either side of the outside rear door, were filled with boxes of canned goods. The floor by the left wall was covered with stacks of large bags of cat and dog food. Tad moved down an aisle between boxes of household supplies and paper goods.

In the center of the large back room was a stainless steel-and-wood cutting table. The other side of the room contained a walk-in freezer, the meat case, and a bathroom. A large sink sat next to the doorway into the store. Tad began by exploring the base of the large table.

Outside, Lance was watching carefully. He peered around the corner, looking toward the front of the store and at the box where Brian was hidden. Fully expecting to get caught, he was still startled when a voice from one of three men behind him said, "Hey, kid. What the hell are you doin'?"

Lance and Tad spun around. Inside, Tad bumped his head on the table and made his way to the window. He saw the men weaving into the back yard and drinking out of their paper bags. Very carefully, he slid the window down, hoping they wouldn't notice him.

"What're you doin'? Answer me, punk!" the tall man ordered.

"I...I...I'm playing hide-and-seek."

"Ain't that sweet? Ain't that sweet, boys? We play hide-and-seek a lot." The young man laughed uncontrollably at his joke and almost fell over.

Another man, older, dirtier than the other two, grabbed him by his arm. Lance tried to pull away. "You just better move your ass out of here, boy, or you're dead. You're dead just like your old man is gonna be."

"What do you mean my old man?" Lance asked, tears forming in his eyes. "What do you mean, Dan?" Getting angry he continued, "My dad's not going to die. He's doing real well in the hospital this time."

"This time," Dan continued, shaking Lance's upper arm. "But his day is comin' and I say good riddance. High and mighty Deiter. Thinks he can throw me off his property, does he? We'll see what he can do now. Maybe I'll pay a little visit to them pretty ripe sisters of yours one of these days right in front of him. Laugh in his damn face while I'm doin' it."

The two men in the background giggled and hooted.

"You keep the hell away from them!" Lance yelled firmly. "You hear me?"

Dan took out a long bone-handled knife, waving it at Lance's throat. "I ought to cut you up for fish bait just for tryin' to order me around just like your old man. But I've got better things to do. I said get outta here and I mean it. Now move and stay alive for awhile."

Lance walked backward, turned the corner, tripped, and fell on the stack of cardboard boxes. "Ow!" Brian yelled.

"Another one," Dan Stark said. "Have to gut them both."

"Come on, Brian. Let's get out of here fast." He grabbed the smaller boy, pulled him running down the short driveway, and headed for the café.

"Tad!"

"Shhh," Lance ordered. "He's okay. Come on. Why don't you know that?"

"I may have to save him, later."

As they reached the café, Lance's mind was exploding with anger and fear. He couldn't go back and get Tad. Did Tad know about the men? Would he come right out in the middle of them?

Tad had watched Dan grab Lance and wanted to jump out of the window and help his friend. However, he knew Dan would spread the word that he had broken into Finney's store. As he watched Lance run with his brother, he felt safer and figured he could wait them out. That was when the back window opened again.

One of the younger men stuck his head inside. Tad had carefully slid under the large cutting table, crawled to the store side of the room, making his way among the boxes of food near the far wall. As one of the drunk men began to climb in, Tad squeezed into a small space behind some boxes next to the wall.

A shelf above him hid him from view. A curve in a water pipe jabbed into Tad's right kidney, but he didn't move. Dan followed the other man through the window. The third man stayed outside.

Although unsteady on their feet, they made their way quickly to the front of the store and came back with several cartons of cigarettes and several cases of beer. They passed these through the back window to the man outside.

"Maybe we ought to take some food," Dan said.

"How're we gonna carry it all?"

"Put it in the cardboard boxes the kids were in. We can take some now, and come back later and get the rest."

"What'll we take?"

Tad slid lower, trying to vanish into the floor. His heart was pounding and his back was killing him. Dan picked up a box from the top of a pile five feet from him. "I don't know. I can't read what's in here anyway. The letters keep moving around," he giggled. Tad felt it was the most evil laugh he'd ever heard.

The man outside yelled, "Hurry up. The jeep just went back to the station. If that kid tells them anything, they'll be right over here."

"If that Deiter kid tells them anything, he's dead," Dan said. "Let's get to the shack."

Dan crawled up on the shelf and began to go through the window, but slipped. His knee slid along the window casing. A tiny metal object was dislodged from the side of the window and fell on the floor. Tad spotted it. The younger man bent down and picked it up. Tad tried to shrink even smaller.

"What's this?"

"What?" Dan asked, finally making it outside through the window.

"This." He showed it to Dan. "I thought you mighta dropped it."

"Ain't mine. Bring it along. Maybe worth somethin'."

As the younger man went back through the open window, Lance was crossing the street from the café to the fire barn. Feeling scared, embarrassed, and furious all at once, he went up to a temporary officer from uptown, who had come on duty that morning.

Lance didn't know him. His voice wavered. "Excuse me. We were playing hide-and-seek behind Finney's Store and some drunks, Dan Stark and two of his friends grabbed me. Dan said he would kill me if I didn't get out of there. Then he said I'd be dead just like my father's going to be, and my father's in the hospital awful sick... and...and I don't know what to do!" Lance began to cry, tried not to, but couldn't control it. "And he said he'd come around now and get my sisters. Then he pulled a large knife on me."

The captain, hearing Lance's story, came down the stairs, wrapped his arm around the sobbing boy's shoulders, and held him close. "Don't worry, Lance. Stark isn't going to touch you or your family. He'd have to go through the entire Lassiter Fire Department and most everyone on the island to do that. Lieutenant, this fellow is a real bad one, drunk or not, and he's drunk most of the time. I think it's about time we took him in. Where did you say he was, Lance?"

"Over behind Finney's."

"Tad's hiding somewhere over there, too, but he's okay now," Brian said.

The captain looked at the little boy. "Tad?"

"I forgot," Lance said. "Tad's hiding over there. We were playing hide and seek with the kids because of the funeral."

"Let's go.   You boys stay right here and don't touch anything."

"We won't."

The captain and the covering lieutenant ran across the street. Jackie, Mickey, and Donsie ran over to the barn to see what was wrong when they spotted Lance.

Tad was just beginning to poke his head out of the window, hoping that the men were gone. Out of the corner of his eye, he spotted the two public safety officers coming fast. He dove into his hiding place once more.

"They may be inside," the captain whispered, pointing to the open window. Cautiously he looked through the window. All was quiet. He motioned that he was going in. Sliding quickly into the room, he peered into the store itself, and then opened the back door.

"Apparently they were in here. They figured no one would be around because of the funeral. They dropped some cigarette packs on the floor. Probably took some beer. Who knows what else? We've suspected him every other time, but this time I think we can prove it."

"Where do we find him?"

"Rumor has it that he has a shack somewhere between Cross and Water Streets, in a large section of thick woods. Mostly blow downs at the moment. We've never been able to find it. I'll put out the word and when someone sees him, we'll pick him up."

He closed the window. "Just in case, ride up the side streets. He's tall with long dark hair. Knife scar on his right cheek. With the other two drunks with him, he should be easy to spot. Don't try to take them alone without a weapon. He may be armed beyond a knife. After I get this window secure I'll make some calls."

The covering lieutenant left. The captain found a hammer and some nails and nailed the window shut. He then locked the back door and walked into the store. After looking all around he went out the front door, locking it behind him.

Tad crept from his hiding place, looked cautiously out the window once more, and walked into the store. Keeping low, he went to the front window. No one was in sight. At the front door he unsnapped the lock, slid through the doorway, and began to close the front door. Mrs. Hall was coming around the corner by the café with several small children. Tad clicked the lock on the door. He couldn't get away. Thinking quickly, he began knocking on the door.

"I don't think the store is open, Tad. The funeral and all, you know."

"Oh yeah, I forgot. I've been playing hide-and-seek and wanted a drink. I'll get one at home. Thank you, Mrs. Hall. You babysitting?"

"How'd you guess?" She smiled. "You certainly look hot."

"Yeah, see you later." Spotting the kids at the fire station he ran over to the steps of the café and yelled, "Goals, one, two, three."

The children all ran over to him at once. Brian asked, "Where were you, Tad? I know you were inside somewhere, but where?"

Concerned that his little brother's psychic powers might cause him problems he said, "You don't expect me to give away a good hiding place do you? I figured Donsie would never find me and I got bored, so here I am, and that's all that matters."

"I wasn't even looking for you," Donsie insisted.

"Let's go home."

"I'm for that," Lance said.

"Can I watch TV now?" Donsie asked.

"You can all watch TV," Tad said with enthusiasm. Donsie and the two nine-year-old boys ran off arguing.

"I want to stay with you, Tad," Brian said.

Tad picked him up and carried him home on his shoulders. Lance walked quietly by his side watching the others race up the street.

"Were you scared, Lance?" Tad asked.

"What do you think?"

"Scared and brave. You really stood up to him."

"He said my father's going to die and he was going after my sisters."

"He's rotten, Lance. He was also very drunk. Don't pay any attention to what he said."

"He meant it, though, Tad. I know he did. That's why I went over to the barn and told them."

"You told them?"

"Of course. How do you think they knew about it?"

"You told them even though I—"

"I didn't tell them everything. And how did I know they were planning to rob the store? I didn't find out until the captain came back and told us."

"I guess it was the right thing to do."

"Besides, I was worried about you. I didn't know if they would get you or not. I had to do something."

"Yeah, I suppose so, but we've had some close calls today."

"What happened to you?" Brian asked. "I didn't know you were in trouble. I always know when you are in trouble."

"Nothing really happened. I went up near Allen's. Their dog almost bit me. He's real scary and mean. That's all. Then I headed back down and saw them with Lance. I saw Dan's big knife."

"You said not to go up there. You shouldn't go in places you don't belong."

"Yeah, I guess I learned a little about that today. That's for sure."

The little boy was very quiet for a moment. Slowly he began, "But…but you said that Lance really stood up to them. If you were up at Allen's, how did you know that, Tad? You must have been close. I felt you close."

Tad blushed and then said, "I was close coming back. I guess I just knew about Lance like you know things sometimes. We're brothers, after all. You know things a lot easier than I do, though, and I care about Lance like you care about me."

"Oh," Brian said, trying to understand. "I guess, maybe."

After the funeral, the island slowly came back to life. Lance told his mother all about Dan Stark. Brian told his mother about Tad almost getting eaten by the dog. Sylvia Deiter called the fire barn. The captain assured her that they would keep an eye on things and explained what he had in mind for arresting Dan Stark. Marge Callant, upon hearing of the situation, decided to call her husband this evening. Contractor or not, he was needed at home.

When supper was finished, Tad and Lance convinced their mothers that they would be all right if they stayed in plain sight. Getting their permission, the boys went to the beach so they could talk. Tad skimmed a stone into the bay. Lance followed with a clamshell.

"Where'd you hide?"

"Under a table, behind some boxes in the back room, next to the meat cooler. Dan began to move some of the boxes to see what he wanted to take, but he was so drunk he couldn't read what was in them, so he left and went into the store itself."

"Where do you think they are now?"

"They said they were going to take it to the shack. I heard the Captain say he thought they had a shack up between Cross and Water Streets."

"But that's all overgrown."

"That's probably why it's a great place. Not many people go up there."

"Well, you won't find me up there anymore."

"We may have to."

"Why would we possibly want to find Dan Stark?"

"Well, as Dan was falling out the window, he knocked something down. The other guy from uptown, the little one, picked it up. It was real small and rectangular. It looked like it was metal. I couldn't see too well, but I'll bet it was the bug. Dan said it might be valuable and they took it with them."

"Maybe it was a cigarette lighter or something."

"No, it was much smaller, and they didn't know what it was."

"They were drunk," Lance reminded him.

"Yeah, I don't want to go near them either."

"Did you see his knife?"

"My heart was in my throat and I almost came out. I thought if I ran by them quickly, you could get away, but then you fell and ran with Brian, so I decided to stay put."

"Super Tad saves the day again."

"Yeah, well, that's when my fun really started. Then, when they left, the captain and that new lieutenant almost caught me. They nailed the window shut."

"How'd you get out?"

"Front door and I almost got caught again." Tad explained.

"Why didn't you use the back door?"

"Oh yeah. I never thought of it. The captain went out the front door and so did I."

"Tad! Lance!"

The boys turned around and looked down the beach. A man in a suit was calling them.

"Who's that?" Lance asked.

"I don't know, but he knows us."

"It isn't Banville, is it?"

"No, I've seen Banville. He's shorter, I think. Be ready to run anyway."

The man caught up to them. Tad was surprised that he wasn't out of breath after running across the sand. The man smiled at them. Tad liked his clothes, his broad smile, and his gray, alert eyes. Lance was ready to run.

"The captain said that you were down on the beach. I'm Carl Linderman. Judy Thompson said I should talk with you. The captain must think highly of you two. He asked me all sorts of questions before he'd tell me where you lived. Finally, I guess I convinced him I'm harmless, because he said you were down here."

The boys looked up and saw the captain leaning against the side of the fire barn, smoking his pipe. Lance waved and the captain waved back. Linderman looked over his shoulder and laughed. "Maybe I didn't convince him after all. Judy did mention me, didn't she?"

"You're a writer who's interested in the old Richards place."

"Right, I am. Now I have to catch the ferry, but I thought you could tell me everything you could about what you heard Mr. Finney tell Mr. Thompson. Judy told me what you told her, but I want to make sure I have it straight. I promise I won't use your names. Do you mind?"

"No," Tad said. "We wanted to tell you because Mr. Thompson wanted to tell you. But it is very dangerous for us if

Dr. Banville finds out, so you have to really promise not to mention our names anywhere at all."

Linderman nodded. The boys told him all about the events of Monday afternoon. Lance told him they thought there must be an electronic bug, in the store. Tad gave him a look that made him just end it there. Linderman looked oddly at Tad, making him feel this man knew everything.

"Are you coming back soon?" Lance asked.

"Yes," Linderman assured them. "I'll be back Saturday to drive Judy and her mother to Judy's aunt's house near Augusta. They want to stay for awhile. I'll come down on the nine-thirty ferry. If you have anything else you want to tell me, why don't we meet then? I've got to catch this boat now."

The boys looked out toward the bay. Tad said, "You still have ten minutes."

Linderman looked at his watch. "How can you tell?"

"I don't know. We just can."

"If you don't mind, I think I'll go. It seems awfully close. I don't like to leave things to chance."

Tad shrugged. Lance smiled and said, "You'll see."

"Maybe, but I like to be sure. Details are important most of the time. See you Saturday."

"Maybe," Lance said.

They watched Linderman run up the beach in his highly polished black shoes. Tad began laughing also. They walked slowly toward the wharf and watched the boat dock exactly ten minutes later. Linderman spotted them. He pointed to his watch and touched the tip of this thumb to his forefinger. The captain continued to watch and smoke his pipe.

CHAPTER SIX

FRIDAY

"No! No!"

A little before five Friday morning Tad woke to the sounds of his brother Brian fighting his pillow in the small bed. Mickey, in Tad's upper bunk, was sleeping through it. Tad got out of his bed, walked over to Brian and gently shook his shoulders. "Brian, wake up," he whispered. "It's all right."

"No!"

"It's okay, Brian. Tad's here. Wake up."

Brian opened his eyes and looked around. His forehead and hair were wringing wet. He looked up at his brother, sat up, threw his arms around Tad's neck, and pulled him down. "You were having a bad dream," Tad whispered.

"Yeah! Me and you were being chased by Dan Stark with a big knife! Lance was there, too. He tripped me and knocked me down. Dan Stark got you and he was going to cut you up! I was trying to get Lance off me so I could save you, but he kept shaking me and I woke up."

"It was only a dream, Brian."

"I know, but it was scary. Maybe my dreams are real, Tad."

"Dan Stark won't hurt me."

"He might!"

"That's ridiculous."

"He might and you know it."

"All right," Tad said, sitting up, "but I don't think he will. As soon as he's seen he'll be arrested."

"What if he comes at night?"

"We're safe here. Everything is locked and safe. Now I've got to get up and do my paper route. You go back to sleep for a little while. I'll lock up and will keep an extra special watch for him. I'll be okay. I have my bike and you know how fast I can go. If he's drunk he'll just fall over."

"Okay. I'll just pretend sleep here. But you watch out. I don't feel anything will happen to you, but it might."

"I'll be careful. See you later in school." He leaned down and kissed his little brother's forehead. Brian grabbed him once more; held him for a moment; and then let go. "Tad."

"What?"

"Make sure you lock the door when you go out."

"I will. I always do."

It was a warm, glorious morning. The sea air wrapped its moist high-tide magic around Tad pulling him toward the wharf. He could see the ferry drifting through the mist-enshrouded bay about eight minutes out. Waiting for the boat, Tad leaned on his bike and pretended that he could walk across the bay. Then he thought about Brian's dream and a shudder went down his back. He jumped forward when a short, skinny, dark-haired boy carrying a fluorescent newspaper bag rode up behind him and gently said, "Hi, Tad."

"Oh, hi, Rick. You scared me."

"Sorry. You looked like you were dreaming."

"Maybe I was. Say, Rick, you know Dan Stark don't you?"

"Who doesn't?"

"Have you seen him since after school yesterday?"

"No, but I don't exactly go out of my way to look for him. Why?"

"They want to arrest him for robbing Finney's store yesterday during the funeral. If you see him anywhere call the barn."

"Can I call you instead of calling the barn? If I call the barn Stark might find out and come get me."

"So you want me to call the barn so he can get me instead, right?"

"Well…nothing personal, Tad. I didn't really mean it that way."

"It's okay, Rick. You can call me or Lance."

The ferry made its turn and slammed the wide wharf hard, rocking both boys. As things settled down, paper bundles flew off the boat. Rick opened his and Tad's quickly with wire cutters.

As Tad was putting his papers into his bag he said, "Rick, Dr. Banville's on your route, isn't he?"

"Yeah."

"What's he like?"

"How do you mean?"

"Well, is he unusual in any way? Does he get angry or anything?"

"No, but I don't see him much. He leaves his money at the door and I leave his paper at the door."

"Did you ever look in his windows or anything?" Tad asked quietly.

"What's that supposed to mean?" Rick's face got very red.

"It's a pretty mysterious house. I'd love to sneak a look."

"I've been in it," Rick whispered.

"You've been in it?"

"Promise you won't tell."

"I promise. Cross my heart. What happened? What's it like?"

Rick finished organizing his papers and knelt close to Tad after looking around. No passengers were waiting or got off this early. The gangplank having stayed on the ferry, ropes were pulled in quickly in preparation for the trip down the bay to the smaller islands.

"It was about a month ago. For a long time I would go up to his house to collect and no one would answer. I'd go back after school and the money would be waiting for me in an envelope. He never gave me any tip. Once in awhile I would stop on Saturdays. I planned to ask him if he wanted me to collect some other day. I was really hoping he would give me a tip if he saw me, but the first time I saw him he said not to bother him.

"I got suspicious and curious, too. I wondered what he was doing in there, but it was too dark to see anything in the mornings. I decided to look in the windows when it started to get lighter earlier, but most of the windows were covered up, and they're high off the ground. I decided to pick a different window every day. Finally, I climbed up on his porch railing to look in a little window that was up high, but not as high as the second floor. I had to lean over a little to see in. When I did, the railing broke. I fell and I got this giant splinter in my leg." He pointed to his inner thigh just above his knee.

"I guess I screamed, even though I don't remember it, but anyway, while I was sitting there trying to get the splinter out, I looked up. Dr. Banville was standing next to me. He was pretty angry, but he didn't say anything."

"How could you tell he was angry?"

"From the way he looked. I thought smoke would come out his ears and flames out his nose. He bent down and looked at the splinter sticking through my pants. Then he picked me up. I thought he was going to drive me home. I don't even know if he's got a car. But anyway, he brought me into the house and put me on the kitchen table. The kitchen is real modern, with a dishwasher and two ovens and everything. Now Tad, promise you won't tell the rest okay?"

"Cross my heart again."

"He pulled my pants down and told me he was going to take the splinter out and that it might hurt a little. I mean, he is a doctor, so I said it was okay and lay back. He gave me a shot and cut my leg a little. I couldn't see and the shot had made it all numb. Then he showed me the splinter. It was about this long." Rick held his fingers about three inches apart.

"Then he washed my leg, and stitched it, put some stuff on it, and bandaged it. When he was all done, he said I could tell my mother and explain what I was doing when I fell. Or I could keep my mouth shut, and keep it clean and bandaged until it healed. I told him I would keep my mouth shut and I thanked him. He gave me some bandages and stuff, and said he would bring me in and take out the stitches in a few days, and if I had any trouble to come see him.

"Then he did a funny thing. He hugged me and didn't say anything. He just held me for the longest time, but don't tell anyone that, Tad. Please? I mean he didn't do anything else. Really. He just hugged me like he was desperate lonely or something. He had tears in his eyes."

"I promise, Rick. I believe you."

"Then he let me go and I didn't tell anyone until now. A while later he checked it and took out the stitches. My leg healed real good and no one knew. The funny thing is that I started to get good tips after that."

"How much?"

"A dollar a week."

"Wow, would I like him for my customer!"

"He's my customer, Tad!" Rick seemed angry.

"I know, Rick. I was just talking. Don't worry."

"Besides, I've seen him once in a while after that, and he acted like he didn't even know me. I mean, wouldn't it be normal to ask me how the leg was? But he acted like he didn't even remember. He didn't want to hold me again either." Rick looked very sad and quickly said, "Not that I wanted him to of course." It was said in a wistful whisper.

"He sounds weird," Tad suggested.

"But he's kind, too. I mean, he didn't have to help me, but he did. And he still gives me a big tip. So he may be a little weird, but he's kind, too."

"I guess so. I've got to go deliver."

"Me, too. See you in school. You won't tell, right?"

"No, it's our secret. Nobody else needs to know."

"Thanks, Tad. I know you won't tell."

Two hours later, as they rode to school, Tad told Lance about Rick and Dr. Banville after swearing him to secrecy. He left out the part about Banville hugging Rick. He figured that was nobody's business, and it could really hurt Rick if it got out. He had trouble enough being really poor, and really dumb, and funny-looking. The kids always made fun of skinny Rick and his fat mother.

"I told Rick to watch out for Dan Stark and call us if he sees him."

"If we tell all the kids, that'll be over two hundred eyes. Nobody on this island can hide from that. Not even Stark."

"I don't want him jumping out at me some dark night," Tad replied, thinking of Brian's warning. "We have to get him. Not to change the subject, but I guess you won't want to go see Mr. Sage this afternoon."

"Of course I want to. I've got six tickets left. How many you got?"

"Seven. You going?"

"No. Mom won't let me go anywhere."

"You can't go through your whole life being protected."

"That's not fair. I'm not hiding from anybody," Lance yelled. Then he was quiet again. "It's just that Mom is going uptown on the four-fifty boat to see Dad. She doesn't want to worry about me. That's all."

"We'll be back by then."

"I told her we just wanted to sell after school today, but she said no and that is that."

"Okay, I'll go alone."

"Not a good idea."

"Five tickets is a good idea, and you have to risk a little in life. That's how you have adventures. A guy has got to have adventures."

"That's usually how we get into trouble, Tad."

* * *

By two-thirty, a heat barrier surrounded the eighth-grade classroom. It seemed as if the humidity had sealed the open windows. No breeze could break through. What a breeze could not penetrate, a wasp could.

It landed on Tad's notebook. Tad raised his heavy Social Studies book to kill it, thought better of it, and decided to watch it instead. Intrigued by its yellow-jacketed boldness, Tad placed his fingers on his notebook very slowly. The wasp crawled toward him. Finally, it crawled across his knuckles with silent tickling feet. It was having an adventure unaware of how close it came to death. Tad figured wasps needed adventure, too.

As the rest of the class was involved with the geography of Asia, the wasp had taken a liking to the geography of Tad's right hand and wrist. Losing interest in the mountains between Afghanistan and Pakistan, Tad took time out for biology. He found it hard to believe that something so small and wildly beautiful could cause such pain. Tad was sure that he and the wasp had a diplomatic understanding that he wouldn't be stung.

It slowly crawled higher up Tad's forearm. Wending its way back and forth through the sweaty light-haired rain forest opposite Tad's elbow, it made it under the shade of his shirtsleeve. Tad began to get nervous. He could no longer see the wasp, but he could feel it.

Lance noticed that Tad was acting oddly. There was a lot of sweat on his forehead, and he seemed to be looking down his shirt. He was squirming slightly.

"Tad, what's the matter?" he whispered.

Tad threw him a painful look, but said nothing. The wasp had almost reached his shoulder. Several of the students, hearing Lance, turned toward Tad.

The wasp began exploring the highlands of his collarbone and was nearing his throat. Tad held his head up high, looking very attentive to Mr. Nelson, who had just asked for attention. This, more than anything, worried Lance. He leaned closer to Tad causing his chair to slide across the highly waxed old wooden floor. As he landed in a pile of humiliation, he looked up at Tad, who was still staring straight ahead and perspiring heavily.

"Lance, what is your problem?" Mr. Nelson asked.

"I'm sorry, Mr. Nelson. I slipped. I think there's something wrong with Tad. I was just trying to find out what it was."

"Be seated, Lance. Tad, is there something wrong?"

The class turned to face him. Tad had turned quite red and seemed to be melting. He continued to stare toward the front. Mr. Nelson walked up to him. A girl near the front of the room began to nervously giggle and was joined by several others.

"Tad Callant, I asked you a question." Mr. Nelson's tone meant business.

"There's a wasp in my shirt," Tad whispered.

The class began to talk all at once. Lance stood up again filled with concern. So did Becky Bridges.

"Class!" Mr. Nelson bellowed.

This new sound weapon seemed to drive the wasp out of his shirt and onto the side of his throat. The class let out assorted gasps, screams, and snickers. As the wasp moved to the side of Tad's neck, Lance jumped forward, slapped it hard, and knocked Tad to the floor. The dead wasp fell onto his knuckles.

"You didn't have to hit it so damn hard!" Tad yelled, rubbing his neck.

"I got it, didn't I?" Lance yelled back.

As Mr. Nelson tried to establish order, the bell rang. There was a sudden rush for the door. "Clean up first!" Mr. Nelson yelled. A few papers from the floor were placed into the basket. Two chairs were placed on desks. The class escaped from the oven of learning.

Tad picked himself up and walked over to Mr. Nelson, who had beckoned him.

"Are you all right, Tad?"

"Yes, sir."

"Just how did it get into your shirt?"

"I was watching it walk around my hand and arm, and it just kept going. I didn't know what to do."

Mr. Nelson motioned for the boys to leave. Sitting down, he looked across the empty mess of a room, shook his head, and wondered if perhaps it was time to retire.

Once outside, Tad and Lance both began talking at once and then began laughing.

"Did...did you see the look on Nelson's face when you clobbered me?"

"No, I was too busy."

"He thought you'd gone crazy. I don't think he saw the wasp at all."

"At least we got out almost on time for a change. Maybe we ought to try that every day."

"Yeah, you get the wasp on Monday and I get to clobber you."

"No, thanks. I'm sorry I hurt you."

"I'm okay. Sore, but okay."

"You have a red hand mark. You still going to see Mr. Sage?"

"Might as well. I won't be long."

"You going up by the pond?"

"No, I think I'll go straight up Central and down his driveway."

"I think it's going to rain. Watch out for Dan."

"Don't worry," Tad called back over his shoulder.

As Tad passed the road to the towers near the pond on his left, and Cross Street on his right he looked into the woods wondering where Dan Stark could be hiding. It started to sprinkle. For the next quarter mile he felt like the wasp was back in his shirt. Would Stark suddenly spring out and start attacking him? Neither Lance nor Brian could save him now. The rain got heavier and the wind had picked up. He ignored it.

Tad realized how ridiculous his thoughts were. Stark didn't even know he had been in the store. He gained control of his emotions by thinking about Judy, and about her canoe somewhere down the stream. And he thought about standing absolutely naked in front of her and how he enjoyed that. He had enjoyed thinking about it over and over, and each time he thought about it the same thing happened, and he enjoyed that, too. "Just like now," he said to no one in particular and reached down and rearranged himself on the bicycle seat.

Just as his dreams were becoming pleasant, he had to get off his bicycle because the hill had become so steep. When he passed Water Street, he felt he was outside enemy territory. The rain had developed into a squall and he had trouble seeing. Soon he was dripping onto the narrow driveway to the old Madison place and shivering a little. It had gotten quite dark.

The front door was open. Tad knocked and laughed at himself. "Dumb. Real dumb," he said and let himself into the house. Walking through the living room, he checked the dining room, and walked into the kitchen. The back door was shut. Spotting a short set of stairs next to the refrigerator, he soon found himself on the landing above the short staircase from the living room. He continued up the stairs.

On the second floor he made a quick check of the four bedrooms and the bathroom. Everything was neat and seemed to be in order, but no Mr. Sage. Starting up to the third floor, he figured he better let Mr. Sage know he was coming. He didn't want to frighten the old man. He stomped on the steps and went up quickly.

The third floor was very bright after the almost total darkness of the second floor. Tad couldn't see Goat Island. The wind was driving the rain against the windows. Mr. Sage's paints and easel were in the same place they had been before. The canvas showed a sketch of a scene beyond the cliff. Tad wasn't impressed.

"Maybe you're in the cottage. Maybe I should leave a note for you, Mr. Sage."

Tad looked for a pen or pencil and one of Mr. Sage's pads of paper. The paint case seemed to be brand new, so was the paint. "What do you mix your paint on, Mr. Sage? There's no palette here." His mother had tried painting and given it up, laughing as her children expressed their opinions of her talent. Tad went down to the second floor. "Where do you keep all those pads? Pencil, here pencil."

There was nothing on the bureau or the tables on the sides of the bed in the only obviously occupied bedroom. Tad spotted a knapsack and looked inside. Mostly clothes. "Why haven't you hung these up, Mr. Sage?" The left-hand side pocket held a flashlight. The right-hand side pocket held an automatic pistol. "What have we here, Mr. Sage? It's pretty heavy. What are you doing, Tad Callant?" he muttered. Realizing what this would look like to anyone stepping into the bedroom, he replaced the gun and decided to forget the note. "Why do you need a gun, Mr. Sage?" He left the room, used the bathroom quickly, and left the old house.

The squall had rapidly moved across the island. Walking through the brambles, he noticed that the front door of the ancient cottage was slightly open. The door to the bedroom where he first met Periander Sage four days ago was closed. Tad placed his ear against it, and hearing nothing, he slowly opened it.

"Nobody home this time." He looked behind the door to be sure. The floorboards behind the door appeared to be cleaner than the others. "You're too curious for your own good," he whispered. "That's what Mom always says. She's got that right, too." He knelt down and pried one of the boards up with his fingers. He couldn't make out anything below.

He pried other boards up. Some large boxes or something were there in the crawlspace below the cottage at the back. Deeper into the crawlspace it was very dark.

Tad wiggled down through the hole he had made. The dirt floor of the crawlspace sloped downward toward the rear of the cottage where it looked like a full grown man could stand up straight. There didn't seem to be anything else in the cellar except some large boxes. It looked like a little of the rock wall had fallen in at the back of the foundation.

"Tad, you are in deep shit if you're caught here," he whispered. He crawled out of the hole and quickly replaced the boards. He wiped off his jeans and noticed that one spot over his knee was ripped a little. "How did you do that?"

He heard voices. Tad wondered if it could be Dan Stark and his friends. He made his way back to the cottage door. Keeping low, he went outside and slowly pulled the door closed. Crawling through the bramble patch he saw Periander Sage walking toward the large house with two men he didn't know. Tad held his breath and waited until they had gone inside.

"You still owe me for the tickets, Mr. Sage." Tad ran to the corner of the large house and then boldly walked to the front door and knocked. One of the men spotted him and pointed. Periander Sage turned, smiled, and beckoned Tad inside.

Sage took out his wallet and handed Tad the money. Tad gave him the tickets. Sage wrote: "Received groceries. Thank you. Come Monday. Another list."

"Okay." Tad nodded toward the men. "Is everything all right?" he asked mouthing the words silently.

Sage wrote again. "Plumbers. Broken pipe somewhere. No water."

Tad remembered flushing the toilet and couldn't remember if he heard it fill up again. Tad nodded and said, "I have to get along. I'll be back Monday. Thank you." On the way out he noticed his wet footprints on the stairs going to the second floor. With a quick, nervous wave, he walked outside.

Reaching his bike, he realized that the men must have seen it as they came down the driveway, but why didn't they mention it? He spotted one of the plumbers heading for the cottage. Tad hid in the wooded area next to the carriage house. The man reappeared. "Why would a plumber go in there?" Tad whispered.

Curiosity was building, but a tiny spark of fear began to grow within him, quickly consuming his curiosity. He wondered if he left wet marks in the cottage. Of course, he did. As Tad burst back through the woods to his bike, the spark grew into a raging monster. Unable to control his shuddering or explain his fear, he felt he couldn't go fast enough.

Almost losing control twice on the wet steep hill, his bike seemed to have developed a mind of its own. It flew past woods and school aiming for home. It didn't stop until Tad was in his own backyard. He went into Lance's house. Lance was watching cartoons with Jackie and Mickey. Life was normal. Everything was okay. Tad took a deep breath and realized how good it felt.

As soon as he could, he took Lance upstairs and explained everything to him while trying to get dry with a towel Lance had thrown at him. Tad put on one of Lance's shirts.

Lance thought about what Tad had told him. He was very quiet for a while. He got up and paced back and forth. Then, as he usually did in situations like this, well not exactly like this, he turned and looked straight at Tad. He was doing his lawyer act.

"We have several things going on here. First, we have Banville, who is weird. He may or may not be a murderer. He did sort of threaten Mr. Finney. He sort of threatened Rick, but not really. First, he sort of threatens and then he pays them money. That's weird. We don't know much about him except he is a doctor, and he was sick somehow, and he works on a project of some kind. Then we've got Mr. Sage, who is weird, too."

"No, he's not. He's nice," Tad said.

"He's weird. Just listen. He may or may not have strange boxes in his little cottage."

"I saw them," Tad argued.

"I didn't. He either has them or maybe he doesn't know they are there. The plumbers may know about the black boxes, but they may not. But they may not be plumbers. Maybe they put all that stuff in there a long time ago, and broke his pipe so they could come back to get the stuff, and then they killed Mr. Sage."

"He's still alive, jerk."

"Possibly."

"You're crazy."

"Okay, but it's possible." He started pacing again. "Then we have Sage and his gun; an artist with no paintings, and no palette; and they must have seen your bike; and maybe your footprints; but didn't say anything about it. If they saw your footprints, they will know everywhere you have been in the house and the cottage, too. Maybe Mr. Sage was their prisoner and they had a gun on him when he was writing to you."

"They didn't have guns."

"It's possible, though."

"Ohhh," Tad said, raising his arms in the air. He threw the towel at Lance and stood up ready to leave.

"Then we have Dan Stark, who is a real problem."

Tad spun around and walked back. "That I agree with you about."

"And he may have an electronic bug which may belong to Banville."

"And then we have other bugs," Tad said. "Wasps, a million wasps flying around looking for revenge. Looking for Lance Deiter, the killer. Buzz." He swung his hand near Lance's head and Lance flinched and threw up his arms.

Checking around his bedroom for possible wasps, he said, "I don't think you're taking me seriously."

"It's your idea I don't take seriously."

"We've got to sort this stuff out. What better way than to use an intelligence unit?"

"Now we're the CIA."

"All we gotta do is get the gang to hang out in the woods up there tomorrow to learn what they can. They can work in shifts."

"Not a good idea, Lance."

"Why not?" His voice rose and cracked. Lance was a little aggravated.

"I don't know. I guess I'd just like to keep it all secret for a little while longer. What if we're wrong and everyone is okay? We'd look awful stupid to our friends, and have a lot of people mad at us, including our families. We promised Mr. Sage we wouldn't say anything about him, and I sure wouldn't want Dr. Banville mad at us, or our mothers."

Lance sat quietly staring at the floor.

"You see what I mean, don't you?" asked Tad.

"Yeah, but this whole thing is beginning to get to me. I'd like to have something figured out. It's a real good mystery."

"Well, let's go back and see Mr. Sage now. Maybe we can get some answers."

"You said you were scared. Are you sure you want to go back?"

"Nothing really bad happened. I was scared, but I don't know why. I just kind of talked myself into being scared. What about your mother?"

"She won't be back until the eleven o'clock boat, and Jackie's going down to rehearsal at the church hall with your family soon. In fact, wait a minute." He walked down the hallway and spoke quietly to one of his sisters. Then he stood at the head of the stairs. The television was shut off. He came back into the bedroom. "Okay, let's go. By the way, my handprint is gone from your neck."

"Wonderful," Tad spat.

The sun was breaking through the clouds over Lassiter. Within a half hour the boys were riding down the root-strewn driveway. Before they got to the house, Tad pointed to where they could hide their bikes. Then they made their way through the bushes to the spot where Tad had hidden earlier.

"The front door is closed," Tad said.

"That doesn't mean a thing. Why are we hiding? Let's go see him," Lance urged.

"Do you think it's all right? You said they'd know where I went."

"Let's do it. Be brave. Besides, Tad, they weren't my footprints." He grinned.

Lance's determination bothered Tad. Lance was never determined about anything except when he acted like some big shot. At the front door, they looked in the window and saw no one. Tad tried the door and pushed it open. They entered the living room. Tad pointed to the stairway. Lance shrugged and followed him. No footprints could be seen on the stairs. Just as they reached the first landing Periander Sage appeared above them. He had his sleeves rolled up and had paint on his hands. He looked ten feet tall. Out came the pad. "Very busy. What can I do for you?"

"You promised that we could see some of your paintings," Tad said. "If this is a bad time, we could come back later."

Sage smiled and motioned them up the stairs. The third floor seemed to be on fire because of the sunlight now bursting through the rhododendron bush and the retreating clouds. Several paintings of the ocean were lined up against the walls. Tad couldn't believe his eyes. He glanced quickly at Lance who was slowly shaking his head back and forth. The paintings were well done and obviously quite fresh.

"How could you get all of these done so soon?" Tad asked, almost to himself.

"Work quite fast," Sage wrote.

"Super fast," Tad whispered.

"May I use your bathroom?" Lance asked.

Sage nodded. Lance went down to the second floor.

"May I watch you work?" Tad asked.

The old man sat down at his easel. His fingers were obviously quite familiar with the brush and his eye with color. Something about the man bothered Tad, but he couldn't figure out what it was. Maybe it was the fact that he was using a well used palette. After watching him for a few minutes, he heard the toilet flush downstairs. He walked around near the canvas so the old man could see him. Sage looked at him with cold gray eyes.

"I have a confession to make. I didn't go right home this afternoon. I was worried about you and I stuck around to make sure you were all right. I saw one of the plumbers come out of the cottage. Is everything okay?"

"Nothing to be worried about. Just a leak," Sage wrote.

"I thought the leak was in the house."

"Water pressure was down. Found broken pipe in cottage. Water everywhere."

"Did you see their truck?"

"Went with them to help get tools. Saw you when we came back."

Lance entered looking troubled.

"Are you all right?" Sage wrote when he saw him.

"Yeah, just my stomach, I guess. We really should be going, Tad."

Tad nodded and turned to Sage. "I really like your paintings. I'm glad you're all right. We'll be over Monday."

Sage smiled and nodded as the boys left. Lance started to talk as they went down the stairs, but Tad put his finger to his lips. Once outside Lance followed Tad back to the bushes.

"What's the matter?" Lance asked. "He couldn't hear us."

"We don't know if he's alone. Besides that, he just lied to me. He said there was a broken pipe in the cottage. I pretended to go along with him, but Lance, there was no water in the cottage when I was there."

"When I went to the bathroom, I really went into his room and looked for his gun. I couldn't find it, Tad. I searched his pack and all over the room real fast, but no gun. Are you sure you saw it?"

"Saw it? I held it in my own two hands."

"Let's go look in the little house."

"He might see us."

"Can't see it from the third floor, and we could say that we wanted to see what the water did."

"There isn't any water. He's lying. But let's go see. I'll show you the boxes."

The boys made their way back through the bramble patch to the side of the cottage. Watching the second floor windows of the big house, they quickly made their way to the open door.

"Boy, I'll say there was water damage in here! What a mess! It sprayed the ceilings and the walls. It's still wet. The floor is covered, too."

"It wasn't like this before. I swear. Really!"

"Let's look for those boxes."

Tad went into the bedroom. Lance followed him in and they shut the door. "You can't tell which boards were cleaned off now that the water covered everything, but I can tell. It's here." He tried to lift the boards. They didn't move.

"What's the matter?"

"Somebody nailed the boards down again."

"I don't see any fresh nails."

"I don't care. These are the boards that came up before."

"Taad." Lance drew out his name. "Are you sure about all this? I mean, you say you saw a gun and there was no gun. You say there are no paintings, but there are good paintings and a lot of them. You say no water. My knees are soaked. Now you say the floor comes up and it doesn't. You say it has been nailed down, but there aren't any new nails."

"Would I lie to you?"

Lance laughed. "Be serious." Then seeing Tad's eyes he said, "I don't know what to think, Tad. I hope you aren't just pulling a big joke on me because I clobbered you. Or maybe I was thinking too much about Dan Stark and you wanted to get my mind off him."

"I know it looks like I'm lying, but damn it, I'm not. I don't know how he knew I knew these things or why he changed them, but I did see them, and I saw them just the way I told you. He must have seen my footprints."

"You didn't hit your head or anything?"

"No!" Tad yelled.

"Maybe the water pipe broke before you came."

"No, it didn't. I was here. It was dry."

"Then the floor and ceiling aren't wet, and I'm seeing things."

"It broke, all right, and it sprayed water all over the place, or someone sprayed water all over the place. Don't you see, Lance? They knew I was here and they knew what I saw, and they fixed it all up to make a liar out of me if I said anything. I'd look stupid. That's what they wanted."

"They did a pretty good job of it, whoever they are. All I see is an old painter who had some troubles with his house. A man who wants to be left alone. And a man who is being bugged by two nosy kids. One of the kids is making accusations that he can't back up."

"Well, he said the plumbers had a truck, and it must have come down on the car ferry and gone back on the car ferry. Let's go ask Jimmy. He should be home by now. He'd remember the truck."

"Okay. What color was it?"

"I never saw it."

"It wasn't in the driveway?"

"No, it must have been out on the road, but I didn't see it there either. Besides, how would Mr. Sage get in touch with the plumbers if he can't talk or hear? I never thought of that before. He'd probably say there were no plumbers at all, and that he fixed the pipes himself. He told me about the truck when you were downstairs. You never read the note and he kept it."

"I bet he'll only say the pipe in the little house broke and he was able to fix it. Let's see if the water is still on."

Lance went into the other room and turned on the water. There was no water. He looked under the sink and turned a valve. Water shot out of a crack in the pipe and covered the ceiling and walls. "See! No plumbers."

"No plumbers," Tad repeated, "and I'm the only one who saw them. Let's get out of here. I'm all mixed up."

"You look ready to cry," Lance said as he shut off the water.

"Get out of here, damn it!" Tad shouted pushing the slightly taller boy toward the door.

"Don't get so pissed. I believe you, sort of. Nobody else will."

As they walked back to their bikes, Tad was unusually quiet. He picked up his bike and rode off without waiting for Lance.

"I really do believe you," Lance yelled, "but I mean it when I say no one else would. So there's no point in using my plan. That reminds me. We have to see Linderman in the morning. Do you want to tell him about this?"

Tad remained quiet as they coasted down the hill. Near the bottom he said, "It just isn't worth it. We can't win anyway. I just want to forget the whole thing."

"Aren't you curious at all?"

"Not anymore."

"What about Banville?"

"Forget him."

"You're kidding."

"No, I'm not. I'm Tad Callant. I just turned fourteen years old last week. I'd like to become fifteen years old. Until today, I liked who I was and where I lived. Someday I may live somewhere else. Someday I may do a lot of things. Joining the FBI or the CIA is not in my plans for when I get older. If I don't plan to do it later, I sure don't plan to do it now. We're in over our heads, Lance. I think Mr. Sage is somehow trying to show us that. I don't know what he is up to, but it is checkmate. I have no place to turn."

"I'd still like to know why all this is happening."

"Find out for yourself."

Until they reached Tad's front yard, not another word was spoken. Tad was hurt and angry. He felt betrayed by Mr. Sage and maybe even by his closest friend. Lance was impressed by what Sage had done, and was more curious than he had been before. Mickey ran down the steps with Brian right behind him.

"You'll never guess what I just heard," Mickey yelled.

"They're gonna get…they're gonna get Dan Stark!" Brian squealed.

"Let me tell," Mickey said. "We were down at the hall and the Captain came in looking for your mother, Lance, but she was uptown. Anyway, I heard him tell Mom that tomorrow they're going to call in the volunteers and go through the woods. They're going to find Stark's shack and arrest him."

"Great," Lance said. "Want to go, Tad?"

"No! I don't know. Maybe."

"They will get him won't they, Tad?" Brian's eyes were pleading, as he looked up at his big brother. He grabbed his hands. Then he pulled Tad down and whispered, "I don't think they're going to find him. He isn't here."

"Sure," Tad said, lifting Brian up into his arms. "They'll get him. Somebody'll get him. That kind of evil guy can't exist in this world too long. Somebody'll get him."

"But I feel inside like somebody maybe already did," Brian whispered in Tad's ear. "But that's dumb. I don't know why I feel that way."

"What do you mean?"

"I don't know. It's like some idea is tickling my brain again. I just don't think we have to worry any more."

"Of course not," Tad said, wondering what his little brother's strange powers really felt this time. "We will just worry about tickling." He began tickling Brian until they were both on the ground wrestling and laughing. Mickey looked on with disdain on his lips and longing in his soul.

CHAPTER SEVEN

SATURDAY MORNING

As Tad approached the Shadik house with the Saturday morning paper, he looked for the prearranged signal. As usual now, the lobster buoy was in the window. Week after week had gone by with old Mr. Shadik blasting him out. First, it was for not knocking on the door to collect for the newspaper. When Tad knocked on the door, Mr. Shadik blasted him out for waking him up. When Tad suggested that Mr. Shadik just leave the money in the doorway, the old lobsterman had shrugged at first. Then he said that he wanted to get the island news fresh, and he couldn't find the real island news in the Lassiter paper.

Finally, they agreed on the signal. If the buoy was in the window Tad would knock. If it wasn't there he would come back later. They also agreed that Tad would take the buoy down to make sure Mr. Shadik didn't forget to do so. Mr. Shadik was pleased with the arrangement and hadn't missed a Saturday to put the buoy in the window yet.

"Haul yourself in here, boy," the familiar raspy voice called. He sounded unusually happy this morning.

Tad opened the door and walked into the dark, cluttered living room. As he took the buoy out of the window and placed it on an old shelf, the slight smell of gas and old cigar smoke made him uncomfortable. Secretly, he wondered why the house hadn't blown up.

The old man turned his wheelchair toward Tad and said, "Sit down. It's all ready." Tad obeyed, wondering what was all ready. This was something new.

Shadik wheeled back to the stove, turned, and came to the table, trying to hide a smile. He lifted a plate from his thighs and placed home-fried potatoes, sausages, fried eggs, and toast in front of Tad. He then turned and took a plate for himself and put it on the table. Wheeling to the refrigerator, he took out a half gallon of milk and a bottle of ketchup.

"Eat up, boy. I know you ain't had nothin' to eat yet, so I thought I'd surprise you." His face burst into a huge smile. His teeth were worn down on one side, giving his face an odd twist. Tad's mouth was open as he really looked at Shadik. He had put on a clean red-and-blue plaid shirt, and clean, but well-worn jeans. His white hair was combed for the first time that Tad could remember. This was a celebration of some kind. It was important to the old man.

"Eat, boy. I was up with the sun, same as you, and we need strength early in the day. 'Specially lobstermen like you and me."

Tad ate. He was surprised at how good it all tasted.

"Now tell me what's happenin' on Feather Island today."

Between mouthfuls Tad said, "They're blowing the horn this morning to get everyone to search for Dan Stark and the guys that hang with him. He broke into Finney's store during the funeral, and he threatened Lance Deiter with a knife just outside the store. He told him his father was going to die, and then he'd get Lance's sisters."

"That bastard should have been used for bait the day he was born. Wher're they lookin'?"

"He's supposed to have a shack somewhere between Cross and Water Streets. I guess they'll look up there."

"Won't find him there. No shack up there unless it's brand new. Up 'til the diabetes took my leg last winter, I hunted that whole section year after year. Nothin' but deer and deadfalls up there. They'd do better over near the towers. Fact is, I think Dan was one of the boys who built the shack there when he was a teenager. Bunch of boys built it. Used to drink up there and use it durin' huntin' season. Hunted out of season, too. Must be where he is now. Ain't no other place 'ceptin' summer places. Can see the shack from Tower One I used to be told. Ain't never been able to make it up to the top floor myself. Too chunky."

"Where is it exactly?" Tad asked. His eyes were shining.

"Know the stream below the pond?"

"Sure."

"Ever been down it?"

"No. We've been in the pond already though. Lance and me. First in."

"Not surprised. Used to be first in myself at your age. Well now, let's see how I can explain it. If you take that dirt road before the pond road you come to the road to the towers. You probably know that. After you cross the stream bridge you go maybe a hundred yards east toward the cliffs. Then you turn north into the woods 'bout another hundred yards. Shack sits in a clearing surrounded by a stand of spruce. Clearing may not be so clear now."

"I'll tell the Captain. Thanks, Mr. Shadik."

"No thanks needed. 'Bout time they got rid of that scum. Deiter's a friend of mine. Stark had no right to threaten his family with him so sick and all. I just wish I could walk. I'd have a new batch of lobster bait. I mean it! How is Deiter anyways?"

"He should be coming home from the hospital sometime this weekend. I don't think he's too good, though."

"Won't last the year. I prob'ly won't either if my son has his way." Tad looked surprised. "Wants to put me in one of them dainty rest homes on the mainland with all of them old biddies always buttin' into my privacy."

In a high pitched voice he said, "'Time to come and have tea with us, Mr. Shadik.' I'd sooner die. He says I can't take care of myself properly. Prop-er-ly, he says. Prop-er-ly. How's that meal, boy?"

"Great."

"There. Anyone who can cook the way I do can take care of himself properly. Used to take care of my son prop-er-ly, but he's forgotten. Prop-er-ly. But then my son would say I shouldn't be eatin' this stuff. Hell, I ate it all my life. Ain't about to change now. Tastes good don't it?"

"It sure does." Tad cleaned his plate.

"Ain't got no more. Can't eat as much as I used to. Don't buy too much at a time. Besides, I have to take care of myself prop-er-ly." He pronounced each syllable separately and prop-er-ly.

"I'm full and I've got to finish collecting. It really was good, and I hope you never leave the island."

"Here's mine."

As Tad reached into his pouch to give the man a quarter in change Shadik shook his head. "Keep it. It ain't much and I ain't got nobody to give anythin' to anymore."

"Thanks, Mr. Shadik. Thanks for everything."

"Now, I've got to get this place clean as a whistle by noon. My pro-per son's comin' on the eleven-fifty boat. Wants to send me to a rest home. Don't ever do that to your father, Tad Callant. Promise me that."

"I promise." Tad was unable to envision his father ready for a rest home. "Is there anything I can do to help you?"

"Nope. I can handle everythin'. 'Specially my son. Besides, I've got Mrs. Holmes from across the street comin' over to put on a show for him. She'll fix up the place just dandy. We're goin' to tell him that we're gettin' hitched. I mean, me bein' a poor widower and her bein' a poor widow, well, we was made for each other. Cost us a lot less with one house. "

"Are you really getting married?" A big smile filled Tad's face. He liked the idea and his mother would love to hear this news.

"Hell no, but we'll tell him that. Claudia and me, we're just goin' to live in sin." With that he let out a big roar. At the same time he farted, his eyes watered, and his nose began to run. Tad burst out laughing and winked. Shadik winked back as Tad closed the door shaking his head.

Tad rode down Main Street where he made two more stops. Planning to stop in at the fire barn, he changed his mind when he saw Periander Sage walking down to the wharf holding onto a sawed-off oar he was using as a walking stick. Tad pulled up beside him.

"Going to town?"

Sage stopped. The boat was five minutes out. Out came the pad. "Ran out of paint."

Angry still, Tad said, "I hope you don't have any more trouble with your plumbing."

Sage looked at him carefully and saw the hurt in the boy's eyes. Tad didn't know whether to yell, cry, or run away. His eyes hit the sandy street.

Sage wrote and took his time. Tad didn't raise his head until Sage handed him the note. "Some things difficult to understand, Tad. You are too curious for your own good. I cannot allow you to be harmed."

"How could I be harmed?" Tad spat out. "I was only looking for you."

"I know. Mistake. Had forgotten extra tickets until I saw you. Cannot explain everything now. Am in no danger, but strange things have happened. Stay out of it. Will tell you what I can, when I can. I promise."

"Who are the men? The plumbers?"

"What men? What plumbers?" Sage asked for his notes back. Tad gave them to him reluctantly. Sage smiled and placed them into his pants pocket. Placing his hand on Tad's shoulder, he gently squeezed, and then, limping a little, he walked to the boat which had docked. It was seven thirty-five.

Tad felt confused, bitter, and happy that Sage had shown some concern for him. His curiosity zoomed again. Sage must have walked into something when he came to the house. That was the only answer. He wondered about Sage's gun though. There were so many questions that he decided to postpone thinking about them. First things first. He rode over to the fire barn.

He saw the familiar figure at the big roll top desk. "Hi, Cap."

"Good morning, Tad."

"I hear you might go after Dan Stark today."

"That's right."

"I was just talking to Mr. Shadik on my paper route. He says there's no shack between Cross and Water Streets. He says he hunted up there last year, but he told me where he thinks the shack might be."

"Where is that?" The Captain put down his pipe and walked over to the map of the island. "Can you show me?"

Tad explained what Shadik had told him and looked carefully at the map. "I haven't been in this section, but it must be about here."

"Yes, I should have thought to talk to Shadik. I always thought that the rumor of the other shack was probably started by Stark himself. We tried to find it now and then. Never did. This information could make my day a lot easier. I'll take a few of the boys up earlier instead of calling everyone out."

"Can Lance and I go? We'd like to see him get caught."

"No. How would I ever explain that to your parents? And no need to let Stark know you boys are involved. He's dangerous enough."

"Yeah, I guess you're right. Well, I better be going."

"Thanks a lot, Tad. I'll thank Shadik, also. We'll try that place first."

Tad started off slowly, but was soon racing up Maple. He jumped off his bike and leaned it against his porch. Tearing through the backyard, he burst through Deiter's back door.

"My, you are in a hurry this morning, Tad. You ready for breakfast?"

"Already had it, but maybe I can squeeze in a little more." He eyed the stove. Pancakes. "Maybe."

"Your mother must have gotten up early this morning."

"I ate with Mr. Shadik while I was collecting. He made me breakfast."

"What did you have?" asked Lance, entering the kitchen.

"Home fries, fried eggs and sausage. He's a great cook."

"Boy, maybe I should come with you next Saturday."

"Well, I guess that puts me in my place," Sylvia said. "I'll have to close down the Deiter restaurant."

"No, don't ever do that," Tad said. "I didn't mean...I mean you're also a great cook."

"Mom, Tad means to say he'll take free food from anyone." Tad punched his shoulder gently.

"Don't be silly. I'm only fooling," Sylvia said.

"Not to change the subject, but Mr. Shadik told me where he thought Dan Stark might be hiding and I told the Captain. They're going to look for him up there first, and then go up into the woods if they can't find him."

"Where are they going to look?"

In one big breath Tad said, "Near the stream out of the pond, halfway between the two ponds, and just in from the tower road on the north side, near a stand of spruce. Old shack. It's complicated."

"Wow, I wonder if Judy ever saw him."

"Judy?" his mother asked. "Judy Thompson?"

"Oh, boy," Lance muttered under his breath. He looked at Tad for help.

"Judy told us that she keeps her canoe near the stream so she can paddle into the pond when no one is around."

"I see."

"I asked if we could watch him capture Dan, but he said we shouldn't get involved."

"That is very good advice. I'm going uptown on the nine-fifty to see your father, Lance. I called him last night and he said he thinks I might be able to convince the doctor to let him come home tomorrow. Now, what are you two planning today?"

"Not babysitting, I hope," Lance stated.

"On Saturday? Would I do that to you?"

"Probably."

"Oh, my poor baby. So put upon." She smoothed his hair out of his eyes and kissed his cheek. "Jackie will stay at Tad's with Mickey. In fact, I'd better get him up."

"Tad and I were planning to go over to the ball field this morning. Some of the guys wanted to start a team again. We don't know if anyone will show up, but we want to get over there by eight anyway. In fact, right away."

"Isn't it a bit early?"

"We planned it that way 'cause all the little kids will still be asleep or watching cartoons. You forgot your glove, Tad."

"I didn't forget. I wanted to tell you about what Mr. Shadik and the Captain said. I have to tell my mom where I'm going and I'll get my glove then."

"Okay."

"Are you sure you don't want more breakfast, Tad?"

"I'm really stuffed. Believe me, if I had room, I'd take the pancakes. I love great cooks." He leaned over and kissed her cheek.

"You're very smooth, Tad Callant, but I'll accept the compliment anyway. Did you compliment Mr. Shadik the same way?"

Tad turned red. "You're pretty smooth yourself, Mrs. Deiter. Come on, Lance. I have to get my glove."

"Meet you outside," Lance told him. "I better kiss her too, or life will get tough."

"Lance!"

Tad left wondering where his glove was and what Lance was up to. Walking into his kitchen he said, "Do you know where my baseball glove is, Mom?"

"You might try one of the hooks above the cellar stairs. I'm on the phone."

"So early?" He opened the cellar door and found the glove right where he had left it last fall. It had gotten a little smaller somehow.

As he came back into the kitchen his mother sat down at the table with a cup of tea and said, "The Captain and some men are going up near the pond to see if they can catch Dan Stark. Now you stay away from there. No swimming."

"How could you possibly know that so fast? Never mind. I don't really want to know. We aren't planning to swim anyway. We're going over to the ball field at the school. We may start a team today."

"Did you have breakfast?"

"Yes, at Mr. Shadik's while I was collecting. He wanted to prove to someone, maybe himself, he could cook good."

"Cook well."

"Well, anyway, his son's coming down to try to put him in a rest home on the mainland. He doesn't want to go, so he had to prove he could take care of himself prop-er-ly, properly. Mrs. Holmes is coming over to fix up the place and they'll fake his son out, so he can stay here."

"It sounds as if you've had a busy morning."

"I take after my mother. I'm surprised you haven't heard about it already."

"What makes you think I haven't?" she said with a large grin. Her eyes were bright and Tad thought she looked really healthy in spite of her constant battle to lose weight. He suddenly realized how much he loved her

"Ah, Mom."

"Now, on your way. I have to get breakfast ready for the kids."

Tad leaned across and kissed her soft face. "You're still the fastest phone in the East, and now I've kissed two beautiful ladies this morning." His mother didn't press the issue.

As he stepped outside he heard his mother ask, "Did Mr. Shadik tell you about the marriage?"

Poking his head back in, he stared at her. "No marriage. They're going to live in sin." He stepped back out laughing and shaking his head in amazement, realizing that nothing got by Mom or Mrs. Deiter, which was a major problem at times.

Lance sat on his steps punching his fist into the palm of his glove. He stood up, threw the ball, and said, "Let's go." Before Tad had a chance to say anything, Lance got on his bike and headed down A Street. At Main he stopped to let a pickup truck go by. Tad caught up to him, wondering what was going on.

"When did you hear about them making a team?" he asked.

"I didn't." He took off fast up Main Street. Tad caught up to him. "I want to see them arrest Dan Stark."

"Damn it, Lance! You can lie to your mother if you want, but you made me lie to my mother, and I don't like that."

"I know. Where can we watch from?"

"Lance, I don't think you're hearing what I'm saying."

"Okay, maybe I'm not. Maybe right now I have only one thing on my mind. Now where can we watch them? I hope they beat the shit out of him."

"Mr. Shadik said he's been told the shack could be seen from Tower One."

"That's beautiful. We can go up there and watch the whole thing, and Stark will never know it."

"Okay, but don't you ever put me in the middle again. I mean it."

"Promise. Let's go."

"Let's go up School Street," Tad suggested. "Your promises smell like shit."

"That's the long way 'round," Lance said, ignoring him.

"I know. We won't run into Cap and the others that way. Besides, I think making a team isn't such a bad idea."

"It'll have to wait until this is over."

Tad hoped it would be over soon. As they passed the school field he half-expected to see several kids warming up, but the field was empty. He could tell his mother no one showed up if she asked. At least it wouldn't really be a lie.

Before long, on the overgrown old road, they approached Tower One. It was a six-story cement tower about sixty feet high. It had been built as a navy observation and fire control tower during World War II. Towers of this sort were built all along the coast. As they approached the massive shaft, Tad remembered all the difficulties they had getting to the top last year. They had grown some. Maybe it would be easier.

The first floor was strewn with beer and soda cans, torn pieces of paper from magazines, cigarette butts and leaves. A set of narrow cement stairs led to the second floor. They raced up and then up another set of stairs to the third floor. Here they found a room similar to the first floor, but with a narrow vertical slit of a window in one wall. No more stairs were to be found. There was only a hole in the ceiling in one corner of the room where a steel ladder had once led to the top. The ladders had been removed about fifty years before, they had been told. A long section of pipe, well used for many years, leaned against the wall. The boys braced it and scrambled up.

The fourth floor was different from the rooms below. Above a four-foot wall there was a large opening on three sides of the tower. They could see for miles. Tad leaned out as far as he could to try to find the shack. "I guess we need to go up another level."

"Can't see anything?"

"I think it must be that stand of spruce over there, but I can't see any clearing."

"Let's go." Lance said. "Hold my feet." He leaned down through the hole. Grabbing the heavy pipe he pulled it up to the fourth floor where it landed with a heavy clank.

"Shhh!"

"I know. I know."

Lance pulled himself up and they braced the pipe above the hole leaning it into the hole above them. Lance started to climb. The pipe began to slip, but Tad jammed his foot against it. Lance pulled himself through the fifth floor hole. Tad placed it carefully this time and climbed it until he could pull himself up. Lance grabbed his wrists and helped him. Within a minute they had pulled the pipe to the fifth level and wedged it above the two holes below them and the stairs below that.

This time Tad went up first and rolled over onto the floor of the top level. Lance followed. Just as his hands reached the floor in front of Tad's face, the pipe slipped and fell to the third floor level. Tad grabbed Lance's forearms. Lance grabbed Tad and slowly lifted one leg over the edge working his way up. They both lay without speaking until Tad with his voice trembling whispered, "Dieter, you always do that. You're going to kill us sometime. How do you do it?"

"I think…I think it's the extra kick I give myself to make sure I get up. Thanks."

"It's a long way down. You weigh more this year. Sometime we might not be so lucky."

Lance peered over the edge, swallowed, and said, "Yeah. My blood and guts splattered on those stairs might save a lot of lives, but I'll pass on that."

"I'll put up a sign making it the Lance Deiter Memorial." From the sixth story the view was remarkable. "I'd really like my bedroom up here," Tad said.

"This would make a great bedroom." Lance looked out over the cliff. "You can see forever. I'd want an elevator against that wall though. Let's see. My bed could go there."

"That must be the shack. Look, Lance. There's the stream, and over there, just beyond that large tree, is the clearing. It really is just a shack. It looks like it's falling apart."

"I don't see anybody."

"Neither do I. What time is it?"

"Eight twenty-five."

"Cap will be here soon," Tad assured him. "I can't see School Street, but look, over by the bridge over the second stream. There's the jeep just pulling up."

"You should have brought your binoculars."

"I thought we were going to play baseball. I didn't need binoculars for that."

"Okay, okay. I said I was sorry. There they are."

Tad could make out four men moving through the brush alongside the stream. He could identify the Captain because of his hat. "They're going to pass it."

Tad wanted to crawl up onto the roof, but he couldn't figure out how to make it up to and over the wide overhang. No way!

That was really a long way down! The men stopped and pointed toward the tower. The boys ducked.

Slowly they rose and peered over the edge. The men had turned back and were headed into the spruces. Tad expected someone to come out of the shack, but no one did. The boys held their breath as the men entered the clearing and went up to the door of the shack. They flattened themselves against the shaky building and seemed to be looking through cracks in the wall. "Do you think they have guns?" Lance asked.

"I don't know. I can't tell. I expect they do. Cap will."

Suddenly, one of the men kicked the door open and they poured in. Lance was sure there was a battle going on inside, but he couldn't hear anything. "What do you think is happening?"

"Wait."

Two of the men came out followed momentarily by the two others. Dan Stark and his friends weren't with them. The men were carrying papers and cans. One man went back inside and came up with a box that they used to carry all the litter.

"Evidence," Tad said. "We better go. Maybe we can beat them back to the station."

"Okay, you go first."

"So I can catch you?"

"I'll go first." Lance swung his legs over the edge. Then he turned, and hanging by his fingers, he swung forward and let go, landing safely on the fifth floor. Tad followed in a well practiced jump. Soon they were on the third floor in one piece except for very sore fingers. Running down the stairs to the first floor, they grabbed their bikes, and raced down the hill until they came to the bridge where the jeep was parked.

"We could wait here," Lance said. "Since Dan Stark isn't with them, the Captain wouldn't mind too much."

"Since Stark isn't with them, he has to be somewhere else, and somewhere could be anywhere around here, so the Captain would still blast us out. Besides, we're not supposed to know that Stark isn't with them. Jeez, Lance! Let's get out of here. We're playing ball. Remember?"

As they were passing the Beach Shop, the tiny island department store on Main Street, the jeep passed them. Tad stopped.

"Why are you stopping?"

"We have to pretend that they captured Dan Stark. If we go bombing in there the Captain will know that we know and he'll be pissed off. We have to pretend that they have him, so we have to be scared."

"How do you think of these things? I'm dizzy just listening to you."

"Easy as falling off a pipe or lying to my mother, I guess."

The boys rode up to the barn and peeked around the corner of the jeep. The Captain spotted them. "Where is he?" Tad asked quietly.

"We didn't get him, but Shadik hit the nail on the head. We have all that's left of the stuff they took from Finney's, and several other stolen items, also. I don't know what went on in that place. It was a mess. They'll probably come back and decide to steal some more. We'll be on the watch for them. We have enough evidence for an arrest on even more charges this time."

"Why don't you put someone up there with a radio? That way you'd know when they came back."

"That's a very good idea, Tad."

"The view from Tower one should be pretty good," Lance offered. "From the top floor you can see everywhere."

The Captain looked very sternly at the boys. He lit his pipe and inhaled. With a sudden twinkle in his eye he smiled. "I guess that probably is a good place. It must be difficult to get to the top since there are no stairs. How did you do it?"

"We used a pipe that was there, but we had to . . . I mean . . . I mean this was a long time ago." Lance stopped with his mouth left open. The four men in the station burst out laughing.

Tad was angry. "You jerk."

"Playing detective can get you in a pack of trouble. Now you boys stay out of those woods for awhile until we get these guys. There is no reason for you to look for trouble. If I catch you in there, I will personally bring you home and tan your hides for your mothers. You understand me?"

"Yes, sir," they both said.

"I'll let you know when we get them. Now run along and behave yourselves. This time I mean it. It's dangerous."

As they grabbed their bikes, their cheeks were burning. Lance looked like he was ready to burst. When they were away from the barn he said furiously, "Don't say it, Tad! I know I was stupid. I am a jerk."

"I was thinking of a few other words."

"What do you want to do now?" Lance asked, hoping to change the subject.

"We could go down and see Mr. Linderman. He said he was coming on the nine-thirty."

"Not a good idea."

"Why not?" Tad asked.

"Two reasons. First, we have nothing to tell him unless we tell him about Mr. Sage. I don't think you want to do that. Second, my mother is going uptown on that boat. If she sees us talking to a stranger she'll be worried all the way uptown. Then she'll try to give me a phone call. If she gets me she'll keep asking questions until I tell her all about him. I can't hold out when she gets going."

"That's all we need. In fact, we better head for the field in case your mother or mine comes along and checks." They headed back to the school field. Tossing the ball back and forth Tad remembered Sage. "I forgot to tell you. I talked with Mr. Sage this morning on my way to see the Captain the first time. He was headed to town for more paint."

"He talked to you?"

"He wrote, like before. I told him I hoped he didn't have any more trouble with his plumbing, and he gave me this funny look."

"Like what?"

"Like he wanted to tell me all about it. He said he'd forgotten about us coming over to sell him more tickets. He said he couldn't explain anything now, but that he was in no danger and he would tell me more when he could. I mean I didn't even mention he was in danger, but he said that."

"Does he mind us coming there?"

"I think Monday's okay. He said we're too curious and he couldn't allow us to get hurt. I asked him who the plumbers were and he said, 'What plumbers?' You were right about that, all right."

"He's really smart for an old man. But you're right. Why would he say anything about us getting hurt? He's a painter. Did he say what boat he'll be back on?"

"No. And I never thought about him saying that about getting hurt. And since when can't old men be smart?"

"The stores uptown don't open before nine-thirty, so he won't be on this boat. That means that the earliest he could be back to his house, if he took Hal's taxi, would be eleven. That gives us at least an hour."

"For what?" Tad sighed.

"I've been thinking," Lance said.

"Something new."

"I still think those boxes you saw may still be under that floor. I want to go back there and see them. Now is as good a time as any."

"Here we go again."

"You got something better to do?"

"This will be the last time. Promise."

"Promise," Lance agreed. "Maybe they're filled with treasure."

"I would like to prove to somebody that I saw what I saw. The floor..."

"Okay, all we need is a large screwdriver or a pinch bar. Maybe both. I've got them at home. No point in us both going. I'll sneak home. Wait for me here on the ball field. That way if I get caught, you won't get in trouble with your mom."

"Don't get caught, but we may not need them. I forgot that the back wall was sort of crumbling."

"I'll bring them anyway. I won't get caught."

"If my mom sees you with them she'll think that we're going to break into the school."

As Lance rode off smiling, Tad waited for awhile behind the ancient school building next to the newer wing. He couldn't be seen from the road. After a short while he began to wonder why he was hiding. Looking at the ball field, he decided that forming a team was really more to his liking than all this mystery. When it was over they would have to really do it. Last year's teams were fun. Phantoms of his team took their places on the field.

Tad ran onto the infield. He would play shortstop or maybe he would pitch. After several trips around the bases to get in shape he walked over to the pitcher's mound, wound up, and threw a ball at the backstop. Racing to get it, he picked it up, pretended to catch it, and ran to first. "Out!"

"Safe by a mile," Lance shouted.

"You wish."

"I brought both. You carry the screwdriver."

The boys once more rode up School Street, keeping a close eye on the almost-hidden summer houses as they passed.

Hiding their bikes when they reached the driveway, they observed the house. It appeared to be all closed up. They quietly made their way through the brush to the cottage and listened until they were satisfied they were alone. Moving quickly and with determination, they went inside to the bedroom and shut the door.

"These boards are really close together, Tad. I don't think we can get the pinch bar between them."

"The screwdriver will leave marks. But maybe I can get close to the baseboard with it." He pried up one board just a little.

"Hold it there. Come this way a little more. Swing the end around. Good. Now let me get the bar in there."

Tad slid down further and Lance followed him with the pinch bar. It soon became evident that they were lifting more than one board.

"It's a trap door," Lance said. They were soon able to lift a section about three feet wide and five feet long.

"This is why we couldn't find the loose boards," Tad sighed. "They nailed them together with these other boards and made a door out of them. The rug covered the places where we could have pried it up easily."

"Let's lift it onto the bed," Lance suggested.

"No, leave just enough room for us to get out. Then if we have to get out fast, we'll be able to cover the hole. Why would they go to all this trouble just to make a liar out of me? It doesn't make sense."

"I don't see any boxes like you said."

"They may have taken them all. I'm going down." Tad slid into the cellar.

"I should've brought a flashlight. Can you see?"

"I can see fine. It was dark down here before, but it looks like they've knocked a bigger hole in the foundation at the back. The ground slopes down so I can stand up back here. The boxes are here like I said. They're just not stacked on top of each other anymore. They're about the size of the trunk in my attic. Larger, I guess. Come on down."

Lance jumped down into the two-foot high crawlspace. It grew to six feet as he walked toward the back of the cottage.

The boys unsnapped the latched cover on the box nearest the opening. Lifting the top, they saw a large rubber bag. Tad found a zipper and pulled it down.

Dan Stark's unseeing eyes stared into Tad's. A small purple hole was placed neatly in the center of his forehead. Tad's mouth fell open as if to mimic the corpse in front of him. The smell was quite powerful. Lance screamed and both boys ran toward the hole in the cellar wall. Not quite making it, they bent over and retched and littered the dirt floor with sausage, home fries, eggs, pancakes, and fear.

Gaining some composure, Tad covered their breakfast with dirt, ran back to the corpse, and began to zip the bag. When the zipper stuck he shut the box and latched it. Making sure, once more that all traces of their visit were covered, he pushed Lance up through the hole. Then wondering about their footprints he started to throw dirt. Finally he went up.

Lance stood wide-eyed and shaking. Tad slid the trap door into place and covered it with the rugs. Picking up the tools, he pulled Lance out of the bedroom toward the door of the cottage. Through the curtained window in the ancient kitchen door, he spotted a plain brown van sitting in Sage's front yard. Three men were walking toward them.

Tad pointed and Lance looked, but did not seem to understand what he saw. One of the men was Carl Linderman. Tad whispered that the other two were the plumbers. The three men walked silently past the door and went around to the back of the cottage. Wanting to run, the boys froze in the kitchen. They could hear the men as they entered the cellar.

"My God, they're ripe."

"One of the bags must be sealed wrong," Linderman said.

Tad knew it was the bag with the stuck zipper. He was sure they would find footprints he missed and would come up through the trap door at any time. He didn't want to get caught out front either.

"This one isn't sealed all the way," said a voice.

"Well, seal it," Linderman said, "and let's get them out of here. We've got to catch that car ferry."

"We can always catch another ferry," the first voice stated, "but if the van smells this bad, we won't even make it down the street."

The boys strained to hear what was going on. All Lance could hear was his heart beating. Tears were in his eyes. Tad saw the three men carrying one of the boxes. He watched them place it into the van ducking out of view as they came back for another. Soon, all three boxes were loaded and the van doors were closed. The three men stood near the rear of the truck talking.

"This has been a lot of work for one little bug. Drop me off below Thompson's on the way to the ferry. I have one other duty to perform." Tad's imagination was working overtime and he shook at the thoughts he was having.

As the three men drove off, tears continued to stream down Lance's face. He sat down and put his head down between his knees. Neither boy spoke. Finally, Tad said, "Come on, Lance. We've got to get out of here."

"I...I don't know if I can. I don't think I can move. I'm shaking too much."

"Come on!" Tad yelled. "If they catch us here we'll end up like Dan Stark."

"I can't."

Tad grabbed Lance's hands and pulled him up. "Come on," he whispered gently. He felt Lance really shaking all over. Tad picked up the tools, put his arm around Lance's shoulders, and guided him outside. Lance seemed to respond automatically when he found his bike.

"Let's go," Tad said.

"Let's go," Lance echoed. His eyes seemed to have a very distant look. Tad was worried about him and wondered if he had flipped out or something. Worrying about Lance kept Tad from worrying about himself. Linderman had killed three men probably just so he could give Banville back his radio, and now he was going after Judy. Not if he could help it.

On the way down Central Avenue, Lance seemed to come back to life. Complaining of a headache and looking very tired, he mentioned nothing about what they had seen. Nearing Main

Street Tad said, "I told you we were in over our heads. I told you it was a bad idea."

"You told me. You told me. I believe you now, so shut up about it. Please, Tad."

"It's not my fault. I didn't kill anybody."

"Neither did I. It's those guys, whoever they are. Damn it, Tad. They're getting away with it. I'm kind of glad because it was Dan Stark, but it's still wrong. We can't let them get away with it. They're no better than Stark."

"You'd look cute with a hole in the middle of your forehead."

Lance shuddered and Tad continued, "They're going to get Judy now too. They're probably going to kill her and her mother. You're right. We can't let that happen, but what can we do?"

"We've got to tell the captain before the ferry leaves."

Tad pondered this as they rode toward the barn. They saw the van sitting in the car ferry line just beyond the fire barn at the foot of the Island Avenue hill. It gave him an idea. "Do you really want to stop them?"

"Yeah, let's go tell."

"If we tell the captain he'll blast us out for playing detective, and if he believes us someone could get hurt or killed. It will be crowded down there. It's Saturday. He might even have to wait for a search warrant. That could take hours or maybe days. I think it has to go to court even, maybe. We've got to show him. We've got to show everybody."

"How?"

"It'll take guts for both of us."

"I haven't got many left."

CHAPTER EIGHT

SATURDAY

A crowd was building toward the wharves. The car ferry was almost in. The passenger ferry was about halfway across the bay. Saturday was an uptown shopping day. Islanders escaped the high island prices by shopping the sales in supermarkets, and large stores on the mainland, and by buying in bulk. Final details for getting their purchases picked up by those bringing cars over and back were taking place in the car ferry line above and below the fire station.

Tad shot up Island Avenue on his bike. Lance headed for the fire barn. Passing Carl Linderman walking down the hill with Judy and her mother, Tad waved, forced a big smile, let out a sigh of relief, and pushed up the hill a little more.

Lance entered the barn. The captain said, "You look as if you've been crying. Is Stark around again?"

"No, not bothering me anyway. Have you seen Tad? He was supposed to meet me here."

"No, I haven't. Now what's the matter, Lance? I haven't much time. I have to get down to meet with the car ferry captain."

"I'm sorry about this morning. I know we had no business up in the tower, but when Tad told me about the shack, we just had to go, and—"

"Here comes Tad now," the captain interrupted, "and way too fast, as usual. Holy Mother!" Jumping out of his chair, he ran to the front of the building just in time to hear a dull thud.

"I'm the one who's supposed to get excited," Lance whispered to himself.

A small crowd had assembled quickly around the van. The driver was kneeling over the boy under the bike by the rear tire. Another man was standing next to him. The captain knelt down to examine Tad.

Lance quietly opened the rear doors of the van and crawled inside. With all his might he braced himself against one of the boxes and pushed at the rear box with his legs as hard as he could. It fell onto the street next to the group of people looking at Tad. Lance jumped down.

"Captain," Tad said, actually more shaken than he expected from slamming into the van, "that box contains a dead man. Dan Stark is in one of the three boxes with a bullet hole in his forehead."

As the captain and the crowd stared from Tad to Lance and back again, Lance opened the box and started to zip down the zipper of the black bag.

"Get away from there, kid!" ordered the driver.

"What's going on here?" the captain asked, drawing his automatic.

The crowd surged in and then back as a head popped into view, lolling to one side like a marionette. Then somebody in the crowd began to scream. The two men from the van ran toward the incoming car ferry. Carl Linderman grabbed Judy's upper left arm and pulled her toward the running men.

The young deckhand, who had just climbed the wharf ladder and was operating the ramp controls, was given instruction to raise it again, and waved back onto the boat by Linderman's automatic. The three men jumped on board waving guns at the people on both sides of the cable strung across the bow. The people began to panic. The three men and Judy headed for the bridge.

Several people, determined to get off, attempted to get over the cable and onto the ramp. The ferry started to slowly back out just as the very rotund Mrs. Morey was trying to get her shopping cart up the extra foot to the ramp. With the lurch of the ferry, Mrs. Morey fell into the water.

The crowd near the van had started to run to the car ferry, partly because of anger toward the men and what they had done; partly because of Mrs. Morey's screams and foul language; partly because Judy Thompson had been forced to go with the killers; but primarily because they didn't want to miss the boat to town.

The captain looked at the boys and then at the bodies in amazement. He told Tad to just sit there for a moment. Then he looked at the ferry, walked inside the barn, and radioed the Lassiter Fire Department, which in turn contacted the police department.

When he came back outside, he closed the bag and the box once more. Another man helped him get the box back into the van. The pumpers were driven out of the station and the van was driven in. As the barn door was closing, the captain ordered Tad and Lance inside the building.

A very wet man came up to him and said, "We got Mrs. Morey out of the water. Four of us fell in doing it. I almost feel sorry for those guys with the guns if she ever gets hold of them. She's okay."

Lance whispered, "He's going to ask us about it. What will we tell him?"

"Nothing about Mr. Sage. I don't think any of this is his fault, and no one would believe us anyway."

"Okay, but what?"

"Too late."

"Now, would you mind going very slowly, and explain this whole thing to me before the police detectives get here shortly on the fireboat? They definitely will question you and they may not be nice about it. Don't leave out one little detail with me. They will probably want your mothers here when they question you."

It was obvious to both boys that he was badly shaken and that his patience with them had run its course.

"We don't really know too much about it," Tad began.

"Tell me everything you do know."

Tad started slowly, thinking his way as he went. He appeared to be scared about telling what he was about to say. "Well, after you told us to stay away from the towers, we decided to go swimming at the pond. We knew it was kind of near the towers, but it wasn't exactly at the towers," Tad emphasized. "And well, to be perfectly honest, we didn't think you'd find out."

Lance listened in fascination, wondering what they did next.

"We swam for awhile. It was really cold. Do you know near the pond that little road to the dam? After we got dressed and were coming out we saw that van. We didn't know who it was. I thought they might be coming to swim."

"I thought it might be somebody making out even though it was daytime," Lance explained, getting into the spirit of the thing. He even smiled at the thought.

"I told him it was too early in the day to make out. Anyway, we got our bikes into the brush and crawled up close to spy on them since we didn't recognize the van. Three guys were there and one was Mr. Linderman, who was a friend of Judy's. At least she thought he was. He had told her and her father he was a writer. You met him the other day when he came down to see us at the beach. He wanted to know all about the old Richards place.

He thought there might be a story in it. We didn't know much except the usual stories. Anyway, they were pulling those black bags out of the brush and putting them into the boxes."

Lance said, "We heard one of the guys say, 'Boy, this one smells bad.' They were having trouble with the zipper on one of the bags. I don't know why we didn't smell it when we went by."

Tad continued: "They got the zipper down. That's when we saw Stark's head with the bullet hole in it. They closed up the bag and shut the box. When they loaded the boxes onto the van we knew we had to get back and tell you, but I didn't think you would believe me. When we saw the van parked out front Lance thought you'd have to have a search warrant, and by then it would be too late. They would be long gone."

"So anyway, when we saw the truck in line, Tad thought up our plan of hitting the truck. And then we both thought of me opening the box in front of you." Lance was happy that he was now telling the truth.

"You feel all right?" the captain asked Tad.

"Still a little dizzy, but okay, I guess. I hit harder than I thought I would."

"Well, stick around. You'll have to repeat it all over again shortly."

"What will happen to Judy and the people on the car ferry?" Tad asked.

"I wish I knew," the captain said. "I don't know if you have been listening to the radio while we have been talking, but the Coast Guard is all tied up with a burning tanker down in Portland harbor. They won't be able to get here. The ferry could get back to the mainland I imagine. The fireboat will probably have a SWAT team on it by now, but frankly, I think they could be more dangerous to the passengers than the three men due to the waves in the bay this morning. You never heard me say that, boys. I doubt they'll use them. We'll just have to wait and see."

"A fat lot of help you are!" screamed the large, deep-throated, mustached Mrs. Morey, as she dripped into the station.

* * *

Three miles away, across the bay, the Indian Bay Lines manager received a radio message: "Indian Bay Lines, this is the car ferry. Do you read me?"

"I read you. Who is this?"

"I am the person who has control of your car ferry. Your crew is under my orders and your passengers are my hostages. I'll put the ferry captain on to confirm this. Then I have something I want you to do. If you do it, everyone will be just fine."

After a rapid question-and-answer session, the ferry captain handed the microphone back to Linderman.

"Now listen carefully. I'm sure by now that you can confirm this with the Lassiter police. Please remember that the future of a large group of hostages and your boat is in your hands. If you do exactly what I tell you within the next ten minutes, there will be no problems. Understand?"

Turning to his secretary, the manager said, "Diane, get on the phone to the cops and find out if they know anything about someone hijacking the Island Queen." Turning back he said, "I understand. What do you want from me?"

"Near the other end of the passenger ferry wharf, in front of the lobster shop, you will find a gentleman sitting in a white Dodge. Tell him the following and write it down, so you can give it to the police. Are you ready?"

"Ready."

"Tell him, 'Fish will fry,' and tell him where we are. He will have a reply for you. Get his reply straight and get it back to me within ten minutes. If you have police on the phone, tell them they should not interfere with him. Any interference will be disastrous."

"I'll do it, but if you are serious about all this, then the police are probably monitoring this channel."

"Fine. Just move."

"I'm sending someone now."

Linderman turned to the ferry captain, "Go to the center of the main channel and cut your engines."

"Are you crazy? This is a busy harbor."

"No one will bother us. I can run this boat without you if I have to."

"Okay, you'll probably sink us anyway," the ferry captain muttered. "We've got little kids and…"

"When that's done, you will go with my two men and get as many passengers as possible locked in the cabin next door. The rest will assemble on the deck below where my men will cover them."

"What about me?" Judy asked.

"You'll stay here in the cabin for the moment. I have something to explain to you."

"I'll bet you do."

In mid-channel, the engines were shut down. Other than a few sailboats and other small craft, the bay was quiet. The fireboat had passed by them and docked at Feather Island. It was now coming back toward them.

Alone on the bridge with Linderman, Judy said, "I don't understand this at all. I don't understand you. After our talk the other day, I thought I knew you. I even liked you. I liked you a lot. Now here you are holding people hostage, kidnapping me, and responsible for three murders."

Linderman lowered his weapon. "Judy, please believe me when I say I didn't want any of this to happen."

"Of course not. No one likes to get caught."

"I mean more than that. I really do like you and your mother. I really was going to deliver you safely to your aunt and uncle. I wanted nothing more than to see you a little happier and safe."

"Why wouldn't I be safe on the island? It's my home. This has something to do with my father's death doesn't it? And Banville. I'll bet that's it. You work for Banville. You do his dirty work. Just what is he up to? And why did Daddy have to die? I hate you!"

"I'm still the guy who sat in your truck and at your table. I can't tell you anything about all this now. I'm just asking you to trust me."

"Whoever you were doesn't count anymore. You came to the island posing as a writer and we became friends. My mother and I welcomed your generous offer to drive us up north. Then, because of two brave boys, you've kidnapped me with a lot of other innocent people. I discovered that my newly trusted friend heads a group of killers. Terrorists! I no longer care about who you were. He's gone, just as my father is gone. Just as my dreams are gone."

"I never promised you more than a ride to your aunt's."

"I know! I hate myself for being so stupid to think that there could be more. I never want to see you again. As soon as I'm free, I'm going to tell the police everything. They'll get you and you'll never hurt anyone again. Those boys were right all along about Banville, my father, and poor Mr. and Mrs. Finney."

"Not quite. And you'll tell none of this to the police."

"Yes—"

"No, not if you value the lives of Tad and Lance. Forget Banville. Your father really did die of a heart attack. If you begin telling your whacked-out theories or any of the stories the boys heard from Finney, you will be wrecking their future and your own.

"None of this can be connected to Banville. You'll only have a court suit on your hands for ruining his reputation. So will the boys. Leave Banville out of it."

"I don't believe you."

"Would you believe me if I said I'll come back and get you if you mention any of that? And I'll kill the boys also? Well, believe it then. Now come with me."

With the fireboat closing off the port bow, Linderman grabbed Judy and pulled her to the door. Outside, several people were making their way up the narrow metal stairs into the small passenger cabin. Linderman pushed Judy into the crowded cabin and had the door locked. Those still on the stairs were sent back to the deck.

Back on the bridge, he looked down at several women and children sitting in front of the cars. He grabbed the microphone. "Indian Bay Lines, this is the car ferry. Do you read me?"

"Loud and clear," the manager sighed.

"Ten minutes are up."

"I know. I know. The kid just hasn't come back yet."

"You know what that means."

"Give me a few more minutes. He should be back soon."

"Two minutes and we start throwing passengers over. I think we'll start with the children first. We'll see how long young Feather Island kids can swim in this cold mid-channel. Get that fireboat on the radio."

"We're already on," a deep voice boomed.

"Back off," Linderman ordered. "Back up the channel where we can see you."

"No deals."

"We have a locked cabin full of passengers. We have women and children on deck. If you do as you're told, everything will be all right. Otherwise, you will be busy searching for bodies."

"What do you want?"

"At the moment we only want you to back off. One of my men just came up from the engine room and says it wouldn't take much to sink this tub. Then again, we could be a lot more spectacular. Using the gas tanks on these cars, we could make it very warm in that passenger cabin."

"He's back!" cried the manager's voice. "The guy in the car said to tell you, now wait a minute, let me read this. He said, 'Fish will fry from five to ten.'"

"That's fine," Linderman said. "Now, fireboat, these people have a fifty-fifty chance of survival. In order to help make it a one hundred percent chance of survival, place the fireboat one mile from here. I would expect that would be about halfway to the lighthouse. Now move it out."

"No deals," the voice said. "I have just been informed that the man in the white Dodge is under surveillance and he hasn't moved."

"Watch him carefully. I assure you that you will know when he has moved."

Voices were heard on the other end and it was obvious that this was a possibility.

"It changes nothing. If you give up now you will not be harmed. Your man in the Dodge will now be placed under arrest."

"That means that you think we're bluffing. I don't make idle threats, gentlemen. It is my understanding that the harbor is forty feet deep here in the channel. The ferry is hardly that high. We have, let's see, seven small children on the deck." Keeping the microphone open, he called to one of his men. "Go below and start a list to port." The man went below.

"You wouldn't."

"Yes, no idle threats, as promised. If you need further proof, tell the officers watching the Dodge to go ahead and attempt the arrest now."

No sooner had the officers in the police car opened their doors than white smoke filled the street. Then the car exploded. As the fire threatened the lobster pound, an officer grabbed an extinguisher while the other radioed the fire department which was already on the way. The officer in the cruiser said, "The car blew up."

"Yes," said Linderman. "Back off. One mile."

The ferry began a slow, but definite tilt. A small child slipped from his mother's hand and grabbed one of the cars. His mother grabbed him.

"We will back off temporarily! Stop the list!" The powerful engines of the fireboat churned and the boat headed down the channel. "You haven't hurt anyone yet. The men you killed were wanted. Give yourself up before a larger mistake is made. We can talk this out."

As the fireboat headed toward the lighthouse, the police officers saw a helicopter coming low across the bay. Assuming it was the Coast Guard, they tried to contact it without success.

They were surprised when it hovered above the ferry, and more surprised when it sent down cables with attached harnesses. By the time they had confirmed that in spite of its markings, it was not the Coast Guard, the three men had been pulled from the ferry. The helicopter then headed back over downtown Lassiter. Moving low among the surrounding hills it disappeared from view. The fireboat headed for the ferry at full speed.

The body of the man in the Dodge was never recovered because the heat was so intense. However, the owner of the lobster pound distinctly remembered a man running through his shop at the time of the smoke screen.

When the fireboat reached the ferry in mid-channel, those officers who boarded were surprised to find that none of the passengers had any great fear of the men. They stated that the men had all acted like gentlemen, explaining that they were sorry for the inconvenience, and that they would be delayed for only a short time. The ferry captain confirmed that before leaving they had started the pumps ending the list.

Those on deck were impressed by the helicopter rescue, but were unable to agree on the helicopter markings. The passengers locked in the cabin, suffering only from claustrophobia, the usual smells of perspiration, intense perfume, and alcohol, were delighted to be let out on deck, and just wanted to go home and get on with their lives.

Judy related what she knew of Linderman the writer, who had become Linderman the friend, offering to help them in their time of mourning. Questions clouded her mind when asked about Linderman the killer, kidnapper, and hijacker of the Island Queen. She began to worry about what her mother must be going through.

As the questioning was completed, the car ferry passengers were brought to town where those who wanted to could remain on board and be taken back to the island free of charge. Also headed to the island were the first summer people taking advantage of the weather to open their cottages, summer people who would leave the next day to return by the Fourth of July. Yes, summer people who came to the island to get away from all the excitement of mainland life. They would carry many exciting tales to work the following Monday, thus making the island an attractive place for others to visit.

After the interview with the police detectives, and very interested TV reporters, Tad and Lance joined a crowd of their school friends and headed home. Marge Callant had been kept up to date by the captain. She made a quick check of her son in the kitchen and sent him back outside to the porch with an ice bag.

There, in all their glory, the boys related what had happened all over again to their harshest critics and their devoted fans. The questions of the children were as sharp and penetrating as those of the investigator, but the subject matter was different. Questions dealt with the color of Dan's face; the size and placement of the hole; whether the bodies were naked; the size of the guns the killers held, and how Lance felt pushing the box of a dead man out of the truck. The partially fictitious story grew as these and many other details were related. The tale was the stuff of legends and the legend grew firm on Tad's front porch.

Mickey, tired of hearing what a hero his brother was—especially from his brother's mouth, reminded everyone that the ferry was still in trouble. The whole group left at once to go down front and watch the action. Brian received his mother's blessing to go with them only after everyone in the group agreed to watch out for him or else.

Seeing that a large crowd had gathered around the wharves, the boys headed up Island Avenue to the heights just above the Thompson house where they could see everything. Brian on his brother's shoulders was the first one to spot the white smoke in

Lassiter. They watched the fireboat turn and head out the channel. Brian was also the first one to spot the helicopter. The group cheered, thinking it was the Coast Guard. Brian said, "It's not the Coast Guard. It belongs to the bad men on the ferry. They'll get away, but nobody will be hurt."

"Did you see the previews?" Lance asked. Everyone laughed until they watched the three men being pulled into the helicopter. When it flew away, they stared in amazement at Brian.

"You're spooky," Lance said.

"I know," Brian sighed.

"Yeah, you really do know," said one of the other boys quietly. "I believe you. I'll always believe you, Brian."

Smiling, Brian quietly said, "Thank you," with a sigh.

Someone above them began to snore loudly and the boys spun around looking up at the house. They began to laugh and stood up.

"It's okay I think," Brian explained. "It's just a friend of a lady named Millie, I think. He was up all night. I don't really understand why. I think they were wrestling or something."

The boys began to roll all over the hill. Brian couldn't figure this out.

"Come on, Brian. We have to get going. Mom'll be worried."

"Okay. Yeah, I guess. She's already worried about you, Tad. She wants you home."

When the passenger ferry docked, the boys ran down the hill to greet the hostages. Brian was perched again on Tad's shoulders. He was secretly happy to have Brian as an excuse to walk slowly.

In the crowd, they found Judy crying and embracing her mother, who was also crying. As two friends of Mrs. Thompson took over the crying for Judy, she turned to Lance and whispered, "We've got to talk." Tad began to ask questions of the hostages to find out what had happened on board the ferry, and to keep Brian away from Judy.

"I know," Lance agreed.

"You and Tad meet me at the pond about three-thirty."

"You want us to swim over?" Lance asked seriously.

"I'll pick you up fully dressed in my canoe at the beach," she said quietly as she turned back to continue crying with her mother.

As the crowd began to disperse when the car ferry pulled out a second time, the van was driven down to the passenger wharf, where the boys watched as the three boxes were placed on the fireboat. The van was then driven to the empty car ferry ramp and the area was sealed off as a crime lab team inspected it. When the fireboat pulled out rapidly and smoothly, its immense wake was the only evidence that it was not flying across the water. The newspaper and televised reports would assure Indian Bay Lines and Feather Island a highly profitable summer.

Later, in her living room, Marge Callant observed the way Tad was moving. She examined a scrape again which the Captain had cleaned and bandaged. "Nothing compared to your usual, I guess. Tell me the truth. How badly did you hurt yourself when you slammed into that truck?"

"You sound just like a mother. I got hurt a little. Maybe a little more than a little. I was going faster than I had planned. I wanted it to look good. My shoulder took most of the bang. I made a little dent in the van though. Maybe my head bounced a little." He felt his head. "No bump though. My neck is sore down into my shoulder. I'll be okay. The Captain checked my eyes. We'll know more in the morning as you always say."

"What I don't understand is why you were up at the pond when you said you were going to be playing baseball?" Lance coughed and Tad slapped him gently on the back.

"Not enough kids showed up, Mom. We decided to do something else. I guess we'll go swimming this afternoon if that's okay."

"The water shouldn't hurt you, but if you get dizzy, or have a headache, or throw up, or anything at all strange you come right home. I mean it! Lance make sure he does. We'll take another look at the scrape, your head, and your shoulder after supper."

"If anything bothers me or my scrape looks funny I'll tell you right away, just like always."

"It's that 'always' that bothers me. You've got to start being more careful in everything. You ride that bike too fast all the time. I just can't understand this week at all. First, we had the fire and the funeral; then Dan Stark and his threats; and now this. This island hasn't had this much excitement in years. They say things happen in threes, so I hope it's all over. I hope my meaning is clear."

"We caused part of it," Tad said, winking at Lance.

"Now what does that mean?" she asked in her very stern voice.

"We're heroes."

"Here we go again," said Mickey raising both hands up in the air from his sides. He and the ever quietly-suffering Jackie walked outside.

"Don't let this foolishness go to your head, young man." His mother lowered her voice and became deadly serious. "If you thought about it at all, you would realize that what you did today was a very stupid and dangerous thing. You caused a lot to happen. Did it ever occur to you how many people you placed in danger? Little children included?"

"Linderman placed them in danger."

"Only because you placed him in danger! You could have been killed! All the people on the ferry could have been killed! How would you feel if children had drowned? The passenger cabin was locked with people in it! It is very difficult to breathe in there like that. You have to accept some of the responsibility, young man!"

"But he was very brave, too," Brian said with adoration.

"No one got hurt but me," Tad pointed out. "Except maybe Mrs. Morey who went swimming and had to climb the ladder." He laughed at the thought. Marge scowled at him at first and then grinned.

"I know, Mom. I really do understand. It was just something we had to do."

He knew what his mother was trying to help him understand. When he saw the three men escape, he secretly felt very nervous about what might happen to the people on the ferry. He was more nervous about that than when the police detective tried to make him change his story. It wasn't until the ferry came back in and Lance talked to Judy that he felt better. He wondered what she wanted, and then figured that she wanted to thank him for his heroic efforts. He went outside to straighten his handlebars and check the rest of his bicycle carefully. And maybe to clear his head a little.

* * *

By three o'clock the two boys, fully clothed, met Judy on the pond beach. Her face was somewhat dirty and tear-stained. "Be careful getting in," Judy warned. "Step into the center and sit down."

"I've been in boats before," Lance told her.

"Yes, but this is a canoe, and you have to know how to act in a canoe," Tad explained.

"Big deal," Lance said.

"I haven't got much time. I'll go around the pond as we talk. My mother and I decided to go to my aunt's tonight anyway. My uncle is coming down to get us this time. I have to be home by four-thirty. Look, I have to talk to you about what happened today. You guys took a big chance, and I'm very grateful in spite of everything. I want you to know that."

"It wasn't anything," Tad said, glowing.

"It may have saved my life in the long run."

"We're sorry that Linderman took you with him," Lance said. "We didn't mean to place you or anyone else in any danger. We didn't think about that possibility."

"There's a lot we don't count on," Judy explained. "It just happens and you can't do anything about it, but accept it. I guess that's one way you have to grow up."

"You're talking about your father, aren't you?" Tad asked gently.

"I guess I am, but more than that. I want you to forget Dr. Banville and everything that we thought he might be involved in. On the ferry I accused Carl of being involved with Banville. He said he had done some checking and Daddy really did die of a heart attack. He said our theories, your theories, were crazy, and Banville would have us in court for damaging his reputation if we said anything."

"That's a lot of bull. We heard Mr. Finney and he wasn't kidding, and we know some other things, too," Lance said.

"But can you prove anything?"

"No, we can't prove a thing, but we're not kidding either."

"I believe you, but a lot of others won't. A court won't be able to do much without proof. If it is all true, it's too dangerous for any of us. If it isn't true, you don't want your folks to lose everything they own because Banville took you to court and won a large settlement. He can probably afford big shot lawyers. Carl said the three deaths couldn't be connected to Banville in any way."

"And you believe him?" Tad asked. "We think Linderman worked for him."

"I don't know what to believe right now. It's all too painful. Someone I loved more than anybody else in the world died this past week. Someone I cared for and trusted very much turned out to be a possible murderer. I don't know. I really don't know. It just all hurts so very much. My poor mother is having all sorts of problems, and I know that you two have gotten into something way over your heads. Maybe what happened isn't connected with my father's death, but you two are connected to all of these horrible deaths. If I'm going away, I want to make sure that you guys will be all right."

"We'll be all right," Tad said quietly. The sincerity in his eyes made Judy's fear melt a little. He looked across the pond and scanned the shoreline. When he turned back to her he said, "These things just happened to us. We didn't go looking for them. Maybe our curiosity led us into some strange stuff, but we didn't think it would be anything like this."

"We haven't said anything to anyone except you and Linderman about Dr. Banville," Lance said.

"When I come back to the island, I want to find you two safe and sound. You hear me?"

"Yeah, when will you be back?"

"I graduate a week from today. I guess we'll be back sometime Friday morning. Maybe earlier. I really don't know. It depends on what my mom wants to do."

She paddled into the beach. "You will try to forget about all this, right?"

"We can try," Tad said, "but it'll be hard. We're heroes."

"You're not indestructible."

Lance stood up in the bow yelling, "We are supermen! We are invulnerable!"

Judy rocked the canoe slightly and Lance fell into the sand.

"Okay, Superman," Tad laughed. "Take care of yourself, Judy, and get some rest. Things will work out. We'll try not to change your island for you anyway."

"I hope so. I truly hope so."

"But I have one question," Tad said quietly, sincerely.

"What?"

"Will you please come swimming with us like we were last time just once? There's so much we want to learn and we trust you. We know you would tell us the truth and show us about girls anatomy and things."

Judy smiled, pushed off, and paddled without looking back.

"I don't believe what you just asked her," Lance said with a very red face. "Anatomy and things?"

"She didn't say no and she smiled. Don't you want to know?" Changing the subject with a big grin he said, "Something else though. These two things have to be connected, Lance. The bug connects Stark and Banville somehow. And Linderman knew about both of them because we told him. Why would he want that electronic bug? I mean, I know he's a reporter or something, but there isn't much we can do about any of it anymore I guess. I suspect that now everything really is over, and we won't fall into any more problems either."

"Don't be so sure," Lance said. He pointed toward the top of the sand hill where Periander Sage stood. He motioned them up. "I think it just happened to us again."

"What now?"

"I don't know, Tad. There isn't much we can do. Has he got his gun?"

"I don't see one." Tad froze his lips as tight as he could when he spoke. "In fact he looks as friendly as always."

"Most dangerous things look friendly."

"Where did you learn that?"

"I think I just made it up. Maybe a wasp and a friend taught me."

"We might as well go see what he wants. We can always run down the other side of the dam and hop on our bikes."

"I suppose. My front wheel wobbles a little though."

As the boys walked toward the old man, he was already writing. He handed the pad to Lance. Tad leaned over and read it with him. "You lied to the police. Van was not here."

"Yes," Tad confessed.

The old man spread out his hands, obviously asking why.

Tad explained, "If we told what we really saw and where we saw it, we'd have to answer a lot of other questions that are very complicated. They would involve you. We'd be in a lot more trouble with our folks. We'd have to tell about the plumbers, and the gun, and how we broke into your house."

"Gun?" the old man wrote. Tad and Lance both looked ashamed with their heads down.

"All right, I guess we better have it out right here and now. Yesterday I went to your house to sell you the rest of the tickets, and I looked all over the place for you. I went upstairs and I didn't see any paintings. It didn't look like you had been painting at all. I tried to find a pencil or a pen to leave you a message. Eventually I looked in your backpack. I found your gun. Then I went to the cottage to see if you were there again. I found the boxes. I'm glad I didn't open them then, since I was alone.

"Later, when I brought Lance back to show him everything, it was all different. You had lots of paintings. Lance checked to see if he could find your gun when he went to the bathroom, but it wasn't there. We snuck into the cottage after we left you and we found water all over the place and the floor was nailed down. Then we checked and found that no plumbers had fixed anything because water shot all over the place when we turned the handle.

"This morning we came back and pulled up the trap door you made. We found Dan Stark. That's when Carl Linderman and two guys came and got them. We were inside the cottage and thought they would catch us. We caught them instead, or almost caught them. And I don't care anymore." He started yelling. "I'm glad it's over and I don't care what you do to us!" Tad's eyes glistened from relief, guilt, anger, and fear. Almost in tears, he stood tall and stared into Periander Sage's eyes.

The old man gripped the boy's shoulders. Tad at first tried to break loose, and then sobbed into the man's chest and let himself be hugged by the old man. Tears slowly drifted down Lance's face, but he kept his distance from Sage.

Letting go of Tad, Sage began to write. "They were already in house when I came first night. Locked me out when you came. I never carried gun. Evidence against me? Promised me they would hurt you unless I cooperated. They were convinced you wouldn't be back."

Lance read the note and a look of disgust crossed his tear-stained face. "When we were alone with you, why didn't you tell us? We could have told the captain."

"I was afraid for you."

"Why did they kill Stark?" Lance asked.

"Don't think they did."

"How come they had three big boxes?" Lance asked.

"Equipment storage. Using house for something I don't know about."

"What about the black body bags? They weren't made for equipment." Tad was sure that the old man would not answer.

"Not sure."

Tad wasn't ready to give up. "But they ran away and hijacked the ferry and got away in a helicopter. If they didn't kill those guys, why did they do all that dumb stuff? Why did they take the bodies in the first place? They could have just left them there. These guys are really organized with lots of money. They even had a helicopter. Who are they?"

"Desperate men. No idea who. Glad they are gone."

"Why didn't they take the bodies off by the helicopter?" Lance asked.

Tad said, "I don't think they wanted to attract attention to themselves."

Sage wrote: "Don't think they'll dare come back. I was followed when in Lassiter this morning. Couldn't go to police. Could go now, but you would still be in trouble. Perhaps we should leave things as they are. No more detective."

"That's a good idea," Lance agreed.

Tad didn't say anything. He just nodded his head and looked troubled.

"Come over Monday. Will give you grocery list. Get back to normal. I have to finish paintings. Glad it is over."

"See you Monday," Lance said.

The man turned and limped into the woods toward his house. Tad noticed how agile he was when he reached the deadfalls. It bothered him. It bothered him a great deal.

As they headed for their bikes Lance asked, "What's the matter?" Tad was too quiet.

"A lot."

"What? Everything seems to make sense to me except the equipment and whether they really did murder Dan Stark or not," Lance said.

"Why would they let Mr. Sage uptown at the same time they were taking the bodies off the island?"

"Maybe they were just stupid."

"They were anything but stupid. They were really organized, even when they got in trouble," Tad pointed out. "They had a helicopter rescue them. And how did Mr. Sage know where we were just now?"

"I think we better do as he says and leave things just as they are. 'No more detective' is maybe a good idea. Everybody is paying attention to us now, and if he thinks we believe him maybe bad things won't happen to us."

"I suppose so, but I would really like to believe him." Tad hesitated, walked further down the path and said quietly, "I like him a lot, or at least I think I do, or I did, or something. But underneath it's all horseshit and horseshit from even nice horses stinks. I've had too much horseshit today. It hurts when you can't trust someone you like."

"I think we both need our fathers at home and well."

"You got that right. Yeah, you got that real right."

"No horses on the island. How do you know what horseshit smells like?"

"No bulls either, but I know bullshit when I hear it. I think I do anyway."

CHAPTER NINE

SATURDAY EVENING

"Tad, you are planning to come down to the hall, aren't you?"

"Aw, Mom, do I have to? I've seen the kids dance."

"I think it is only right that you should. They all came to your shows. I'll buy you a ticket. Maybe refreshments?"

"It wasn't that. I just wanted to watch TV and relax."

"You've certainly had a busy day. How are your shoulder, and your arm, and your head, and anything else you haven't told me about?"

"Okay. I told you everything so far over and over!"

She looked at her son carefully. "You didn't go swimming, did you?"

"No."

"Why not? Was something the matter?"

"Well, sort of. Judy was paddling around the pond in her canoe, so we couldn't exactly swim. She gave us a ride and that made up for it. I feel sorry for her, I guess."

"Poor Judy. She's going to graduate soon. It's a shame her father couldn't have seen that. He was so proud of her. She will be the first to graduate from high school in her family in years."

"He probably wouldn't go uptown to see it anyway."

"Tad Callant! What a horrible thing to say of the dead! Whatever made you say such a thing?"

"I don't know. From what I saw of Mr. Thompson, I just thought he wouldn't like graduations or big ceremonies like that.

I mean, he seemed to want to stay on the island. He never worked uptown or anything."

"There was enough work on the island with all the plumbing and electrical work the summer people needed, and many island people, too. Although, I must admit, I was always a little worried since he wasn't licensed and always wanted cash. But that has nothing to do with Judy's graduation. Of course he would have gone. He was always so proud of her. I don't know where you get some of your crazy ideas sometimes."

"I didn't mean anything by it, Mom. I liked him okay, and I'm sorry he's dead and all. I really do feel sorry for Judy. She's going up to her aunt's tonight. In fact, I guess she's already gone. Her uncle was coming to pick her up."

"Her mother's going up?"

"Yeah, I hope they make it this time, but I guess she will now that Linderman isn't around."

"Linderman?"

"Yeah."

"Yes."

"Yes, Carl Linderman. He was the guy who hijacked the ferry this morning. He was going to drive Judy and her mother to Augusta."

"You're quite sure of this, Tad?"

"Sure. Linderman was a new friend of Judy's and her father, too. Judy said he was on the island looking for ideas for a book and maybe to invest some money somehow. Judy even drove him around the island. They thought he was their friend. He went to the funeral with them."

"I was wondering who that young man was. No one seemed to know. Judy told you all this at the pond?"

"Well, some of it. We saw him before and wondered who he was and asked around."

"You are your mother's son. I guess he will write his story in prison. That poor girl. To lose her father, and then to be deceived, and so hurt at this time. What is the world coming to?"

"Judy will be all right."

"Well, she's young. I certainly hope so. We'll have to have them over to supper when they get back from Augusta."

"Great."

"Fine, now get ready. Put on your new shirt. The Deiters will be here soon. Tell Mickey I've got his shoes all ready."

"But I didn't say I wanted to go."

"Of course you did. Now get upstairs and tell Brian to come down so I can comb his hair. Comb yours, too, and wash your face. Put on your good shirt."

"Ah, Mom, you already told me."

"Sometimes you have to be told twice. I always want to be proud of how my children look in public."

As Tad reached the top step of the stairwell which led from the kitchen to the boys' bedroom, he couldn't believe his eyes. Mickey was standing in the middle of the bedroom in green tights.

"Are you really going to wear those?" He put his right hand over his mouth and his eyes danced all around the room.

"Shut up, Tad. Don't say a thing. Not one thing."

"Tights! Mickey's wearing tights! Mickey's wearing tights!" he chanted.

"I'm an elf. It's part of the dance. It wasn't my idea."

"He dances good, too," Brian said from Mickey's top bunk.

"And I'm gonna wear this long shirt anyway, so the tights don't really show anything."

"Put on your hat," Brian said, passing it to him.

"Is Jackie wearing the same thing?"

"Yeah, we're both elves."

"And you two guys are going to stand in front of the whole island, and I have to watch you?"

"I'm going to watch him," Brian said. "I think he's great. Mrs. O'Dell said that I can take lessons next September, just like Mickey, and Jackie, and Donsie. Then I can be in the show next year."

"So don't say anything else, Tad."

"I have just one more thing to say."

"Don't say anything," Mickey warned.

"But I wanted to say—"

"Not one word."

"I just wanted to say Mom has your shoes ready."

With a sigh of relief, Mickey started down the stairs.

"And you're really cute," Tad yelled after him.

"Mom!" Mickey wailed.

"Tad Callant," his mother yelled up the stairs. "That will be enough of that, young man. You have a very short memory. You don't remember that show three years ago. Brian, get down here so I can do your hair."

"What show?" Tad hollered, changing his shirt.

"The Christmas show. The one where you danced to all those Mother Goose poems."

"What was Tad?" Mickey asked. "I forgot."

"Mom! No!" Tad yelled.

"What was he?" Mickey urged.

"Yeah," Brian said, "what was he? I was too little to remember."

"I remember, I think," Donsie said, as she entered the kitchen, also dressed as an elf.

"You were only five," Tad yelled down the stairs. "You couldn't remember anything."

"I remember lots of stuff, and I'm only five," Brian pointed out.

"But I do remember. I even know where there's a picture of you. I'll go get it."

Tad flew down the stairs with his shirttail hanging out of his jeans. Mickey and Donsie were going through the middle kitchen drawer where the photograph albums were kept.

Donsie pulled out a large red album and put it on the kitchen table. Marge blocked Tad's way and danced him back to the stairs. Brian crawled through their legs laughing, and reached the table as the kitchen door opened. Mrs. Deiter, Lance, and another elf filed in. Seeing the action, they went over to the table.

"Here it is!" Donsie squealed.

"Mom," Tad yelled. "Mom, get that picture. I'll…let me get it…move, Mom…NO! Let me at her."

"A girl!" Mickey yelled. "Tad was a girl! Now I remember. I was so embarrassed to have a brother who was a girl. No wonder I forgot!"

"Mary had a little lamb," Donsie explained. "I knew I remembered it."

"Yes," said her mother. "Mary got sick just before the show and Tad was the only one who could fit into her costume. He knew everyone's dances and songs and did very well."

"And a sweet little girl he was," said Sylvia. "Just look at that angelic little face."

"A real angel," Lance sighed, clasping his hands to his chest. Jackie and Mickey followed his example.

Tad swung his mother around, started for the picture, and grabbed Lance instead when Donsie closed the album and put it back in the drawer.

"That's enough, now," his mother laughed. "Get upstairs and finish changing."

Glad to get out of the crowd, Tad carried his beet-red face up the stairs with him. Lance helped him.

"Did you have a real lamb?" Brian called after him.

"Tad was a girl!" Mickey chanted. "Tad was a girl!"

"I'm going to kill that kid."

"I'm glad I never took dancing lessons."

"How did you get out of it? Every kid since the creation of the island has taken dancing lessons from Mrs. O'Dell. Cave kids took lessons from her."

"That's when my sisters were taking piano lessons. Mom thought I had real talent. So I took them, too."

"I remember. You didn't have real talent."

"I know, but I got outta taking dancing lessons."

Twenty minutes later, after walking as slowly as they could to the St. Peter's Church hall a hundred yards down the street, Tad and Lance gave their tickets to Mrs. O'Leary at the door. In the hall, occasional heads were poked through the curtain as stage lights were flashed on and off amidst muffled giggles. A general murmur accompanied by pointing and loud laughter made it a warm, excited audience. Tad led the way down the left side of the chairs until they came to two boys from their class sitting on one of the ventilators.

"Your mothers made you come, right?" David asked.

"Yeah," Tad said, lifting himself onto the edge of the ventilator.

"Ours too," moaned the other boys together.

As Mrs. Landers began to warm up the crowd with a medley of show tunes on the piano, Tad jabbed Lance in the ribs and pointed toward the door. Dr. Banville was coming to the show. He was alone. Walking to the rear, he passed right in front of the boys without looking at them. He took a seat near the back of the nearly full hall.

"What's Banville doing here?" Lance whispered.

"Maybe he likes to watch little kids dance."

At seven o'clock sharp, the lights went out and the hall was black. The stage lights came on and Mrs. Landers changed to an overture. The curtain opened with jerks and tugs. A group of Celtic dancers began to do their thing. Lance watched the dancers with the other boys. Tad watched Dr. Banville.

As the music changed, elves and fairies pranced into position and began a tap routine well known to Tad. His feet began to move. He turned and watched Mickey and Donsie. He would never admit it to them, but he was proud of his brother and sister. They had the routine down perfectly. Jackie wasn't too bad either.

A group of younger soldiers followed. Tad's eyes turned back toward Dr. Banville. He was gone. Tad tried to search the back of the hall, but it was too dark to see anything. He couldn't be seen anywhere. Tad nudged Lance who looked at Banville's empty seat.

"Where is he?"

"I don't know. Maybe standing up back."

"I can't see."

"I know. Let's walk back there."

At the back of the hall they couldn't see him or his silhouette in front of them. Lance pointed toward the exit along the wall across from where they had been seated. "Let's check."

As they slowly approached the exit, Tad spotted his mother and she spotted him. Thinking he was leaving the show, she gave him a look which stopped him in his tracks. Both boys became glued to the wall by their mothers' stares. As the women turned back to the dancers Tad and Lance were still unable to move.

From where he was standing, Lance was able to slowly open the exit door. Looking through the crack he could see Banville standing outside. Tad slid over next to him. Suddenly, red sparks shot through the air to the parking lot behind the building.

"It's a bomb!" Lance said too loudly.

"It's a cigar," Tad said, smiling at the people in the crowd near him.

The man who threw the cigar bomb opened the exit door and came through quickly, bumping into Lance.

"Excuse me," Banville whispered.

"Sorry," Lance said.

Banville moved back to his seat and continued to watch the show. The boys followed his example. When it was over he congratulated the children and Mrs. O'Dell, and moved outside with the crowd. The boys stayed right behind him.

"Lance," his mother called, "where are you going?"

"We just want to see the boat come in and we'll be right home," Lance called, proud of his quick thinking.

"Make sure you are. By nine."

The boys followed Banville down Maple Street and turned onto Main. Suddenly, Banville stopped and turned, causing Lance to bump into him.

"Sorry again. Since we're headed the same way, perhaps I should introduce myself. My name is Doctor Banville. You must be the Callant boy who ran into the truck this morning."

"No, he is. I'm Lance Deiter."

"Ah yes. You pitched one of the dead men out of the truck. Don't look so surprised. You are quite the celebrities. Everyone is talking about you. That was certainly a brave thing you did."

"Thank you."

"They say you saw the men load the bodies over at the pond. I'm afraid I don't get around the island much. Where exactly is this pond?"

Lance explained and Banville asked, "Were they in the pond?"

"No, on the little road that leads up to the dam to the west of the pond," Tad said. "Why?"

"It just seems like an unusual spot to hide bodies. They say you had been swimming there. That means, I presume, that most of the children swim there. The chance of being seen with bodies seems highly probable, if you follow me."

"Not really," Tad explained. "First, we're early this year and only a few boys go swimming this early. It's kind of a contest. We were the first ones in. Second, that whole area is loaded with brush. It wouldn't be such a bad place, but we really don't know if they hid the bodies there. We only saw them loading them there."

"I see. That certainly was a fine bit of work."

"You live in the old Richards place, right?"

"Why, yes. Now I'm surprised."

"I've seen you once or twice before and wondered who you were, so somebody told me. I also heard you were with Mr. Thompson when he died."

"I only wish I had been. Perhaps I could have helped him. Perhaps not. I was called down after they found him. It was a sad, sad, horrible fire."

"Dr. Banville, there is something I would like to know, but you may think I'm being rude. I really don't mean it that way," Tad said.

"No, please, go on. What is it?"

"Well, sir, it's about that house you live in…well, it's always been pretty mysterious. I mean, all my life there have been all sorts of stories about it having secret stairways and a secret passage to the ocean. Is that true?"

"And smuggled treasure, too," Lance added.

"And I guess my real question is, well, what do you do there all day?"

Banville laughed a nervous laugh. "You want to know if I'm a pirate. First of all, I don't think you're rude. I certainly understand not only your curiosity, but also the curiosity of the entire island regarding that grand old house. There are no dungeons or secret passageways that I have found. I do have some very deep cellars, one of which, I assume, was a wine cellar. It is my understanding that smugglers did use the house at one time over a hundred years ago. I would assume that is where all those stories came from. The story I heard that made the most sense to me was that the smugglers used large baskets placed down over the cliff.

"As to your other question, I am sure that is on the mind of a great many of the islanders, also. When a new person moves in, and is hardly ever seen, stories are bound to begin. Actually, I was very ill several years after I began my medical practice. I was hospitalized for some time. When I got out, I needed a place to recuperate for a couple of years. I found this place and I'm doing just fine."

"But if you just started your practice, how could you afford to buy a house like that and live in it all these months without working? My dad works all the time and we would love a larger house, but I've lived in mine all my life. I'm sorry. Now I'm asking something that is none of my business. I'm really sorry, Dr. Banville."

"I see. You are the curious one, aren't you? Well, I guess my secret is out. You see, I come from a rather wealthy family, and I was able to purchase the house for almost nothing. The town of Lassiter owned it after the prior owner passed away. Apparently no one wanted it. When I knew I was going to be laid up for awhile, I applied for a grant to work on a special project. I was given the grant and I use that money to live on while I am here. I work on my project when I want and rest when I need to rest. Tonight, I felt the need to get out of the house, and to do something entirely out of the ordinary. Spring fever, I guess."

"What is this project?" Lance asked.

"The project is very complicated."

"I'd give anything to see the house," Tad offered, grasping at the seconds before Dr. Banville left and they had to go home.

"I'm afraid I have to turn here," Banville said. "I'll see you boys around sometime."

The boys moved toward the wharf. The boat was still a few minutes out. "Was that an invitation?" Tad asked.

"I don't think so, but he seems to make sense and seems like a nice guy."

"He doesn't seem like Mr. Finney described him."

"I wonder what he had when he was sick," Lance said.

"Probably some strange tropical disease where his face was covered with mold, and worms crawled out of his ears and nose. Let's go home. This has been the strangest day of my life."

"It certainly affected you in strange ways. Worms crawling out his ears." Lance smiled, and then shook his head.

* * *

One of the privileges of being first-born in the Callant household was that of staying up late on Saturday nights. Tad had watched his programs and was now sitting on the large floral slip-covered sofa drinking a Coke. He was all wrapped up in the power of his lies. His interview had made the Eleven O'clock Channel Six News.

He was fascinated by the action, the courage, and the danger spread all over the news. But it was his creative talent that both fascinated him and made him feel guilty at the same time. He remembered getting angry at Lance for involving him in a lie earlier in the day. Now here he was on Portland TV telling a whopper to the world. Nobody would ever believe him again if the truth ever came out. The reality of that possibility shook him to his very being. He looked over at his mother's chunky body filling the recliner. Her snoring shook the entire room. "Mom."

"What? Are you all right?" She sat the chair up straight.

"Yeah, you missed my interview."

"Oh, I'm sorry. It's been quite a day. I'm sure I'll catch it tomorrow morning. They usually repeat the big stories. She remained still for a moment, letting the dizziness pass, and then leaned back again.

"Did you call Dad?"

"He was out in the field. I didn't want to call his pager, so I just left a message for him to call tomorrow."

"When I was born was he around?"

"He was as nervous as a herring in a mackerel tank. Yes, he has been around for the birth of each of my beautiful children."

"He really wanted children then?"

"Tad! Yes. Yes, he wanted each of you very badly. He loves you very much."

"Does he? He's never home. It doesn't seem like he cares. I mean, it's not just me, but well, how about you? How do you know he doesn't have a different woman each night? I'm sorry, but maybe he has a whole other family." Tad really was sorry he said it as soon as the words left his mouth.

Usually quick to correct her son, Marge hesitated and then said, "Is that what you truly think?"

"I wonder about it, sometimes. I guess I believe he's got another family that he loves a lot more than he loves us. Other times, I see him in a bar after work with girls all over him."

"It's probably just your hormones doing the thinking instead of your brain. He just hates to be tied down. He travels from job to job to make his money. You have to admit that he is very generous. We live quite well."

"No, we don't."

"Don't be foolish."

"We don't, Ma. Look at our furniture. It's old. The TV is as old as I am, so is this couch even with its beautiful slipcover you made. That rug is ancient and almost bare. We don't even have a computer."

"We've had this conversation before. We have no need for a computer."

"Everyone has a computer. You could e-mail everyone, even Dad. I could use it for school. Like I said, we're just too poor."

"We make do quite nicely. Your father is just an active man."

"That's what I'm afraid of. Don't you ever wonder what he's doing and who he's with?"

"I love your father very much. I trust him and he trusts me."

"But doesn't caring make up part of a marriage? He doesn't care about us."

"Tad, how can you say these things?"

"I feel them, Mom." Tad stood up and paced on the threadbare rug. "I feel them a lot real deep down. It's easy to run away and build things. It's hard to stay and deal with all the everyday problems. I love you so much and I'm just so proud of you. But there are things I just don't know how to handle. I just need to talk to Dad about them, and damn him, he isn't here. The captain's more like a father to me than Dad is."

Tad folded his arms across his chest and slumped back down on the couch, feeling very guilty and exposed. Then he shoved his hands deep into the pockets of his jeans with his head down feeling ashamed of saying what he truly felt. Marge got out of her recliner with effort and sat down next to him. He leaned back into her and wiped his eyes with his shirtsleeve. She put her arm around him and held him close.

"There are times when I do get so cross with him," she said. "Oh, I get so angry with him, but I do trust him, Tad. I know how hard he works and I don't let my imagination run away with me. There is great danger and great fear when you worry that way, and most of the time you're wrong. I think the time has come for you and your father to take some long walks together to talk things out. He needs to understand how grown up you are. He needs to hear your fears and your other feelings. He needs to know how much you love him. And Lord knows, shy man or not, he needs to tell you how much he loves you."

"Shy? Dad isn't shy."

"He's not one to speak his heart, Tad. But when he does, it's so beautiful. When he does, you will know why I trust him, and why I love him, and why I miss him even more than you do."

"It'll never happen, but I'm willing to try I guess, so maybe he will, too." Tad was quiet for awhile, just thinking. His mother smoothed his hair. "You know, Mom, none of us really speak about what we really feel. I mean, except for Brian, we kind of play a game with each other. Sometimes we talk kind of mean to each other and make fun of each other. Most of the time we're just saying what each of us is used to hearing. Set the table. Sort the clothes. That's my program. Don't put the crayons on the radiator. Don't do this. Don't do that. Tad's on my side of the couch. Tad was a girl. We just say the things that keep the family moving or to tear each other down. Why is it so hard to say what we really feel if we really love each other?"

"Love is a powerful force, Tad. Sometimes though, we mix it all up. There are times when we feel we will hurt someone we love if we tell what's in our hearts. Sometimes we are afraid we will be hurt if we tell what we feel. After awhile it just builds up and eats at us. Then problems begin.

"It's kind of like it's a big, invisible wall that keeps us apart when it should bring us together. Sometimes it's like we get hurt because we really don't trust the other person to understand what is so important to us deep down. Sometimes it's like their feelings are in a foreign language, even though we talk the same language. We need to risk walking through that imaginary wall, so we can see the trust that's already there just waiting for us. We need to trust."

Tad was quiet for a minute thinking about what his mother had said. "Sometimes, with Lance, the wall shifts a little, and then surrounds us and kind of protects us instead of keeping us apart. Our problem is that we don't know that wall too well. I think the wall, somehow, is love. It holds us all together like we're inside a big bubble, but we're each inside our own bubble, too, and that keeps us apart at the same time. It lets me be me, but the other one keeps us together, too. It holds both our bubbles. In a family there are lots more kinds of bubbles."

"My, my, aren't we getting philosophical."

"I think about these things a lot. It's nice most of the time. Trying to make sense of everything. Most of the time, it's hard because a lot doesn't make any sense at all, but I feel it and know it's true. I just don't talk about it because I think nobody will understand and will make fun of me. Maybe I need to risk a little more."

"Young man, you have risked more than enough for all of us today. Look at the time. Look at the time! It's off to bed with you. How is your shoulder? Take off your shirt. Show me again if you have any bruises. Have you truly told me all of the places you got hurt? You have to do that. I am your mother after all. Turn around. Are you hurt here?"

"Mom!"

CHAPTER TEN

SUNDAY

Sunday morning dawned cool, clear, and quiet, promising that the weekend would end peacefully. Gulls gently flew in and captured the rocks on the back shore. Hermit crabs trudged across the deserted beach. Starfish began to move among the pilings below the wharves. The jeep sat patiently in front of the fire barn. A night of special dancing was over. A night of friendly singing at the legion hall was over. The lights behind the picket fences were now out.

As the spirits of Henry Thompson and Harry Finney walked down Island Avenue, they saw an island they had forgotten about. So used to the hustle and bustle of this community, they were surprised that such quiet existed. The dawn air became as velvet wrapping around their souls. The warm breezes wandering through the pines had spotted them and nestled in close to them, like a purring cat with nothing better to do.

As they reached the beach and turned east the windows of the small shops and cottages stared down at them, wondering why they were about. Henry and Harry said nothing, but smiled. The rising sun reflecting from the same windows winked back at them. At the other end of the beach, the schoolhouse sat patiently waiting like a pregnant father, knowing the time was near, but not quite yet.

The grass on the ball field did not bend to their step, and welcomed them in awe. In the stream, Henry bent down to caress the old canoe he had used as a boy. The canvas wrapped around his hand, urging him to climb aboard one last time. The memories of the pond with its gleaming wet bodies, laughter, and cool water jumped up and down between the two men who were now free of their own. The summer people in the awakening summer cottages did not see them pass, but the cycles of the opening and closings of these houses begged them to join in the memory building for a while longer.

At the top of the bluff, the men took one last look at the island which had been so good to them. Then, they jumped high into eternity. Spinning out past Keelscrape Island, spinning high up over Goat Island light, spinning higher than good old Jon Seagull ever dreamed, they went in search of their new homes further out where Mrs. Finney waited.

Young Brian Callant, coming back from the bathroom, looked out the window, and seeing them pass, waved, and crawled in with his older brother.

Tad grunted as Brian snuggled in close and then whispered, "You okay?"

"Yeah, I just saw Mr. Thompson and Mr. Finney leave the island and I got lonely."

"You were dreaming. Go back to sleep."

"I'm okay now." With that he pulled the blanket over his shoulders a little more and shut his eyes. "Anyway, they waved at me."

A little while later Tad said, "Who waved at you?"

"Hmmm?" murmured Brian.

Now wide awake, Tad said, "You said they waved at you. Who waved at you?"

"Mr. Thompson and Mr. Finney," Brian whispered.

"You are weird."

"I know, but it's okay. It's just the way I am, and I know stuff other people don't know about, so it's good." he explained. He looked into his brother's matching dark blue eyes and asked, "Tad, what's it like to die? I don't know much about that."

"Why ask that?"

"What's it like, Tad? I think I should know, but I don't."

"I don't know. I haven't died yet."

"But what do you think it's like?"

"I can only guess." He paused. "I have thought about it some," he whispered so as to not wake up Mickey. "Once, when Mom's crocuses came up through the snow I thought about it. I know that sounds dumb, but it's true. I mean, there they were, looking so beautiful, and yet so stupid in the snow. They just didn't belong there, but there they were so alive and yelling to everyone that spring was coming. And then spring came and it was great, and beautiful, and more and more flowers came. Everything turned green and alive again, but the crocuses had disappeared. One second in life they were more alive and beautiful than anything, and then they just disappeared. They didn't whimper or cry or anything. They just seemed to know that it was okay to do all that they did. It was natural to come in the snow, and it was natural to disappear in the garden with all the new flowers. It was no big deal."

"Did the other flowers miss them?"

"I suppose so, for a little while, but the other flowers became so wrapped up in their own lives, and their own beauty, that the crocuses became a memory. The loneliness and the pain of losing them became a memory, too. I guess on a rainy, foggy day it came back and hurt for a while as they remembered either seeing them or hearing about them, but it was okay when the sun came back."

"It's like the dew was the flowers crying all night," Brian whispered.

"Yeah, I suppose that could make sense," Tad pondered, "but the sun helped them out and the flowers lived happily again."

"Lance and Jackie will cry, Tad."

"What do you mean?" Tad asked, wishing Brian hadn't said that.

"When their father dies, they'll cry."

"What makes you think he'll die?"

"I don't know, but he will, this summer. I guess I just know it."

"If he does die, they'll cry and we'll probably cry with them, and it'll be okay."

Brian sniffed and his warm tears fell on Tad's neck as his brother wrapped his arm around him. Trying to hold back his own tears he said, "Why are you crying now?"

"Just getting into practice I guess," Brian shuddered. Tad pulled his little brother closer, and joined him with tears, wondering why fathers and crocuses had to disappear at all.

* * *

Later, sitting on Lance's back steps, Tad hesitated, and then asked, "Is your father coming home today?"

"Yeah, and my bossy sisters, too. Mom's already gone uptown and they're all supposed to come back on the two-fifteen. They're up at my aunt's now."

"How is your dad?"

"He's great, I guess. Mom says he's still very tired, but he should be getting better."

"It will be good to have him up and around."

"Yeah, I really miss him. I missed him even when he was here. He was so sick."

"I know what you mean. I wish my dad would come home. He's supposed to come back soon, but it's been so long. He left in November, and came back for Christmas, and then he stopped back in February. I wish he'd just stick around."

"There must be work around here he can do."

"I guess there is, but when you're one of the bosses for a construction company that big, you have to go where they need you. Mom says the money is real good and he sends us stuff, but it's just not the same."

"I've seen more of my father than you have of yours, but seeing my father sick all those months is the same as not seeing him at all. At least you know your father will come back. I don't know if Dad will ever get well."

Remembering what Brian said, Tad's top teeth toyed with his lower lip. Suddenly he stood up. "We're a couple of big babies, feeling sorry for ourselves. Let's face it, when you get right down to it, each of us has to stand on our own two feet anyway. Let's do something."

"What?"

"I don't know. I want to do something different."

"What?"

"I don't know. Maybe take a hike up to the other end of the island somewhere."

"Like up near Dr. Banville's?"

"No, not really. Just a hike through the woods. We haven't been up that way for a long time. It must be . . . I don't think I've been up there since last winter."

"You mean the day you decided to slide down Island Avenue on your sled and you drove Old Hal and his taxi into the snow bank."

"He sure yelled at us that day. He used words I'd never heard before. I still don't know what some of them mean."

"Yelled at you, you mean. I never went down."

"You were chicken."

"I was smart. You're the one that got into trouble,"

"Well, how about it? Let's go up. We don't have to go near Banville's. We can go up near Finney's and cut up through the woods."

* * *

Finney's ruins had been carefully examined by youthful island archeologists all week long. Finding little of value, the two boys headed into the woods. Hiding their bikes in the brush, they searched for the path they had taken during the winter.

"It's all grown over or something, but I think I know where it is anyway," Lance said pointing.

"So do I. Let's head up to Cabbage Pond."

Walking quickly through the tall pines on a soft floor of pine needles, the boys came to a meadow where blueberry bushes were just starting to get their leaves. Occasional furry sumac bushes and large old pines blown down by the winter storms blocked their way.

"It always looks so different in the spring than in the winter," Lance remembered.

"I should hope so."

"You know what I mean. The path is almost impossible to find. In the winter all the guys make a path so you can find it, but now everything looks just the same. Let's head over toward those trees."

"You always make that mistake. That heads toward the other little pond. Remember? Last winter you went there and waited for us. We were already skating and about to head home when you finally showed up."

"Froze my ass off. I wonder why I do that. I won't do it any more, now that I know."

"That's what you said last winter," Tad laughed. "Look, the water tower is over there on our left. The trees we want to aim toward are almost straight ahead. See? That tall pine and the two shorter ones."

"Oh yeah, I know that. I think you told me last winter."

"I did and I'll probably have to tell you this winter. You don't even follow the path when it's in front of you."

Making their way across the meadow, the boys came to a thick stand of spruce. In a clearing they found an old campsite littered with plastic forks, empty soda cans, and a wet sock. "Pisses me off," said Tad.

"We could pick it up."

"Not today. More important stuff to do."

"Banville," Lance muttered to himself as they pushed on. "I knew it. I just knew it."

Approaching Cabbage Pond, knowing it was getting close to summer, knowing it was very warm, and knowing there was no snow, the boys were strangely disappointed and oddly surprised that the ice had melted.

"Do you remember when you almost killed me here?" Tad asked.

"I never did."

"Three years ago. You were being a real wise-ass and grabbed a handful of cat tails. Then to be funny you hit me in the face with them."

"They don't hurt. They just bounce off."

"No, they burst open into a bunch of little feathers and flew into my nose and mouth. I couldn't tell anyone, I couldn't breathe and I couldn't get them all out."

"Oh, yeah. We were wondering if you were going to die. I kept trying to get you out of the cloud, but they kept coming with you. Some of the kids waved the stuff away."

"Yeah, and I coughed, and coughed, and I couldn't inhale. I knew I was going to die."

"You lived. You're alive. Don't relive it, Tad. I said I was sorry and I was. It was a stupid thing to do. But it hurts too much to relive bad things."

They skimmed a few rocks across the shallow water and moved ahead into the woods on the other side.

"Which way now?" Lance asked quietly. "As if I didn't know."

"Summer people live up that way. They may be here now. They won't want us wandering into their backyard. Let's go that way." He pointed to the right.

"That will take us up across the street from Dr. Banville's property I think."

"It might. As long as we're this far, we might as well walk by."

"Why didn't you say so in the first place? All this has been a waste of time. We could've been there a long time ago if we pushed our bikes straight up Island Ave. But no! 'Let's just take a little hike,' he says. 'Let's go see the pond,' he says."

"I really wanted to see Cabbage Pond again."

"At least we could have ridden down the hill."

"I did that yesterday, if you'll recall. And I really didn't want to today. I just want to take a little look. Just a peek."

"Just a peek!" said Lance. "Just a peek in his windows."

As the sun rose to its eleven o'clock height on that June morning, Tad and Lance finally spotted Upper Island Avenue which ran east and west across the top of the bluff. They also spotted the tall iron fence across the road from them. The fence stood tall around two sides of the two acres of the Old Richards Estate. The edge of the tall bluff protected the other sides. Walking casually across the road, Tad's heart was pounding with eagerness.

Lance felt guilty about being here. Tad grabbed the bars of the old fence, looking at the ancient overgrown gardens. Lance walked along the road very slowly, knowing they looked suspicious. No one else seemed to be in sight though as Tad joined him.

"I had forgotten how really bad it looks," Tad said. "But if you use your imagination you can almost see how beautiful it must have been." He stopped and stared a moment more, shut his eyes for about thirty seconds, and suddenly yelled, "Come on!" He raced alongside the fence toward the house.

Lance, thinking they had been spotted, spun around, tripped over his own feet, and upon picking himself up, ran after Tad. He wondered who they were running from. He was more amazed to see Tad run through Banville's gate and again yell, "Come on!"

"What are you up to now, Tad Callant?" Lance muttered. "First, you scare the shit out of me, and now you do it all over again. What are you up to, Tad Callant?"

Tad waited on the other side of Banville's gate. "Hurry up. This place is a gold mine."

"I don't get it."

"Oh, for cryin' out loud, Deiter, use your head for something other than a peanut butter container. Look at this mess! It will take hours, weeks, to clean this yard out. Then we'd have to keep it nice after that. Dr. Banville says he comes from a wealthy family. Maybe he'd be willing to share some of that wealth with us. We could work by the hour. He obviously isn't planning to do anything about it or he would have done it already. If we sell him just right, we could make a bundle, do a favor for him, and keep an eye on him all at the same time."

"Up until you said keep an eye on him I thought you might have a good idea. But Mr. Finney said he was moving out."

"Maybe not yet. He said a month. Remember? I think he did anyway. Come on. Don't be chicken. It won't look right."

"Okay."

"You knock and I'll talk."

"Now he's a poet. Poems written by the hour. Just line up here. We need the money."

Lance knocked. No one came to open the door. He pressed the bell. A very disturbed-looking Banville suddenly stepped outside. Both boys took a step backward and were surprised when his scowl disappeared as he pleasantly said, "Why, Tad and Lance, good morning."

"Good morning, Dr. Banville," Tad replied.

"What can I do for you, boys?"

"Lance and I were walking by when we noticed your gardens. They're quite overgrown, but they must have been beautiful gardens in their day."

"Yes, yes, I believe that they were." Banville looked toward the garden and a dreamy look spread over his face. "There are old photographs in the house. Yes, the gardens were quite beautiful. This was a showplace. Lots of important people visited here. Even governors and United States senators I believe."

"That's what we thought. How would you like to see it looking like that again?"

"I don't think that's possible."

"We formed a landscape company last year, and we have a lot of experience. We would be willing to clean that mess out for you and make it look real sharp again."

"No, I…"

"We're efficient workers and hard workers, too. You won't find better on the island, even among the adults. We wouldn't goof off or anything and we wouldn't bother you when you were working on your project or resting. Dr. Banville, we want to get lobster licenses this summer. We had hoped to win some money for selling the most tickets in the school raffle, but it looks like Becky Bridges has won. We really need a job. We're not afraid of work, sir."

"I give up."

"You mean we're hired?" asked Lance.

"First, we had better talk wages. How does six dollars an hour sound?"

"Seven fifty an hour sounds a lot better," said Tad. Lance felt six dollars sounded like a gold mine.

"Six seventy-five."

"Tad?" asked Lance.

Tad rubbed his chin. His eyes scanned the sky and he looked very serious, very shrewd, and very determined. "Very hard work. Seven."

"Tad!"

"Okay, seven it is, then."

"Is there someplace where we could safely store our tools?"

"Yes, there is a barn you can use."

"Then it sounds like a fair deal. That was seven dollars apiece, correct?"

"Each."

Lance felt he was going to faint. He thought he and Tad would split the seven dollars.

"May we begin this afternoon?"

"That's fine. I don't really know what's out there. I'll need to spend some time there. Begin in the front yard. Leave the large bushes for now. Clean out all the weeds and trash and we'll have a start. How often can you work?"

"Every afternoon after school; all day on weekends; and during the summer."

"Well, slow down a bit. You talk your hours over with your parents. They may have some other ideas, and don't forget to save some time for fun. As you pointed out, this is a very demanding job. You keep track of your hours. From the time you walk through the gate until you go through again. Give it to me at the end of the week. No Sundays except for today if you want. I'll check on you from time to time to keep you honest."

"We'll be back as soon as we get our tools."

Banville went back inside. The boys walked calmly through the gate to the top of the hill. Then they burst down the middle of the hill, screaming with joy. As he drove up the Island Avenue with three passengers, Old Hal had to swerve to the right, almost hitting a telephone pole. He let off more than a little very colorful steam out his window.

Stopping to pick up their bikes near Finney's cellar hole, they pumped down Island Avenue and around the corner by the fire barn. The captain, seeing them coming, cringed, stood up, ducked, weaved, moved the bikes with his pipe, watched them make the corner, settled back into his chair, and finally began to breathe again. He wiped his forehead with his handkerchief while his heart slowed down to above normal and he wondered what they were up to now.

In Tad's kitchen Marge Callant's voice chased them down the cellar stairs, "What are you two up to now?"

"We got a job," Tad yelled. "We're going to be gardeners."

"Lord help us! Here we go again. Gardeners, now, is it? Who did you con this time?"

"Dr. Banville."

"Dr. Banville?" Marge looked down the dark stairway. "You mean to tell me that you've been bothering that poor man?"

"He isn't poor. He's rich. We just happened to be hiking up next to his house. We went through the woods to see Cabbage Pond. We haven't been there since last winter."

"Get to Dr. Banville, please." She moved down to the bottom of the stairs and sat down.

"Well anyway, we found ourselves up on his road when we came out of the woods. We weren't really sure where we were. But right there across the street was his huge overgrown garden just staring us in the face. I suddenly thought of a way to make money. He's from a very wealthy family, you know. Anyway, we suggested that we could put his poor garden back into shape and he offered us six dollars an hour."

"But Tad talked him up to seven dollars," Lance said very quickly.

"Each," Tad put in.

"And we get to keep our tools up there, and work on Saturday and every day after school."

"Tad, do you really need money that badly? Isn't your paper route enough?"

"Not really, Mom. Not if we want to become lobstermen, and besides, Lance doesn't have a paper route."

His mother didn't look convinced, so Tad continued. "That garden really needs help, and it's something we can do. You ought to see it. It must have been beautiful. Governors and U. S. senators used to hold parties in it, but now it's all overgrown and neglected. It's part of island history, Mom. We can make it beautiful again. It can be the garden spot of the island again, Mom. People from all over will come to see it, and they'll be begging for us to work for them for years and years."

"Your love of beauty has not done much for our place. Our lawn and garden could use your expert help as well. You may have noticed the dirt lawn we have in front of the house is so bare that it has uncovered the tree roots."

Lance's head began to spin trying to figure that out, but Tad persisted, "Oh, I will, Mom. I'll plant grass and keep the kids off it until it grows. I promise."

"With all the tools up at Dr. Banville's and you spending every spare minute up there, how do you intend to make our house a garden spot?"

"You're making it difficult for me, Mom. If Dad were here I bet he would let me do it."

"Don't you start that with me, young man. Don't you dare start that with me. I haven't decided you can't do it. I just want you to remember our yard."

"I will, Mom. I promise."

"All right, get cleaned up for lunch. By the way, Lance, your mother wants you to meet the two-thirty boat."

"I will, Mrs. Callant. Mom already told me. I'll help Tad up the hill with the tools and the mower. Then I'll come down and meet the boat. Is Jackie coming down?"

"I'll send him down. Don't be late."

"We won't. I'll take Dad's old watch," Tad said.

"Don't lose it."

The boys followed Marge up the cellar stairs. Tad whispered to Lance, "It always works when I mention that Dad would let me."

"No, it doesn't," his mother reminded him from the living room. "I had already made up my mind that you could do it."

Tad winked at Lance and they washed up.

After lunch, the islanders saw the boys wearing huge work gloves, pushing a lawn mower, and pulling a wagon filled with clippers, rakes, gasoline, saws, and shovels. By the time they had turned from Main onto Island Avenue, the word was spreading about their good luck. Other boys joined them to ask if they needed help.

By the time they had reached the heights near Cross Street, everyone was winded. By the time they had reached Water Street, their knees became rubbery and the crowd had thinned out. By the time they had reached the Thompson house, they rested under a convenient oak. Only three boys from high school stayed with them.

"You know," Lance said, puffing, "this…this may not be such a swift…a swift idea after all."

"We'll make it."

"I'm sure glad I don't have to do this every day," said the tallest boy who was also the fattest boy.

"Let's go," Tad ordered. "See you guys."

"Already?" Lance said pulling the wagon close to him.

Tad got up and looked up the hill. "Here, I'll pull the wagon for a while. You can push the mower."

Lance pretended the steep part of the hill was the top of Mt. Everest. One step at a time without even using oxygen brought them to Banville's gate. Tad pulled out an oil can and oiled the gate until the squeak disappeared.

"We're getting paid now," Lance said, massaging his calves. "What time do you have?

"Just one-ten. I'll write it down, too. Don't forget that you have to leave early. When you leave, write down that time, too. I'll keep track of my own time."

"I know. I won't gyp anyone. What'll we do first?"

"I guess we could start here in front of the house like he said. I think my mower will be able to take care of the small brush and the dead grass here. The good stuff hasn't started to grow much yet. Why don't you start near the fence and rip out the tall dead stuff, so we can mow it?"

For the next hour, the boys transformed the immediate front yard into something they thought Dr. Banville would be proud to own. As they were raking the cuttings into a pile Lance spotted the boat starting across the bay. "I've got to leave soon."

"I'll finish this," Tad said. "Then I think I'll keep going along the fence a little bit doing your job. I'm getting beat, though."

"Okay, see you later. I really want to see Dad."

"Yeah," Tad said, looking wistfully toward the boat.

An hour later, Tad looked at his watch and stood up. He looked along the fence and muttered, "With the brush this thick, we might not be able to see the end of the fence for months. Lots of hours. Lots of hours." He was smiling as he walked back to get the rake and was surprised to see Rick standing on the other side of the gate when he turned around.

"Hi, Rick."

"Heard you had a job up here."

"Lance and me."

"Even after what I told you?"

"He seems okay."

"Need any help?"

"Not right now, but we may."

Rick's face went through several contortions as anger made him wonder what to say. Finally he said, "He's my customer, Tad."

"What's that supposed to mean? We're not selling him papers. Are you sore or something?"

"Yeah, I guess, kinda." He looked down at the ground, unsure how to continue. Then he looked at Tad, hoping he could help him.

"Why?"

"You know."

"Because he didn't ask you to do this job?"

"Partly."

"He didn't ask us either. He didn't want anybody. I had to talk him into it."

Rick's mousy eyes brightened a little and then he turned away. Staring at the ground again he said, "He could have asked me. He is my customer, you know."

"Damn it, Rick, is he your paper customer or your garden customer?"

"You know."

"He's still your paper customer, Rick, and you know what? You know what? He's my garden customer. So just get off my back about he's your customer. You don't own him, you know."

"I just wondered why he didn't want me. Just forget I said that. I didn't mean it."

"I understand, Rick. I really do. He's your friend, but he isn't my friend though, and like I said, it was my idea not his. He's my boss now, so I have to get back to work."

"See you then," Rick said in a friendlier way. "Lots of work here."

"Yeah," Tad said, his features softening as he shoved his adrenaline through the rake and spread it on top of the brush around him. Raking up the piles into one large pile, Tad wondered about Rick's odd behavior. He had known Rick for years and he had never acted this way before. Why was Banville so special to him? "Hell," he whispered, "probably nobody else ever hugged him. He doesn't have a father either. Might as well join the club." Maybe they could use Rick after all. Tad thought it as he went to look in the barn and sheds.

Two of the sheds were off to the right side of the house. They were large, but in poor shape. "Need to be torn down before they fall down," he whispered. The small barn behind them, on the other hand, although in great need of paint, was in good shape. The roof actually looked new. The loft was empty, as were several stalls on the main floor.

Tad assumed correctly that the islanders had helped themselves to anything not locked up when Old Man Richards died. He hoped they wouldn't help themselves to his tools. Pulling the wagon and the mower into one of the stalls, he spotted two steel doors near the end of the barn in another stall. He walked over and tried to open the left-hand door. It was locked. He opened the right-hand door and found a stairway going up into the loft. At the top was another door, which opened into a large room filled with enormous gears and a great deal of machinery that he didn't recognize. It all appeared to be rusty. Tad figured that, up this high, it was some elaborate pulley system to store things in the loft. "None of my business anyway," he whispered to himself.

As he walked out of the barn, he pulled a large door closed. It slid on wheels across an inside rail above the opening. A voice called from the doorway of the house. "Would you like a cold drink?"

"Yes, thank you," Tad said, surprised and grateful.

Banville held a small pitcher and a glass. Pouring lemonade into the glass, he said, "You've done a remarkable job already."

"We started along the fence for a way, but it's going to take some time."

"I'm very pleased. Was that my paperboy I saw out here?"

"Rick? Yes, it was."

"Was he surprised that you had this job?"

Tad wondered where this conversation was leading. "Yes, he thought you had asked us, and I guess he was a little hurt for some reason. I told him that it was our idea, but he really seems to want to help."

"Would you want him to help?"

"He's a good worker, and, well, he could use the money, but it's not really necessary, Dr. Banville. I can handle Rick."

"Well, if you feel it would help you, go ahead and hire him. I'll leave it up to you."

A beeping sound came from Banville's pocket. He pulled out a pager and clicked it off. "Time to get back to my project."

He took the empty glass from Tad and went inside. As the door closed, Tad thought he heard Banville talking to himself.

"This is going to be a very interesting job," Tad said quietly. He walked through the gate that didn't squeak any more. Taking out his notebook, he marked the time, took one last look at the yard, and walked proudly down the hill.

CHAPTER ELEVEN

MONDAY

After changing from their school clothes into work clothes, which were in fact last year's school clothes and a little tight, Lance asked, "What are we going to do about Mr. Sage?"

"What do you mean?"

"We said we'd take his grocery list today, but we have to work."

"I don't really want to go to Mr. Sage's anymore, Lance."

"I don't either, but we did say we would do it. Maybe we should, one last time."

"Okay, but let's make it quick. I want to get to work. I wonder when he'll pay us."

"He said the end of the week, so Saturday probably."

"Is Finney's still open?"

"Yeah, my mom said that Marty took his vacation from his other job early, and is going to keep the store open for awhile. I wonder what he'll do when his vacation is over."

"Probably sell it if he owns it now, or quit his other job and come down here. My mom says there's all kinds of legal stuff that needs to be done."

At Sage's house, Tad found the front door locked and ran to the kitchen door. A note was tacked to the inside door. "Tad and Lance. Thank you. Tell delivery boy I'll be here about four-thirty. On bluff painting. – Sage"

"Odds or evens to go to the store?" Tad asked.

"Odds, two out of three."

Throwing down their fingers three times it was decided that Lance would go to work while Tad delivered the grocery list. Tad took off saying, "Keep going along the fence."

Lance pulled out of the driveway and tried to pump up the hill, but even standing it was impossible. It was just as steep on the east side of the island as Island Avenue on the west side. Getting off he said, "At least I can ride across the top and ride down when we're done."

On Upper Island Avenue as he came to Banville's fence, Lance noticed how very long it was. He realized that their job seemed like another impossible task. It wasn't until he reached the gate that he realized that he had no idea where Tad left the tools. He began with the sheds and then headed for the barn. Pushing hard, he was jolted when the barn door opened only about a foot and stopped abruptly.

"Probably just a dead body," he said to no one in particular.

Squeezing inside, he quickly found the problem. One of several wheels on the top of the large door had slid off the track and jammed. He tried to lift the large door, but it was too heavy. After finding the tools, he grabbed the work gloves, a rake, and clippers and began work where Tad had left off. He had worked about twenty minutes before he saw Tad push his bike over the crest of the hill in front of the house.

"Where've you been?"

"The store was packed and I had to explain to Billy that he shouldn't go right away. That hill seems to get steeper and steeper. You know I really could have killed myself going down there Saturday."

"You're telling me? I watched you part way. I thought you might knock the truck over. Come over to the barn. One wheel slipped off the track and the door is stuck." He waited as Tad wrote down his time. "I think we can both lift it."

They examined the huge door. With one of them on each side, and with a good deal of effort, they lifted the door enough so the wheel was above the track.

"Okay," said Tad, who was inside, "go slow. Come this way just a little. Too much! Back a little. Okay, lower it gently." The wheel wobbled, but held. Lance tried to open the door again and it slid easily. All the wheels stayed on the track.

"That ought to hold it," Tad said. "We'll really have to treat it gently. I sure don't want to strain a gut lifting that damn door again. Let's get to work."

An hour later, a familiar figure poked his head through the bars of the fence. "How's it goin'?"

"Hi, Rick," Lance said. "It's going fine, but it's hard work. See how far we've come?"

"You doin' the whole garden?"

"We hope to."

"Take a long time, just the two of you."

"You want to work, right?" Tad asked.

"Can I?" His eyes brightened and grew large in anticipation.

"I can work it out, but you only get six-fifty an hour and I pay you."

"What are you doing?" Lance asked.

"Six-seventy-five and Dr. Banville pays me. He's my customer."

"I don't know. But I'm the foreman and you'll do what I say or you're fired. You got that?"

"Dr. Banville pays me, though. Right?"

"Yeah…yes, come on in. I'll keep you on my time list and you don't work here unless I say or Dr. Banville asks you to. We work after school and Saturdays, but not Sundays. You got that?"

"Okay, as long as Dr. Banville stays my customer."

"And stop yapping about your customer. He's your customer. He will always be your customer. When you have a white beard he will still be your customer, so stop talking about it."

Rick walked down to the gate all smiles. Lance remained standing with his mouth open. Finally, he said quietly, "Tad, you can't do this. There's more than enough work for all of us, but you can't do this. You can't promise another kid he will be paid unless you're planning to take it out of your pay. Don't plan to take it out of mine because you won't get it. Just because you feel sorry for him doesn't mean that you can do this."

Tad looked at the ground while his best friend was talking. Then Lance was totally confused as Tad lifted a large smile. Tad hollered to Rick, "Go over to the barn and get a rake and start raking this stuff up into a pile.

"Rick and I had a go-around about this yesterday after you left. He told me I was stealing his customer and all that. I hate that whining. It's stupid. So I talked to Dr. Banville about it, and he said it was up to me whether I hired him or not. Now Rick probably thinks that if I hire him, I won't get Dr. Banville's permission, and then, not only will his pay have to come out of my pay, but that Dr. Banville will get mad at me and fire me. Then Rick will have my job and Banville will really be his customer for the garden, too. Now, I don't want to make an enemy out of Rick just because he isn't too bright, so no matter what he figures, I've got it covered. Dr. Banville will pay him, we get help, and I'm his boss. We all stay friends. He stops whining. It all works well."

"Rick wouldn't think like that. You said it. He's not too bright. But you do scare me sometimes. Someday they're going to put your brain on display at Harvard or someplace, as the most devious, complicated brain in the universe. They will sit around and watch the little wheels turning and the little gerbil running around and—"

"Wheels!" Tad exclaimed.

"Wheels!" Lance echoed, running after Tad toward the barn.

They were surprised to see the barn door wide open and Rick coming out with a rake. Tad checked and saw the wheels still on the rail. "We had some trouble with this door before," he said to Rick. "That wheel came off and the door stuck. It's real heavy, but we managed to get it back on. We figure we better be gentle with it."

"It's a good thing you told me. I just gave it a shove."

Tad and Lance stared at each other.

"Let's get to work. I'll take the mower and go along the section we already pulled up, and if I can, I'll make some paths. Then it will be easier for us to clean out each patch. Lance, you might as well keep going. Rick, you rake that stuff into piles and then help Lance."

"How come I don't get to use the mower?" Lance asked quietly, as Rick began raking.

"My mower. You want to mow?"

"Not as long as I know I can."

"You can, but you're beginning to sound like Rick."

"You're beginning to sound like a boss." In a low voice he said, "And 'my mower' sounds the same as 'my customer' to me." It was Tad's turn to stand there with his mouth open.

In another hour, the yard near the house began to look less like a jungle and more like a manicured front yard. All three boys were sweating and covered with dirt. Tad rubbed his face with his shirt and yelled to Rick, "Bring the gas can. I'm putting the mower away."

He pushed the mower toward the barn. The boys followed with various tools. In the barn, Lance flipped his gloves into the wagon and said, "That was a good afternoon's work."

"Yeah, and only three acres to go."

"We have all summer."

"I know," Tad said, "but I like to finish what I start, and this looks like we'll never finish. I have a dream of what this place can look like, and it will take a long, long time to do."

"I just dream of getting something to drink," Rick said.

"We'll have to bring up canteens or something," Lance agreed.

"Let's close up and get going," Tad said. He pulled the barn door shut very carefully and the boys walked to their bikes.

At the gate Rick yelled, "Wait a minute. I forgot to put away the rake." He grabbed it and ran back to the barn, shoved the door open, and stepped inside. Tad and Lance heard Rick yelling, "Oh no! Oh no!" This was followed by a scream.

They turned and watched the large door fall with Rick behind it. As they raced inside, screams seemed to come out of the floor beneath the door.

"He's under it!" Lance shouted.

"Lift! Let's get it off him."

"It's huge."

"I know and a lot heavier this way."

They tried to lift the side, but it was too heavy for them to hold, and get Rick out at the same time. Muffled screams continued. They held up one corner and tried to figure out how badly Rick was hurt.

"Maybe we can get the wheelbarrow underneath a corner," Lance said.

"How? I can't hold it while you get it."

Suddenly, out of the corner of his eye, Tad saw a shadow burst into the barn. It tore the door from their hands and flung it to the rear of the room in one motion. The door landed almost upright against the stalls behind them. The man went over to the boy who was still screaming and skillfully checked him.

"Mr. Sage!" Tad yelled.

"How?" Lance puzzled.

Suddenly, Dr. Banville entered the barn and bent down over the boy. He spoke quietly. Tad and Lance explained quickly what happened. Dr. Banville checked the boy's eyes, ears, and mouth. He worked down his body, asking Rick questions and making him wiggle his fingers and toes. Rick calmed down immediately in Banville's presence. He was shaking, but didn't seem to be in too much pain.

"I think you will be fine, Rick. Your thighs took most of the blow from one of the cross beams. They will be quite sore for several days. I'll call the taxi to take you home. In the meantime I will call your mother. Let's see if you can walk." Badly bruised and frightened, Rick got to his feet. His walking was unsteady, but he was happy to be on his feet.

"The door is so large that when it fell, the air below served somewhat as a cushion. As you can see, there are three large beams that run horizontally at various levels. You were lucky. Only the middle one hit you. Thank goodness you aren't tall enough to have had your head under the top beam. I don't know how it could have fallen. It's a good thing you were here, sir."

Sage began writing: "Painting nearby. Saw the boys running. I am deaf mute. Expression on their faces said trouble. Sheer luck."

Tad looked at the door more closely. The crossbeams were rough-cut four by fours, which went the entire width of the twelve-foot wide door. After calling Rick's mother and the taxi the two men went to lift the door back toward the front of the barn. It was obvious that it was incredibly heavy. Tad and Lance helped them place it back on the track. They couldn't believe that Mr. Sage had picked it up and thrown it so easily.

"How could he do that?" Tad asked. "How could an old man throw this door like that?"

"Adrenaline," Dr. Banville said. "In an emergency, that chemical can, in some instances, make us all supermen for a very brief time."

"Amazing," Lance said. "You mean he took drugs or something?"

Too amazing, Tad thought.

"No, it's a natural chemical we already possess." Turning to Sage he said, "Sir, do you feel all right? I am a doctor. The door was very heavy. Shall I examine you?"

Sage waved him off and wrote, "In good shape. Not in any pain. If develop pain, will come see you. Have to get home to receive delivery of groceries."

He walked over to Rick, placed his hands on the boy's face, and looked into his eyes long and seriously. Then he began to smile and Rick smiled also. Sage fluffed his hair and walked out.

"Are you boys all set?" Banville asked.

"Yes, thanks, Dr. Banville. We're already late for supper," Lance said.

"Dr. Banville, it's okay if I work for you, isn't it? Tad said you would pay me six-seventy-five an hour."

Banville looked at Tad, who grinned sheepishly and then looked at the ground.

"I left that up to Tad."

"But you're still my customer, right?"

"Of course, and your friend, Rick. I'm so glad you're all right. Now, come sit on my front steps and wait for the taxi. Perhaps we can do a little better than six-seventy-five." Tad snickered to himself. Banville continued, "That was quite enough excitement for me, I'm afraid." He went into the house without looking back.

As the boys reached the top of the hill, Tad waved to Rick and, seeing Mr. Sage limping across the bluff, said to Lance, "Go ahead. I'll catch up. I have to see Mr. Sage for a second."

Lance waited for Tad, sensing his strange need to be alone with Mr. Sage.

Tad ran and pulled alongside the old man, stopped, and faced him. "Mr. Sage, I took your grocery list to Finney's and gave them your message. They probably already delivered it."

Sage smiled and nodded. Tad continued, "That was a good thing you did back there. Rick could have been hurt very badly, but I don't believe you saw us running. And you couldn't have seen our faces. I didn't even know you came into the barn. I don't know how you knew, but you couldn't have seen us. I just want you to know that. I won't tell anyone, but I don't really trust you anymore. I hope that you can trust me enough soon to tell me what the heck is going on."

Sage began writing furiously, finished, began to hand the note to Tad, then took it back and wrote some more. "Thank you for patience, loyalty. You are very brave, very kind, and caring under circumstances. More than most. You are unusual boy. I promised tell you sometime, and will try very hard to keep promise. Late now. Be very careful working for that man."

Tad wasn't sure how to take the last sentence. Banville didn't appear to be anything like what Mr. Finney or Linderman described. Did Sage have special knowledge? Was there a hidden meaning in this last sentence? Should he ask? He said, "I am always careful with people I don't know and some that I do know."

He turned and left. As he reached Lance he picked up his bike and they rode down the hill as slowly as they could. "Did he say anything special?"

"He said we should be very careful in our work."

"We have been so far. We haven't broken or fouled anything up yet. The door wasn't our fault."

"No, but he meant to be careful working for Dr. Banville."

"How does he know anything about Banville? Maybe he's weird like Brian?"

"Psychic, not weird."

"You call it what you want and I'll call it what I want."

* * *

After supper, Lance decided to spend the evening with his father. Tad and his fishing pole went down front to the old army dock. He hoped that the mackerel would be running. The dock had been built during World War II as a place to unload the materials and equipment needed to build, supply, and maintain the lookout towers and gun emplacements on the eastern shore. These in turn had protected Lassiter harbor, and protected naval craft as they refueled in the bay.

The two towers still stood. The gun emplacements had been filled in. The old army dock remained partially functional. It was a place to unload fuel and heavy supplies, and vehicles like the fire engine that were awkward, illegal, or impossible to bring over on the ferry. Only the central ramp was safe and maintained. The rest of the very large dock was a huge maze of rotting timbers and poles. It was from these that the island boys enjoyed fishing.

Tad made his way across the maze to his favorite spot in the northwest corner. He had fished here since he was nine when he was accepted by the older boys on the dock. His mother didn't know about it until he was twelve. All the island mothers were for demolishing the dangerous hazard. Just about all island fathers had fished there. They examined it each year, and made a cast or two into memorable, often happier days. Some even spent an evening here later with their sons.

Tad cast his jig with skill and reeled it in with a slow, jerky motion. He cast again and again, becoming convinced there were no mackerel in this part of the Atlantic.

Within the hour boys seemed to grow out of the huge timbers. Agile as sand fleas and surefooted as snails, they hopped the beams until they found a safe place of their own. Suddenly, within an eye blink their shining jigs appeared to multiply. Hundreds of herring were shimmering this way and that in the reflection of the setting sun as they swam around the old timbers running from the mackerel.

Soon Tad felt a yank, yanked back, and reeled in his first mackerel of the season. There was a yell from another boy and yet another. Excitement among the group rose to a fever pitch.

A gull settled on one of the taller poles looking for a free meal. Others silently joined it, sharing the excitement. Tad cast in again and slightly noticed someone casting close to him from

Lance's spot. Another yank and he was reeling in another mackerel. The person next to him was reeling one in also.

"Bet I can catch more than you can," Becky said a little too loud.

Tad didn't say anything. A hush fell over the whole wharf. The boys took a look to assure themselves of who had dared to say what they had just heard. Then they continued to cast and listen intently.

Sitting next to Tad was his ticket rival, the smartest girl in his class. Sitting next to him in a plaid shirt and blue jeans, her Dutch-cut blond hair shimmering like the hundreds of herring in the fading sunlight, was someone who had dared to challenge Tad Callant. SHE had dared to challenge the present, undisputed, King of the Timbers. Sitting next to him was a GIRL who had dared to break the age-old rules. SHE hadn't even asked permission, as all newcomers had to do. SHE hadn't followed the rules. SHE had simply appeared, and had DARED to cast into this section of the male-owned ocean. The boys watched carefully, judicially. What would the KING do?

Tad didn't know what to say, so he said nothing. The contest was on. Some unwritten rule was being created here. None of the boys knew exactly what it was, but it permeated the atmosphere as sure as the mackerel permeated the water and devoured the herring below. What was the King's strategy? This was definitely a contest to decide the future of MANkind on the island. This was a contest about a HOLY TRADITION. The status quo of the entire dock was at stake. The STATUS QUO OF ISLAND HISTORY was at stake. The pressure was INTENSE! Some boys forgot to cast. Some almost forgot to exhale.

Within the next half-hour, as the word had flown around away from the timbers, more and more boys had come over to examine the contest and the contestants. Tad had twelve mackerel. Becky had ten. Becky got another strike. Tad reeled in with nothing following his line. He immediately cast again, reeled in slowly, using what had unfortunately been known for years as the Callant-Jerk. Was the pressure getting to HIM? Nothing happened! Becky's infectious laughter and quick comments punctuated the hush on the dock. Tad grinned in spite of the pressure and the sweat dripping from his forehead.

Becky cast again. Tad cast again. Another yank on the line and Becky was even with Tad. More boys without poles and some girls came to watch. The dock became crowded as males of all ages were now drawn to the dangerous timbers near the northwest corner. Some men were smoking intensely as they watched from the ferry dock, unable to head home after getting off the ferry a half hour before.

As another ferry came in, the jeep stopped and turned around as it usually did on the wharf. The lieutenant took one look at the army dock and didn't bother to wait. He drove up the hill and then down to the central ramp where he parked with blue lights flashing.

"What's going on out there?" he called.

Everyone except Tad and Becky turned and looked and turned back again. No one said anything. The lieutenant made his way cautiously across the rotting timbers and hollered, "Is anyone hurt out there? Did anyone fall in?"

One of the boys hollered back, "It's a contest to see who can catch the most.

A small boy hollered, "A GIRL is fighting the KING!"

An older teenager said quietly, "That timber you're on is a bad one."

The lieutenant, suspecting that the boy knew what he was talking about, froze. He backed up slowly to a timber that looked safer. Unsure of which way to reach the kids, he yelled, "This dock is dangerous. You kids have been told year after year to stay off. Most of the time you spread yourselves out and we don't say too much. But getting together like that is very dangerous. With all that weight in one place that whole section could cut loose. Clear out of there, and I mean now!"

The crowd moaned and some made obscene gestures behind friends so the lieutenant couldn't see them. Those without poles or good excuses began to move off faster than others. The sun was setting, reflecting off the shimmering bay, but it was a tie. No one moved too quickly. Tad cast again and reeled in slowly. Becky obediently got up, picked up her catch, and began to move off. Tad pulled in another mackerel and hollered, "I got one."

The moaning and groaning changed to cheers. If the lieutenant hadn't been standing there, they would have been all over Tad. Instead they walked off the dock chanting over and over, "Tad beat Becky! Tad beat Becky! Girls LOSE! THE KING RULES!" The disgrace of losing to the girls in the raffle had now been avenged.

Tad, a hero once more, picked up his fish, and began to move off. Becky was waiting for him on the central ramp. "You cheated," she said quietly.

"I did not."

"Yes, you did. We were told to get off and you kept casting."

"Being told by someone not in the competition doesn't have to end it. I'm getting off now. It had to end sometime, and I would have beaten you anyway."

"I've been fishing as long as you have, Tad Callant, and I know as many tricks as you do. You might not have won. I even have some suggestions I could give you about the Callant Jerk."

Tad knew she was right about some of what she said. Now that the crowd was ahead of them he said quietly, "You kept up to me until you quit. I guess that's good for something, and you can fish from the wharf now. No other girl can do that."

"Wait and see."

As they walked past the lieutenant, Tad said, "We can still fish here if we spread out, right?"

"Don't tell anybody I said that. The minute you crowd around, we'll be after you. The timbers are getting very dangerous. You know that, Tad."

"I understand, but we know which ones are still okay. We really do. We study them."

"That's quite a catch you have."

"Want some?"

"Are you trying to bribe a Public Safety officer?"

"That's probably illegal. I've got more than enough. Kind of heavy and I'm awful tired. May I drop a few off when I pass the barn?"

"Do what you want, but don't tell the captain I know about it."

"Right," Tad said, smiling. Becky noticed, not for the first time, the beautiful dimples near his lips.

The lieutenant walked back to the jeep and drove off. Becky and Tad walked up the path to Island Avenue. "Where's Lance?" Becky asked.

"He stayed with his dad tonight."

"I hear you're working up at Dr. Banville's."

"Yeah, we're cleaning up his yard. It a big job, but it can be a beautiful garden just like it used to be years ago."

"You'll make it look great, Tad. You always do the right thing."

Tad turned a little red, and for the second time that day shivers went up and down his spine. These were different though. Near the fire barn Tad said, "Well, I've got to go home now. I'll drop off a few mackerel to keep them off our backs."

Becky pulled three fish from her string. "Give these to the captain, too. Maybe we can keep them really happy." With that, she ran off.

Tad stood there for a moment, watching her. With his hands full of wet fish the King of the Timbers knew that something new had been added to his life.

CHAPTER TWELVE

TUESDAY AFTER SCHOOL

Leaving school, Lance was unusually quiet. He had hardly spoken to Tad all afternoon. Now he walked home with his hands clenched and his head hanging low. Tad ignored it for a while and finally said, "What's the matter with you, anyway?"

"What's the matter with me?"

"Yeah, what's the matter with you?"

"Nothing's the matter with ME!"

"What's that supposed to mean? Are you angry?"

"I'm not mad at you, Tad."

"Well, what's the matter then?"

"You really want to know? You really want to know?" He stopped and looked Tad in the eyes.

Tad saw a great sadness sitting there and wasn't sure what had happened. Wondering about Lance's father, he finally said quietly, "Yes, I really want to know."

"All right. I'll tell you." Lance continued to walk.

Tad waited, and then followed him up the well-worn path through the woods between School Street and Central Avenue. "So tell me."

"All right. If you really want to know, it's because of the stupid way you acted today."

"What way did I act?"

"Stupid, that's how." Lance's head hung lower as he walked.

"I didn't act stupid, Lance."

"Yes, you did. Ask anybody."

"What? What did I do?"

"What about first thing this morning on the playground?"

"What about it?"

"Just think, Tad. Try to remember if you can think at all."

"I'm not playing guessing games. Now what are you talking about?"

"You really don't remember, do you?"

"All I remember is I went to school, got the ball like always, and we played kickball. Then the bell rang and we went in, like always."

"Who did you pick first for your team?"

"You, like always."

"No, you didn't, Tad Callant." Lance stopped and stood in front of him. Tad pushed past him. Lance caught up to him. "You picked me second. Who did you pick first?"

"Oh…oh, is that it?"

"Who did you pick? Come on, say it."

"Becky."

"Who did you walk into school with?"

"Becky."

"In math, who did you pass the note to?"

"Becky, but—"

"In social studies you changed your project. Who is the head of your new committee?"

"Becky, but I—"

"At lunch recess, what blond girl chose you for her team?"

"Becky. All right. All right. I get the point."

"You have a point on your head."

"She's a good kid, Lance. I've always liked Becky."

"She's just a girl!" Lance spouted without meaning to.

Now Tad stopped and grabbed his arm. "You're jealous."

"I am not. You acted stupid."

"That's what it is, Lance. You're jealous. You're mad because I paid more attention to her today than I did to you. That's it. Huh? Huh?"

"That's not all of it." He continued walking rapidly. They crossed Central Avenue and continued on the path to F Street.

"But it's most of it," Tad insisted. "Hey, we're best friends, right? Hell, we're family. Why are you upset?"

"I'm not upset about anything."

"Well, you're mad at me for hanging with Becky a little."

"That's true enough."

"Well, don't worry about it."

"You mean you won't hang around with her anymore?"

"No, I don't mean that. I like her a lot, but you're my best friend and always will be. Is that good enough?"

"It's pretty good, but I'd feel better if you'd forget her."

Tad was quiet as they walked. When they reached E Street, he said. "You'll get a girl friend sometime. Wait and see. Did I really make a fool out of myself?"

"Yeah, you did. All the guys were wondering what was wrong with you."

"What did they say?"

"Oh things like, Tad's flipped for Becky, and stuff like that."

"That's crazy."

"You should have seen yourself. You looked at her all day." Lance kicked a rock across D Street. Tad kicked it into the woods and was silent for a few seconds.

"Did I really?" Tad asked on C Street.

"What?"

"Look at her all day?"

"Yeah, you did. We all watched you. It was embarrassing."

"Wow."

"Yeah, wow. The guys were calling you the King and Queen!"

The boys avoided the tiny frog pond where they normally pegged a few stones on the way. They cut through the path between B and A Streets before Tad spoke again. "Do you think she'd do it?" he almost whispered.

"What did you say?"

"Do you think Becky's cute?"

"I thought…I thought you were never going to pay attention to her again."

"I never said that."

"Then the hell with you," Lance said, as he ran off toward home.

Tad ran after him, tackled him near the Deiter's hedge, rolled him over, and pinned him down. Then he realized that Lance had been crying.

"Let me up," Lance said quietly.

"Not until you listen to me."

"I've listened to you enough. I've listened to you for years. Years, Tad. Now let me up. It's over with us."

"You can listen some more."

Lance tried to scramble away and got one arm free. He swung and hit Tad hard in the mouth. Tad grabbed his arm and held it firmly. Blood from Tad's lip dripped onto Lance's chin. Lance looked him square in the eyes and said, "What would you do if you had Becky like this?"

"I'd probably kiss her with my bloody damn lips." Lance squirmed and Tad gripped him harder as he licked his lips. "Understand this, Lance: I want to start going with Becky. I can't stay a kid all my life. Understand this, too: I won't give up on you, Lance. You're part of my family and I'm part of yours. We've been together all our lives. Nothing can break our friendship. Nothing. I'm not going to give up on Brian, or Mickey, or even Donsie. And I won't ever give up on you. Do I have to say it? Okay, I love you, Lance. I mean it when I say I won't ever give up on you. I'm just not like that. You know that. You have to know that! You're feeling sorry for yourself, and if anyone is acting stupid, it's you."

"You're right," he whispered. He wiped his chin with his sleeve. "I am acting like a jerk. I guess I'm just afraid of losing you, too. Really afraid, Tad. I can't lose you. You're my anchor. I'm afraid of losing you and my father. I'm all mixed up right now."

"Isn't your father better?"

"I don't know. I guess I expected him to come home from the hospital all better. I know that Mom told me what he'd be like and all, but I guess I wanted him the way he used to be. He's weaker than Jackie, and that's pretty weak. The pain is gone mostly and he's sleeping, but damn it, Tad, I just know he's never going to be right again. I haven't said that to anyone else, but I know it."

"He might be."

"Oh sure, he might be. I hope and hope. For months I've hoped. I've even prayed about it, but it's just wait, wait, wait, and nobody seems to be able to make him better. Not even God.

"Even Dad thinks he might be getting better, but then he knows he's not. He talks about what we're going to do when he gets well one minute, and then he starts talking about how to handle this type of thing this way, and that type of thing that way. It's like he knows he isn't going to be around and he wants to cram the next five or six years until we grow up into a few weeks.

He's driving us crazy. He even talked about things I have to remember when I get my driver's license in a couple of years. Even I don't think about that yet. Not much anyway. "Then he gets so quiet. He just sits there and doesn't say anything at all. That's the worst. He's so scared for us and I think...and I think for himself. I just know he's going to die and I don't know what to do about it!" Tears began to pour out. "I can't do anything right," he shuddered. Then he whispered, "Please don't leave me, Tad."

"I won't! You're right about one thing though, Lance. You can't do anything about it. You've got to accept that. When my dad went away, I tried everything to keep him here, but nothing worked. I realized that I couldn't control everything. Just like Judy said. Not even the things and people that mean everything to us. You've got to do the same, Lance. Have you talked with your mother about this?"

"No. She acts so strong, like everything is going to be okay, but I've heard her crying at night sometimes."

"Maybe that's what all of you should do."

"Ask my mother about it or cry?"

"Both. I don't know why, but I feel like you should both cry, and your father, too, and Jackie and your sisters. You should all cry together."

"For how long?"

"For an hour? How do I know? The whole family in the living room, all crying together because your dad is going to die. For a week, maybe kinda celebrate his dying, and his life, and just cry together. I mean we all die sometime. Cry until the water gets up to your knees. I don't know. It just seems to me that if you all feel that way, then instead of hiding it from each other, you should all tell each other what you really feel, and cry it out together. Maybe once. Maybe a thousand times. Then, when you're all cried out, you could maybe start accepting whatever is going to happen, and together you could handle it. I bet even your father would feel better."

"That's awfully hard. We hide a lot from each other."

Tad stooped down and said, "I know it sounds dumb, but something told me to tell you that. Sometimes it's awful hard to tell the people that are closest to you that you care about them. I can do it with Brian, but I have real trouble with Mickey, and especially Donsie. I know I should, but it's awfully hard. I don't know why."

"You always know the right thing to say, Tad. Right now the picture of you telling Mickey you love him makes me laugh."

"I'm not trying to make you laugh, you jerk."

"I know, but what you said makes a lot of sense, even if we can't do it. I get the picture of you coming in my back door for breakfast, and when you open the door a wave of water from our tears pushes you back into your yard."

"Yeah, and when I ask your mother what's for breakfast she says, 'Get your pole and catch some of the pancakes that are floating around.' I go upstairs to wake you up and I have to swim underwater. When I reach your room, there you are, sitting in your wet bed as usual."

Lance leaped for Tad, but Tad was up and racing toward his house. He ran around the large maple tree that separated their yards. Lance grabbed for him. After three trips around the old maple with both of them laughing, Tad said, "I give up. I give. I take it all back." He sat down under the tree and Lance sat down next to him, shoulder to shoulder.

"We're losing time."

"What do you mean?"

"Banville's."

Tad jumped up. "I forgot! Go change!"

Lance looked at their clothes. "I don't think it will make much difference."

Entering his house, Tad saw a note on the table: "Gone to Joanie's. Back by four. Brownies are for supper. Have an orange instead. Love, Mom."

Tad changed quickly, grabbed a brownie, and started out the door. Seeing Mickey, Brian, and Jackie coming into the yard, he put the brownie into his pocket and walked out.

"Mom's at Joanie's. You guys behave yourselves. Understand? I have to go to work."

"We will," said Brian.

"Some work, pulling weeds," Mickey sneered.

"For seven bucks an hour," Tad boasted.

"Probably below miminum wage," Jackie smirked.

"Minimum. You better check that out," Tad said getting on his bike. "Oh, and by the way, I love you guys." He rode off.

"What did he say?" Jackie asked.

"He said he loved us," said Brian. "But I know that. His lip was bleeding. Lance did it, but they're okay now."

"He's up to something," Mickey said. "We need to watch him very closely. Very, very closely."

* * *

At Banville's Tad took out the mower once more. Lance said, "I'm sick of the fence. That'll take forever."

"Want to mow?"

"Not yet. I just need to do something different. I'll start clipping some of those big bushes by the fountain."

"Don't cut any live ones."

"I won't. Is Rick coming?"

"No. I asked him in school when I wasn't looking at Becky." Tad smiled. "He said his mother wasn't mad or anything, but wanted him to rest his legs for a couple of days. He told her that we had warned him about the door. She talked to Dr. Banville about it and she really likes him."

"I'll bet he gave them money."

"Maybe, I don't know." Tad started the mower and Lance started clipping. The brush was thick. The work went slowly. Tad started with thin weeds and the thin brush. Every time he started on the thicker brush, the old mower, although powerful, wanted to die. He leaned it back and it roared back to life. He attacked again and again.

Lance found the brush by the fountain just beyond the house more difficult to cut than he had anticipated. Each piece seemed to be like rock. As he snapped through a piece, his knuckles banged together.

"You guys are certainly doing a magnificent job out here." Lance jumped at the voice. "I'm sorry. I didn't mean to frighten you."

"You just surprised me, Dr. Banville."

Tad, seeing Banville and Lance talking, shut off the mower and came over to them.

"I was just saying to Lance that you boys are doing a fine job. It certainly is a lot of work."

"It is," Tad agreed, "but we're getting it."

"How is Rick today?"

"Walking funny and complaining a lot, but he's okay. He's smiling about having the job. His mother wants him to rest his legs for a few days," Tad said.

"Yes, I suggested that to her again last evening when I called. Rick made light of his injury, but she knew when he walked in the door that he was in pain. Mothers always do."

"That's for sure," Lance laughed nervously.

"I see you speak from experience. By the way, I'm just on my way to the boat. I won't be back until late. Just put your tools away when you're done and I'll see you tomorrow. Be careful with that door. Tad, your lip is bleeding."

"A little disagreement. Nothing to do with work. It'll be okay. We're going to work for just a little while longer. We were a little late today, but we still have to be home in time for supper."

"I understand. Put some ice on it this evening. You just keep your hours and give them to me when you get paid on Saturday as I said. Don't feel you have to work all day on Saturday. I think a few hours will be quite enough, and remember not to work on Sunday."

"Sounds good to me," Lance said.

"Me too," agreed Tad.

"Well then, I'm off. I'll see you tomorrow."

Banville walked across the yard and down the hill. Lance went back to work. Tad started the mower, ran to the gate, and walked cautiously to the top of the hill. In a few minutes, he ran back.

"He's really going."

Lance looked up and saw the boat five minutes out. "He better get moving."

"He'll make it. Come to the top of the hill."

Carrying the clippers, Lance followed Tad, wondering what was going on now. He saw Banville almost at the bottom and walking very fast, running a few steps, and walking again.

"Stand here until you see him get on the boat, but keep down."

"I'll just turn on my telescopic eyes."

"Just watch for his red blazer. How can you miss him?"

"What are you going to do?"

"You just watch, and when the boat leaves, make sure he's on it. If he misses it, find me fast. I'll be checking the windows."

"Here we go again. Now who's breaking the law?"

"I've got to find a way in. It's the reason we're here."

"I thought we were here for the money."

"That too. Just watch." Tad ran back to the house and tried the front door, which was locked. He tried climbing up to several windows in the front. They were impossible. On the east side of the house near a strong ancient vine he found one unlocked.

Lance found him. "He made it. They pulled in the ramp and then pushed it out again."

"Give me a boost."

"As usual. This isn't a very good idea. In fact, it's a real lousy idea. We can be seen from the street."

"No one's on the street."

With Lance's boost he was through the window. Reaching outside, he grabbed Lance's hand and helped him walk up the side of the house.

They found themselves in a very large and very dark living room. It was filled with lots of furniture covered with very dirty sheets. It was obvious that none had been touched for many years.

"This place is creepy," Lance whispered.

"Let's find the kitchen. Rick said it was really modern. So did Mr. Finney."

Opening a door, they found themselves in a spotless hallway which ran back to the kitchen from the front door. The spacious kitchen was as modern and clean as Rick said it was. From the large kitchen windows which wrapped around the corner of the house they had a broad view of Lassiter, Indian Bay and Keelscrape Island right behind them across a narrow channel.

"This section sticks out like a tower," Lance said.

"There must be a pantry here somewhere."

"You hungry?" Lance asked. He knew he was.

"We have to find all the food that's supposed to be here."

Lance opened a door to a little room with cherry paneling. It had many shelves covered by beveled glass doors. There were several wide drawers below. "This must be for dishes and stuff, but it's empty and as dirty as the living room."

"I think this is the pantry back here," Tad said from the other side of the kitchen. "But there's nothing here, but more dirt."

Lance opened the refrigerator. It was empty except for a cold drink and cookies from the store. "This is ridiculous. Where does he keep all his food? Let's try upstairs. We can check the other rooms down here after. Where are the stairs?"

"Near the front door, I think."

In the shining hallway they found shining stairs leading up to an equally shining hallway. Three doors were closed on each side of the hallway that ran to the right and the left of the stairs. A large bathroom was found in the tower which they figured was above the kitchen.

"Wow, twelve rooms! You take the left," Tad said.

Opening the first door, Tad was amazed. The room was empty except for a bed and an empty chest. The bed contained only an old mattress. It hadn't been touched either. The next room was the same except that it had more furniture. At the end of the hallway, Tad hollered, "It doesn't make any sense. These rooms haven't been touched in years. Lots of old furniture in good shape, everything is antique. The kitchen and the hallways are just for show in case anybody comes inside. That's what it is! It's all for show! But where does he live? Why buy a beautiful old house like this and not use it?"

"And where is his project? Where does he sleep?"

Racing down the stairs, they checked two other very large rooms on the first floor each with a beautiful bay view. They were filled with very old fine furniture, which also had not been touched except by mice and the setting sun.

"We better get out of here, Tad."

"I know, but where the hell does he live?"

"How about the cellar?"

"I was afraid you were going to say that."

"I don't really mean it," Lance explained.

"I know, but it may be our only chance. Let's go a little way down. Leave the cellar door open."

"What cellar door?"

"I don't know. Maybe it's the other door in the kitchen."

In a moment they stood in front of the open door looking at each other. "This is it," Tad said.

"Turn on the light."

Halfway down the stairs, Lance said, "You don't believe in vampires, do you?"

"No, definitely not. No, I do not. No." The cellar also looked unused. There were several benches with old tools scattered here and there, and hung on the wall.

"Definitely not, maybe," he whispered. "There are supposed to be wine cellars below this, and maybe the passage down to the bottom of the cliff."

"Wine cellars below this cellar?"

"Let's look for the door to the wine cellar and then we'll leave."

They found another door. Tad opened it and confirmed it was another stairway. No light switch could be found. "That's it. We'll have to keep some flashlights here somewhere. Wait, there's one hung up here on the wall."

"Let's get out of here, Tad."

Suddenly frightened, Tad said, "Yeah, I'm for that. We can try this some other time."

Back in the kitchen, Lance shut the cellar door and they headed for the window in the living room. "Wait. Wait," Tad said, "the cellar light. I'll get it. No mistakes." He ran back and shut it off.

"Tad! Lance!"

"Did you hear that?" Lance asked.

"Becky?" Tad asked.

"Tad! Lance!" Becky called again. She was outside.

"What'll we do?"

"Can you see her?"

"Yeah, she's over next to the mower. You and your dumb girlfriend! She can see us no matter how we leave the house. It's too steep to get out in the back anyway."

"Don't start."

"Remember what you told me about how you almost got caught at Finney's?"

"Won't work."

"Yes, it will. It's simple."

"Just remember that it's your idea."

Opening the front door, Lance stepped out where Becky could see him. He turned back and said, "Thanks for the drinks, Dr. Banville."

"Yeah, thanks," followed Tad. "It was getting hot out there. We have to put the tools away. See you tomorrow. Oh, hi, Becky. What are you doing here?"

Tad shut the door making sure it was locked. Smiling widely he looked again at her and forgot everything else.

"You were inside?"

"Just in the kitchen. Dr. Banville gave us a cold drink."

"What are you doing here?" Lance asked, trying too hard to sound pleasant.

"I just came up to see if you wanted to come to a clambake we're having Saturday. Mom is having a lot of her old friends down from uptown and they don't have any kids, so she said I could ask some. I decided to ask you first."

"Yeah, that would be great."

Surprised, Lance said, "Both of us?"

"Of course, silly. And I promise I won't tell."

"You won't tell what?" Lance asked.

"I won't tell that you were in the old Richards place. I promise I won't."

"We were just getting a drink," Lance said. "Nothing wrong with that."

"I know that's what you said, but I saw Dr. Banville running for the boat."

"Oh, boy," Lance said.

"You and your ideas, Deiter." Tad's face had turned bright red.

"I won't tell anyone if you'll—"

"If we'll what?" Tad asked, somewhat hopeful.

"If you'll take me in there the next time you go in."

"Oh, boy," Lance said.

"We don't know if we'll get a chance to go back in," Tad said.

"Why were you in there?"

"It's a long, long story, but let's just say we were just curious. We didn't take anything or anything like that. Really."

"Oh, I know you guys wouldn't do anything like that. I don't want to either. I'm really curious, too. I've heard so much about it that I want to see it. What's it like?"

"What's it like?" Tad echoed, looking at Lance. Lance gave a shrug saying that all was lost anyway. "It's got a beautiful kitchen. All modern. My mom would love it."

"And lots of old furniture. Antiques."

"I want to see the dungeons," Becky said excitedly.

"Dr. Banville said there weren't any dungeons. He said there were wine cellars, but it was dark and we didn't want to go down to them."

"Next time we'll bring flashlights," Becky decided. "I hear that a secret passageway goes all the way down to the water and there's a secret entrance to the ocean."

"Yeah, I know, but nobody's ever found it, and Dr. Banville said that wasn't true either."

"Promise me you'll take me next time anyway."

"We can't really promise that, Becky. If we decide to go in again, it will probably be when we're working. We don't know when Dr. Banville will be away. Besides, it's dangerous."

"Tad, I don't mind danger."

"Oh, boy."

"Will you stop saying that, Lance?" Becky took Tad's hands gently. "If you are here and I am here, and if Dr. Banville goes away, will you promise to take me in with you, if you go?"

Tad's mouth suddenly turned very dry. "All right, but that's a lot of ifs. No other promises, because I really don't know what's going to happen and we have to be very careful."

"Are you going to hang around all the time and wait?" Lance asked angrily. "We have work to do and it'll look funny."

"He's right, we really do have work to do."

"I know and I won't bother you, but a promise is a promise, even with a lot of ifs. Maybe Dr. Banville could hire me, too. I can work as hard as you can. Right now though, I have to get home to supper."

"We'll just put the tools away and ride down with you," Tad said. Looking into her beautiful eyes, he still held her hands.

"Wonderful, I guess I know who puts the tools away," Lance muttered to himself.

Halfway down the hill, Tad seemed to wake up from a dream. "Wait, stop!"

"What?" Becky and Lance said.

"My dad's watch is missing."

"I don't remember seeing it. Are you sure you had it?"

"I had it. I recorded the exact time when we came through the gate. I guess I forgot to record when I left. I kind of remember hitting it when I tried to open one of the windows or the barn door or something. I think I know where it might be. I better go back and get it. We don't want Dr. Banville to find it in the wrong place. It shouldn't take more than a few minutes."

"Is it in the house?" Becky asked in anticipation.

"No, and it's ridiculous to climb this hill if you don't have to. I'll be right back like I said."

Tad pushed his bike up the steep section once more. At the top, he left it at the gate and ran over to the unlocked window. Quickly scanning the plants and vines that surrounded it, he found nothing. He ran to the other windows. Nothing. He decided to look in the barn.

"What's keeping him?" Lance asked.

"Maybe we'd better go back and help," Becky said.

"I'll wait a few more minutes. You can go home if you have to. The boat's coming in and maybe Dr. Banville will be on it, but I guess it would be crazy to go uptown and then right back down. We'd better wait and see."

"Let's ride down to Finney's. Then we can see better and get a head start to get Tad if we see him."

Keeping his eyes to the ground, trying to retrace his steps, Tad entered the barn. He saw nothing and knew he had to go back inside the house.

Ten minutes later as Lance watched the boat dock he said, "Okay, Banville isn't on the boat. Tad must've gone back into the house by now. We'd better go back up. If he left the watch in the house, it could be anywhere."

"I want to go in anyway," Becky said.

Fifteen minutes later they both called for Tad and searched around the house. There was no answer.

"Where's his bike?"

"Probably in the barn, just in case Banville got by us. Tad always thinks ahead. We better put ours in there, too."

After searching the building without finding anything, they ran around the house, calling him. "I don't get it," Becky said. "What window did you guys use?"

"Over here, but where would his bike be?"

"In one of the bushes maybe. There are enough of them around."

At the side of the house the window was still open. "I know I closed that window."

"Then he did go in. Give me a boost."

"I always end up giving boosts. Remember to help pull me up."

"I will."

Lance was surprised at how agile Becky was. He watched her crawl through the window. When she reached down for him, he grabbed her arm using it for support as he climbed the ancient vines. Once through the open window he shut it behind him.

"Linderman!" Lance gasped as he turned around.

Becky was struggling in the arms of another man. "Let . . . let her go!" Lance kicked Linderman in the shin as hard as he could and broke free. Trying to pull Becky free, he blacked out.

"Tie them up and put them with the other boy. Then bring in their bikes. We'll have to work very quickly now. There will be people looking for them soon."

Becky was carried, still struggling, into the hallway and down the cellar stairs. Linderman followed with Lance over his shoulders. In the cellar, as Becky was being tied, she began to yell, "You leave us alone you big apes! We're just kids and you don't know the people on this island! They'll all get you for this. You just signed your own death warrants!"

A piece of duct tape was placed over her mouth. The same was done to Lance. Becky spotted an unconscious Tad in a similar condition. All three were seated on the floor next to an ancient workbench, which was very solid and very high. A man brought down their bikes, and placed them next to Tad's. He disappeared through a doorway to another stairwell just as

Linderman had before him. A single light bulb over the bench was left on.

Becky struggled to stand by inching up against the bench. Using the edge of a vise, she managed with great difficulty to pull part of the duct tape from her mouth. She scanned the bench for something to cut the ropes holding her. There was no way she could reach anything.

Looking at the two boys, she had no idea how long they would be unconscious. Maybe they were dead. "That's ridiculous, Becky," she whispered to herself. "If they were dead, why would they tie them? I've got to get help." Hopping over to the stairs, she sat down on the second step and made her way to the top, one step at a time. The door to the kitchen was open. Becky saw no one. Hunching backwards into the kitchen, she stood with difficulty, and hopped into the hallway. That was when an armed lookout in the living room spotted her.

CHAPTER THIRTEEN

TUESDAY EVENING

By five o'clock, when Tad hadn't come home, Marge fended off her other three hungry children and sent them to wash. By five-fifteen she was angry. At five-thirty, Sylvia called and sent Jackie over. Happy to take on any responsibility for getting their brothers in trouble Jackie and Mickey went looking for them. By six-fifteen, Marge Callant was frantic. Sylvia had already called her twice.

Brian came back into the kitchen, wrapped his arms around his mother's ample waist, and said, "Tad's all right. He's asleep."

That was enough for Marge. She had never understood Brian's unusual ability to know things other people didn't know. It was considered a gift by her people. Her uncle Clyde had the sight, but her family considered him very strange and had little to do with him. Strange how folks say one thing and practice another, she thought. Brian's words comforted her, but why would Tad be asleep?

"Where is he?" she asked Brian.

"He's someplace with a workbench and three bikes. Lance is with him. He's asleep, too."

That was all it took. She didn't know whether to trust Brian in something this serious, but she found she couldn't discount it either. She dialed Sylvia. "I'm going down to the barn."

"I'll go with you."

"Perhaps one of us better stay, in case they come in. Wait a minute, Mickey and Jackie are coming in."

"We couldn't find them," Mickey said, out of breath. "We looked all around Dr. Banville's. Nobody is home and the tools are all in the barn. No bikes though."

"Sylvia, no sign of them."

"Send the kids over here. One of the girls can care for them. I'll be down as soon as I can."

Hanging up the phone, Marge said, "You kids go over to Jackie's and stay there. I'm going down to the fire barn. If Tad and Lance come home, send them down. Thank you for searching for them, boys. Get along now."

Walking rapidly down Maple Street, her mind raced with possibilities. Finally, she found one that made sense. If Dr. Banville wasn't home, maybe the boys decided to go swimming. She tried to keep Brian's statement out of her mind, but it kept creeping in like a poisonous gas, and it frightened her. By the time she had reached the fire barn, she was convinced that they were in real trouble.

"Marge," said the captain, "what's wrong?"

"Tad and Lance didn't come home for supper and it's not like them. I sent Mickey and Jackie up to Dr. Banville's where the boys have been working for the past few days, but they couldn't find them. He isn't home and the boys' tools were all put away in the barn. Now it could be if he went away they went swimming and forgot the time, but Sylvia and I are very worried. It just isn't like them."

"What time was Tad supposed to be home?"

"Five o'clock."

The lieutenant, who had been standing next to the captain, said, "I'll take a trip around. I'll check the pond first."

"The boys had their bikes."

"Sit down here, Marge." He pulled out his chair. "Please, sit. I'm sure the boys will turn up. I'm willing to bet that it's not the first time they've been late."

"No, but Tad's always managed to let me know. Since his father left, he has always been very concerned about my feelings."

"If they don't show up soon, I'll call some men together and we'll conduct a search."

Sylvia Deiter showed up five minutes later looking as worried as Marge, who explained to her what was being done.

"The lieutenant just stopped me to make sure they hadn't come home. I can't imagine what's happened. They've never been this late before."

The phone rang. As the captain listened, his face was no longer calm. "Hang on, Mrs. Bridges." Turning to Sylvia and Marge, he said, "Becky is missing, too. It seems she went looking for the boys to ask them to come to a clambake. Mrs. Bridges hasn't seen her since. She's been calling all over. Have either of you seen her?"

"No."

"Mrs. Bridges, I have Marge and Sylvia here. They are missing Tad and Lance. The lieutenant is checking a few places. Did Becky have her bike? . . . Yes, I see. I'll get back to you. . . . No, why don't you stay there in case she comes back. That's right. Yes. Yes. I'll call you just as soon as I know anything. Please do the same."

The captain turned to the radio. "Base to unit one."

"Unit one, Cap."

"We have another one. Mrs. Bridges just called. Becky is missing. She went up to Banville's about four-thirty to invite the boys to a clambake and hasn't been seen either. She also had a bike."

"She and Tad had that contest catching mackerel last night. They may be back down on the army dock. No sign of anyone at the pond. Plenty of tracks, but no clothes or bicycles."

"Stop up at Banville's and see if he's home yet. If he's not, ask around and see if anyone has seen him or the kids. I'll check the wharves with the glasses."

"Ten-four. Out."

The captain grabbed his field glasses and walked out of the station. With an experienced eye he examined the army dock, the marina, and the two ferry wharves from top to bottom. There were plenty of children, but not the children he was looking for.

Walking back into the station, he picked up the phone. In the next few minutes he called his mobile eyes: Hal's taxi, the two oil companies, the plumbers, and Jimmy, the bread man and ticket-seller for the boat. Receiving negative replies and promises, he called the storeowners. Finally, reluctantly, he called some shut-in women known to be concerned with all that went on outside their windows.

"We have a little news," he said to the mothers. Turning again to the radio he said, "Base to unit one."

"Unit one. I was just about to call you. Dr. Banville is not at home. The house is all locked up. From the looks of the yard I suspect the boys were here today. Some of the grass has been freshly cut."

"Ten-four. I made some calls. We now have an informal search going on. I did pick up some information: first, Lance and Becky were seen heading up Island Avenue after the five o'clock boat came in. Dr. Banville went up on the three-fifty. No one has seen him come back. I checked the waterfront, but you might want to swing down there and talk to the kids. I'm going to wait just a little while longer and then call for a search."

"I'll check the cross streets and then swing down and talk to the kids. Out."

"Base out."

Turning to the mothers he said, "I have to ask a silly, but routine question. Were either of your boys going out with the Bridges girl?"

"No," Sylvia said. "At this point I doubt that Lance even thinks in those directions."

"Up until last night I didn't think Tad would either, but he was on cloud nine when he came home from fishing. He said that he and Becky had a contest. I suspect he caught more than fish."

"Yes, that's what I felt, too. They dropped some mackerel off here on the way home. It was a gentle bribe to let us know the kids still wanted to use the army dock. We go through it every year. They were both already on cloud nine by then. I wasn't sure why."

"What I don't understand is why Lance was with Becky without Tad?" Sylvia said.

"And why were they headed up Island Avenue at that time unless they went to find Tad?"

"Well, we'll find out," the captain said. "I am quite sure the word has been widespread by now. They didn't take the ferry. Jimmy confirmed that, so they have to be on the island. It's simply a matter of finding where."

The phone rang. As the captain put the receiver down he said, "That was Marty. The boys brought Billy a grocery list from Mr. Sage yesterday afternoon. Billy wondered if they might be up there."

"Mr. Sage?" Sylvia asked.

"He's an older deaf mute renting the Madison place. An artist. Apparently the boys met him when they were selling raffle tickets. I really don't know much about him except that he's working on a commission to do seascapes. As a matter of fact, all I do know about him comes from Tad and Lance." Picking up the microphone, he called the lieutenant.

"One."

The phone rang. "Hold on." Answering the phone he listened, then said, "Okay, Marty. Thanks." Turning to Marge he said, "Marty just wanted to be sure that I understood it was yesterday Tad brought the list in. This isn't the first list they've brought down for him.

"Unit one, check out the old Madison place where Mr. Sage is staying. Marty called to say that the boys have brought grocery lists to him from Mr. Sage a couple of times recently."

"Ten-four. I've checked all of the cross streets and talked with some of the kids. It appears that Tad was somewhat infatuated with Becky all day in school, but no one has seen them. They're all out looking now. I hope we don't get anymore lost kids on my account. I told them to go home."

"After you check Sage's, you better check all of Upper Island Av and Island Av again. Check house by house. Check all around Banville's again."

"Are you calling out the boys for a search?"

"A few more minutes. Out."

"Okay, Cap, out."

"I just can't sit around here," Sylvia said. "Neil will be quite upset. I better get home or he'll be down here, too."

"Let me know if the kids are a handful, Sylvia. I'll stay here for a bit longer."

A half hour went by before the jeep pulled into the yard. Getting out, the lieutenant said, "I think you better call them in. Marge, do you recognize this?"

"It's Tad's father's watch. He was wearing it. Where did you find it?"

"Near one of the windows on the side of the Banville house. I was walking around the house and spotted it caught in some bushes about four feet off the ground. The window near it was locked, and as near as I can tell the house is all locked up. I doubt they were able to go in even if they wanted to.

"The boys' tools are in a barn near the rear of the house. At least I assume they are their tools. An old red mower with green paint dripped on one side?" Marge nodded. "There are no bikes anywhere. I checked through all the brush. I checked on Sage. The house was open so I went in, knowing he was deaf. He has been doing a good deal of painting. There are seascapes all over the third floor. I couldn't find him though.

"There's a little cottage on the property. Looks like it had a recent water leak, but nothing out of the ordinary. I guess that's where the boxes on the ferry were."

The captain confirmed that.

"There's an ancient gate near the rear of the house that's frozen open in front of the ledge, but nothing out of the ordinary there either, and nobody down below.

"I checked all of the cottages on Upper Island Avenue and they're all secure. When I found the watch I figured I had better come back and make sure one of the boys had it. It'll be getting dark soon."

With that report, and the sun beginning to set, the Captain called the Lassiter Fire Department on the radio. Moments later the horn blasted out a single mournful wail. It was a rare call. It was a call that meant unusual trouble. Marge shuddered at its sound and shuddered again a few moments later as the horn wailed another single blast.

The station began to take on an amazing transformation. It became cramped with people willing to help. The Captain explained the situation, even though the people assembled were already quite informed. Groups were assigned their areas. They knew what to do. A special telephone tree prepared for just such an emergency went into effect, and those houses were taken off the list of houses to be searched.

The Captain handed out the keys he had to the summer houses. Those summer houses without keys were assigned to a special group who had done the task before. They knew all the tricks, many having learned them as teenagers, and the summer people never knew their houses had been checked inside and out.

The towers, the dump, and the ponds were given to another special more agile younger group. Another was given the entire waterfront. It was decided to save the denser woods and swamp areas until all the other groups had reported back, providing the manpower necessary for the task. All children who arrived were sent home. Few, except the younger ones, bothered to go, and listened from behind the parked vehicles outside. It was going to be a very busy evening on Feather Island.

When the station quieted down, Marge called Deiters' and asked to speak to Brian.

"Hi, Mom, you wanted me?" He had never gotten a phone call before. "Is it really you, Mom?"

"Yes, Brian. I'm still down at the barn. Now, honey, I want you to think about Tad. Tell me if he's still asleep." Brian was quiet. Marge wondered why he was unsure if it was her on the phone.

"He's waking up. Me, too. Tad has a headache and he can't move too good. He's with Lance and Becky Bridges. It's pretty dark where they are, so I can't really tell where he is, but it seems like he's down in a cellar. That's all, Mom. Is it okay? I know I'm weird, but I hope it's okay?"

"Oh, Brian, you aren't weird. You have a wonderful gift and I love you very much. I'll let you know when we find them. Bye."

"I'll know anyway," Brian yawned. "Bye."

Marge wasn't sure how to approach this with the Captain. It would affect Brian's future on the island no matter what happened. What if he was wrong? What if he was right? She decided not to say anything. The Captain had overheard the conversation and knew what was on her heart. "Is Tad all right?" he asked quietly.

Marge took a deep breath, and without thinking about it anymore, said, "He's waking up and has a headache. He can't move too well and may be in a cellar. Please—"

"Just between us, Marge. Just between us. I welcome the information."

"Thank you." Her eyes filled with tears for the first time, but she remained reserved and in control. "He's with Becky and Lance."

* * *

Tad woke slowly, finding it difficult to focus his eyes and surprised that he couldn't move. He was more surprised to see Lance and Becky tied up and gagged. Realizing he was in the same state, he sat up quickly and became painfully aware of the headache he had.

His neck hurt also and his muscles were stiff.

Becky looked at him. Lance seemed to be unconscious. As he looked around the dimly lit cellar, Tad recognized where he was and became frightened. He had no idea of what time it was and remembered his watch was missing. How long had he been here? Was anyone looking for them?

Becky was angry. The man upstairs had carried her down, kicking. He had tied her to the bench and she couldn't move. She was glad to see Tad awake. She had been worried about him. As Tad looked at her and she looked at him, she wondered if that was going to be the extent of their conversation for the rest of their lives. Suddenly she remembered that Tad could still hop. He wasn't tied to anything. She lifted her feet up and down and nodded toward the large vise on the bench.

Tad had assumed he was tied the same as Becky was, but now he tried to get up. He found that with some effort, although he was stiff, he could stand by bracing himself. He hopped over to Becky and tried to figure out what she meant. It was obvious with her grunting and nodding that she meant the vise, but he wasn't sure what he was supposed to do with it. He turned around and backed up. His fingertips found the tape on her mouth and tore it off.

"Ow! Damn it, Tad. That hurt!"

Tad shrugged and moved in close to her face. Becky grabbed an edge of the tape with her teeth and yanked. Some of it stuck on her lower lip. Tad gripped the outside of the tape with his teeth and pulled it off gently. As he dropped it, he took advantage of the situation and kissed her on the cheek.

"As long as I have you captive, I might as well do it. I've wanted to do it all day. You're so beautiful. Sorry about the sticky fat lip though."

"We don't have time for any of that stuff. Besides, your lip is still bloody. I know these guys didn't do it to you. I saw it before. What happened?"

"I ran into something hard. It'll be okay."

"I almost made it outside, but they have a guard up there. He brought me back down here and tied me to the bench. There's no point in trying to get out that way."

"How did you get here?"

"We came looking for you, and when we couldn't find you we thought you had gone inside. Some guys grabbed me and then pulled Lance in. How about you?"

"I went into the barn and here I am. Did you recognize them?"

"No, but Lance called one of them Linderman. He kicked him hard in the shin. Another guy used karate on him and knocked him out. They didn't do anything to me."

"They're the guys who had the bodies and hijacked the ferry."

"You're lucky they didn't kill you."

"That's what I was thinking. How long have you been here?"

"At least an hour. Our parents must be pretty worried by now."

"That's for sure, but we can't think about that now. We've got to get untied. See if you can use your teeth."

Tad turned around and stood up. Becky pulled and pulled at the knots. "It's no use," she said. "It'd take hours, if I could do it at all."

"I'll look around."

Tad looked through the many old tools on the bench. Those he could reach were all in piles. Off to one side was a rusty old sickle. Using his teeth, he pulled it over to the edge of the bench.

Spitting out the dirt, he tried to get his hands up to the edge of the bench, but it was too high.

Turning around again, he gripped it with his teeth once more and pulled it over the edge. It fell onto his sneaker, almost cutting into his instep. Working himself down to a sitting position he grabbed the sickle with his hands and tried to place it in a secure position. It kept falling. He slid it back to Becky. "Can you grab it somehow?"

"Maybe you can wedge it between my feet with your hands."

With Becky's directions he was able to do so, and he began working on his ropes.

"Move your hands a little to the left. That's it."

The blade was dull, but it worked. After a few minutes a strand was cut through. Tad had to cut a second strand before he could move his wrists at all. Finally, with one last pull, the rope fell apart. Tad immediately proceeded to cut through the rope binding his legs and turned toward Becky's ropes.

When she was free, they both noticed Lance watching them. Tad moved to him, cut his ropes, and quietly explained their situation. Lance pulled off his gag.

"It's Linderman. I tagged him good, but he got me, too, I guess. I'll never be the same."

"I guess life isn't all bad then," Tad said smiling. "We can't get out the front. Becky tried. If they've gone down into the wine cellar we might get caught, but we don't have any choice. Maybe there really is a passageway to the bay. If there is, maybe they went all the way down. That way we can hide. Then when the guard from upstairs comes searching for us, we can escape."

"Lot of ifs," Lance pointed out.

"Maybe if we all went upstairs at once, the guard couldn't get all of us," Tad suggested.

"Does he have a gun?" asked Lance.

Becky nodded, "Automatic rifle, like in the SWAT movies."

"We'd never stand a chance," Tad said.

"Do you really think he'd shoot us?" Becky asked.

"I don't know. They knocked me out without caring that I was a kid, and they did the same with Lance. Of course, they're really pissed at us. Yes, I think they would shoot us without even thinking twice about it. They must be desperate for some reason. We can't take that chance."

"Well, there's no place to hide here," Lance said. "It seems that the only thing we can do is try to find a place in the wine cellar."

"Linderman and another guy went through that door over there a long time ago."

"That's the door to the wine cellar, at least we think it is, but we couldn't find a light," Lance reminded them.

Tad opened the door slowly and peeked around the edge. "It's as dark as it was before, and I still can't find a switch," he whispered.

"Use my light," Becky said handing it to him.

"Where did you get that?"

"Off my bike."

"I never thought of that. Get ours, Lance."

"Oh sure, get this, get that. Go into the cliff and find us a way out, Lance," he muttered. "Get killed for us, so we can escape while they deal with slicing your body, will you, good fellow? You didn't even say please."

"Whining doesn't become you, Lance," Becky said. "You're too smart to whine."

Lance looked at her in surprise. A smile spread over his face and he pulled the lights off their bicycles.

The stairs were wide rough slabs of rock. The walls were carefully fitted rocks covered with condensation. The stairs curved to the right. The three young teenagers started down. Tad closed the door behind them, wondering if they would ever see daylight again.

As they slowly followed the curve they saw that they were coming down to a very large, dimly lit room filled with row after row of slanting shelves. Many of the shelves had cobweb-covered bottles placed on them. No voices were heard and they saw no one.

"If we can't get out, at least we can party," Lance said.

"Shhh."

Tad took the lead and led the trio back against the wall which formed the base for the stairs. "If they come down they won't see us. Stay close," he whispered.

"I saw them come down here, so there must be another door somewhere," Becky said, pointing out the obvious.

"Like this one maybe," Lance said as he opened a door below the stairs. "Nope, just a large closet. Nothing here except coats and stuff. We can hide here if we have to, I think."

Tad had followed him in. The boys examined every inch of the closet. "Look in the pockets, Tad." Lance said. "Maybe there's a key or some money or something."

"Nothing in this one, but it is one heavy coat. I wonder who wears this. It's too big for Dr. Banville. Feel this thing." As they lifted it they heard a click in the wall. A narrow door opened inward. Lights came on in a slightly curving, stone-carved passageway about twenty feet long. Leaving that door open, they crept along the stone hallway. Becky followed. At the other end they found an intricately carved door.

As Lance opened it slowly a bright light blinded them for several seconds. When they were able to see, they were amazed. It was a large comfortable, living room with recliners and couches. The bright light came from a strange sort of window built into the cliff at the other end of the room.   They found a kitchen as modern as the one upstairs. A large table and six chairs separated it from the living room.

In two other rooms off the living room Tad found bunk beds. A modern bathroom was off of that. Tad made immediate use of it, but decided not to flush. Becky went into the kitchen and found a pantry filled with food. Lance opened the refrigerator and said, "Wow!" Opening the door next to it he found a room with two freezers and a large pantry. "Look at all this food!" he yelled as he started going through the shelves.

"Shhh," Tad said. "They may be around."

"So this is where they keep it," Lance said. "Let's eat."

Becky whispered, "Over here is the laundry."

Tad said, "Back there is a room with beds. I counted eight beds being used."

"There're men in them?" Lance turned white.

"No. They're all made. There are eight knapsacks hanging up. There's a bathroom, too."

"Where?" Lance asked in desperation.

Tad pointed. "Don't flush."

Tad and Becky found cookies and sliced meat, which they began to devour. Lance came back and said, "Cookies, great. Hey, what's this door over here?"

"Be careful," Tad ordered.

Becky disappeared into the bedroom. When she returned she said, "It's insane to stay here. Besides, I flushed. If they saw what was in it, they would definitely know we had been here."

"We can't get out above," Tad said. "What's that door go to, Lance?"

"I...I don't really know. It's like a...I don't know, maybe a large refrigerator? Nothing really in it."

As Tad walked over he was hit with strong medicinal odors. Two large white metal tables containing many small drawers of different sizes and shapes below stood empty and spotless. Large lights, dark now, stood above them.

"It's like a hospital," Lance said. "Like when I broke my arm a few years ago."

"I don't like this one bit. We better get going," Becky said.

"Maybe we'll find other stairs that go up to the house. Maybe we can get out," Tad said.

"Well, we didn't see an elevator anywhere, Tad. We never checked out if the old one in the barn really works. It wouldn't be fun to have a door open and be faced with rifles, all firing at us. There'd be blood and brains and guts all over the walls. I'm going back for some of the food in case we get stuck in here."

"Enough, Lance!" Becky exclaimed. "Let's get going."

"Wait just a minute. I want to see one more thing," Tad said. "I hope I'm wrong, but there are floor drains here, too. I hope...I hope I'm wrong. It's insane." Tad raced back to the two freezers and opened the first one slowly. "Empty except for wrapped and sealed packages. There's writing on them I can't figure out. Must be hams or beef or something." Moving to the next one he stood silent and motionless with his mouth open. Tears formed in his eyes. He shut it and spun around. "SHIT!"

"What?" Lance asked.

"Tad?" Becky said.

Unable to speak again, Tad stood silently and just shook his head. Becky opened the second one and came face to face with a nude young girl about seven or eight. Another body was below her in the freezer. She didn't touch either of them. Tears formed in her eyes also. Lance caught a glance and froze. Tad shut it.

Entering the passageway again they waited and listened. Nothing could be heard except Lance ahead of them chewing cookies. Tad and Becky moved cautiously. Lance ran back to the kitchen. He grabbed the rest of the cookies, opened the refrigerator, and came back with a gallon of milk, cheese, bread, and bologna. He felt brave, smelling it just to be sure.

"Somehow I don't think Dr. Banville is going to pay us if we get out of here, so this food is definitely ours. We worked our asses off for it. Want some now?"

"I'm not hungry," Tad said. "I'm definitely not hungry. How can you be hungry?"

"I didn't see anything in the freezer. I saw nothing. Everything is okay. These cookies and meat are the only real thing here. There is nothing wrong. I'm not scared anymore. Everything is fine."

"Neither am I!" Becky whispered. "Let's get out of here." She grabbed Tad's hand. "Please, get me out, Tad."

"Yeah," Tad whispered.

"You're the one that wanted to see dungeons," Lance pointed out. "Maybe you'll have your chance. We aren't done yet. Maybe they have guys around here who have been tortured, and have been hanging on the walls for years. Oh, shit, what am I saying?"

"Shut up, Lance. Just shut up. We are done here," Tad said.

They moved slowly back through the dimly lit passage heading back to the wine cellar. Becky pointed out occasional small holes in the left wall that let in air, but no light. The air was somewhat musty compared to the air in the room. Tad realized they must have had some sort of air conditioner going in the living quarters. Otherwise, it would be difficult to live down in the cliff because the strange windows in the living room didn't seem to have any way to open them. Tad remembered the rusty machinery in the shed, and wondered if it was just painted to look rusty. Was it for the ancient metal elevator they had seen, or for something else? They headed back to the wine cellar.

CHAPTER FOURTEEN

TUESDAY EVENING

By eight thirty, as the units of searchers began to report back to the station, Marge was feeling helpless. With the return of each group her hope crumbled. Each unit was questioned in detail. The Captain pressed them to be exact. All comments were recorded. Group after group was sent back to double-check where a possibility might still exist.

Marge Callant called Sylvia to see if Brian was all right and if he had any more to say.

"Brian's asleep now. He was exhausted. The last thing he said was that Tad was awake and they were looking all around in a big, dark room. He wanted to sleep and I let him. Does any of that make sense to you, Marge?

"I think he's trying to help us as only a five-year-old can. He's trying to assure us that they are okay."

"Neil and I are coming down."

Marge hesitated when she hung up the phone. Deciding to chance it she told the captain.

"I'm not sure what to do, Marge. Let's wait a bit more."

By eight forty-five, Sylvia and a very weak Neil Deiter entered and asked what was being done. The captain explained. Neil nodded, as he sat exhausted, examining the large island map.

By nine o'clock, most of the units had returned, some reporting their findings for the second time. They stood around smoking, expounding theories, and waiting for the last units.

"Coming through! Coming through!" Claudia Holmes' high-pitched voice squealed with as much authority as she could muster. She pushed Nick Shadik's wheelchair into the station.

She was drowned out by Shadik's booming voice. "What the hell's bein' done about them boys and little Becky?"

Several people started to talk at once.

"Wait a damn minute." He rolled himself over to the vinyl-covered map and said, "Somebody show me." He placed his glasses on the end of his puffy nose and squinted. The lieutenant showed Shadik exactly what was being done, which units had returned, and who they were waiting for.

"I heard somebody found Tad's watch up at the old Richards place."

"That's right, Mr. Shadik," the lieutenant continued. "I found his watch on a bush up there. The strap was broken."

"No one has checked the old Richards place, even though you found his watch there? Don't make much sense to me to search the whole island when it's pretty obvious."

Several people, including Marge and Sylvia, pushed in closer, wondering what Shadik knew that they didn't. "We were waiting to check all other possibilities, hoping that Dr. Banville would come back to the island."

"Tad and Lance been workin' for this Banville, I'm told."

"That's right," Marge said. "Cutting brush and mowing. Why?"

"Well now, I may have this all wrong, but seein' as how I'm just an old cripple, and all you capable people have been runnin' your asses off instead of thinkin', you could just humor me and hear me out, I suppose."

With that, everyone quieted down. Shadik winked at Claudia and she placed her hand on his right shoulder. "I know Tad as well as I know anybody on this island anymore, I guess. He's my paperboy and we talk a lot. That boy has a lot of guts. A lot of guts, a lot of adventures, and a lot of mischief. He's an awful good kid and smart as a whip, but he takes a lot of risks that maybe he shouldn't. His curiosity gets the best of him. Really good mind. I know…I know, you want me to come to the point and I'm gettin' there. Important to know him though.

"Now it seems to me if I was Tad, and I was workin' for this here Banville fella, who none of us knows a whole hell of a lot about I might add. Anyway, if I was workin' for him and he left and went uptown, and left that great big temptin' house sittin' there with me there in the yard…well, it stands to reason I might be a mite curious."

Men, who had been curious about that house for years, stood around nodding, intrigued by Shadik, and by their own fantasies.

"Now if you add in stories about secret passageways, and dungeons, and hidden, smuggled treasure, and everythin' every boy on this island has grown up with…well, I can tell you, Tad Callant, and any boy worth his salt, is goin' to take advantage of the situation. Nothin' is goin' to keep him out of that house lookin' for the truth.

"I ain't sayin' he'd steal anythin' or break anythin' like a lot of kids on this here rock. A lot right here in this room over the years included." A ripple of laughter broke the tension. "I'm not sayin' that at all. Tad wouldn't do that. He's been brought up right."

Marge turned red and wiped her eyes. "Lance is the same way, probably. Don't know him as well, but Tad likes him. Always has. Don't know too much about Miss Becky neither, or why she was there, but I'm just sayin' they'd go explorin'. I know I would, and Tad's got the same type of mind except he's a lot brighter than me. He'll get off this island and will do well. But that makes him even more curiouser.

"Now, if the lieutenant found his watch up on a bush like I heard, that means he must've had his hand up there for some reason. And if the bush was near a window, I think the reason is obvious."

"I did find it near a window, but it was locked."

"Locked now, from the inside prob'ly," Shadik pointed out.

"We have one or two other problems with what you say, Mr. Shadik," the captain interjected. "First, we can't find the kids' bikes. The other is that Becky and Lance were seen at the bottom of the hill without Tad after the children were supposed to be home for supper. They could be anywhere, or so we thought before the search."

"If Tad went into the house, Lance would have followed him. I don't know why he was with Becky. I don't give a monkey's spit for what makes sense or don't make sense at this point. I don't give a damn for bikes or no bikes or what some busybodies think they saw and made up. I tell you those kids are in that house. They've gotten themselves into some kind of trouble. You say you haven't checked there, and I say you better do it soon."

"All right," the Captain sighed. "What you say could happen, I suppose. It's worth checking. The summer section will go up with the Lieutenant and check. The rest of you better stick around in case we have to check the woods."

"Although I think Shadik may be right," Neil Deiter said quietly, "if my son is in there, I don't want his life threatened by a riot of curiosity seekers. I would like to go up and wait, but I think the captain is right. The rest should wait here."

"You folks can ride in the jeep, Neil. Marge, why don't you come, too."

"We better all go," someone yelled.

"No!" the captain ordered. "Stay away from there. If they are in there, we'll get them out. Wait here. The lieutenant will report in on the radio."

As the jeep and a few cars left, the crowd thinned out just milling around outside. Slowly, several other cars left in various directions, so as to appear that they were headed home. By the time Claudia pushed Shadik outside, the station was empty except for the captain and old Murray.

"Damn it," Shadik said. "I give them the idea and they leave me behind. How the hell am I going to get up there, Claudia? You can't push me up that hill. No one can."

Young Dale, who had been using the bathroom, came out of the building zipping his fly and said, "Where'd everybody go?"

"They've all gone to search the old Richards place and I can't get up there. I gave them the idea and they left me. You have your truck, Dale?"

Dale looked around and said, "Nope. I guess the guys took it." He thought a minute, smiled, and said quietly, "I know what we can do." He bent down and whispered his idea to Shadik and Claudia, and the three of them headed out. With Dale pushing Shadik they were all giggling like children.

The phone rang. The captain was standing out front. Old Murray answered. It was one of Lance's sisters, wondering if her whole evening was going to be spoiled because she had to babysit. In the background he heard the two nine year olds yelling defiantly. Old Murray took the cigar out of his mouth, took his time, blew a perfect smoke ring, and said, "Well, honey, my best guess is that it sure as hell is. Have a nice night."

Becky's mother called as she had every fifteen minutes and said she was driving up with the rest of the island. They could contact her at the old Richards place. Old Murray was about to tell the captain when the search party from the towers reported back. They had found nothing except some of their sons and daughters drinking beer on the third floor. They were not happy and were headed home with their kids. The waterfront unit reported in with negative findings.

The captain yelled, "I'd better get up to Banville's before they begin to tear the place apart. You comfortable covering the phone, Murray?"

"Sure, go ahead up there. Probably torn it to pieces and emptied it out already, but at least you can cover your ass, and say you tried to stop them. Reminds me of the time back in '67, or was it '68?" Murray began, as he always did, with his telling of the many battles fought on the Lassiter Fire Department. The captain left, leaving him alone. Old Murray didn't care. He just sat there talking to himself and waiting for the horn to blow.

"We'd got a tip and captured a very large Mary Wanna plant from some kids in the middle of the island. They didn't know we had grabbed it we thought. Held Mary captive in the back room of this very station waitin' for the cops from Lassiter to pick it up. Then the next mornin' we got a call 'bout a house fire way out on the point. We took everything and everybody. False alarm! So back we all came. But when we got back old Mary Wanna must have gone dancin' because she was nowhere to be found from that day forward. The old Richards place is just gonna be toast. Toast I tell ya. But go if you want. As usual I'll stay here and handle everything. Be crazier than hell up there anyway."

The captain and the waterfront unit found Island Avenue clogged with cars and trucks. Nothing could get through. They couldn't get close to the house, so they got out and walked the rest of the way up the hill from Thompson's house.

People and cars littered the whole area of the bluff across the front of Banville's long, long fence. They were being kept off the property by members of the volunteers under orders from the lieutenant. At the gate, the captain was told that the search group was already inside.

He was greeted at the door by Danny, one of the best summer section men he had. "They were in the cellar, Cap," he whispered. "Bikes are there and we found some used duct tape and ropes. It doesn't look good. I was just coming out to call you. Radios don't seem to work from down inside."

"Dan, make sure absolutely no one outside finds out about this. Keep them out of here. I'll use Banville's phone to call the Lassiter police."

"I better show you the way first. There's something funny going on here. This house isn't being lived in. Kitchen and hallways are the only clean section of the house. Kitchen's so clean there's nothing in it."

The captain hurried down the cellar stairs where he met the lieutenant and five men. "Brief me." He was shown the ropes and bikes and the old sickle on the floor.

"They must've gotten free. The question is where are they now? We were just about to go down to the next level."

"Go ahead. I'll go up and use Banville's phone to call it in. If I use the radio they'll be all over us. It seems like everyone's carrying a scanner."

The lieutenant led the men down the stairwell into the wine cellar. Seeing the glowing smiles, he reminded the men that they were to leave all evidence alone, even if it was old web-covered wine bottles. Not long after their descent, a few of the men deserted and went back up the stairs. Their jackets appeared fuller than they had before. No one cared.

"Search everywhere," ordered the lieutenant.

The three children hearing the commotion in the wine cellar and not knowing who was out there hid in the hallway with their backs to the closet door holding it shut.

CHAPTER FIFTEEN

TUESDAY NIGHT

High above and outside, George, one of the fire department volunteers, sensing the impatience and urgency of the rapidly growing crowd, made his way to the front door of the house. Spotting Danny he said, "What's the news? They need news or they're coming through."

"I don't know. They've gone deeper into the cliff. I haven't heard anything from them at all."

"I'd better bring in some of the boys and check on them."

"Who's going to keep the people back?"

"They'll probably behave themselves and you're here to stop them. I'll only take a few guys."

"I'm here to keep everyone back, but if they make up their minds to come in, there isn't anything I can do against all of them."

"Everyone understands that, Dan. Be creative," George smiled at his old friend.

George went back to the crowd and called over a few friends. Everyone was asking for some word. He offered none and ignored most. Two men tried to grab him. Some pushing led to angry comments arising from feelings embedded deeply years before.

Danny heard the shouts and observed the jostling. He knew the extra men had their hands full and would not be looking for the captain. He didn't have much time, but he was determined to do the best he could. Then he had an idea. "Be creative. Well, why not? Why the hell not?" he said smiling.

More of the crowd burst through the front gate. Only the iron fence slowed down the entire tide descending toward the front door.

"Hold it, folks," Danny said quietly, but firmly at the door. "This is still private property. A careful official search is taking place inside."

"What the hell is going on?"

"I don't really know. I'm sure the Captain'll let us know when he knows something."

"What if he can't? What if he's been killed or something?"

"What did he say?" someone in the back of the crowd asked.

"Says the Captain's been killed," said another.

"Kids too, I imagine."

"The Captain's been killed and the kids too," rippled through several other voices all at once. The word then spread like wildfire in a breeze among the good inhabitants of Feather Island. Their usual calm, but curious demeanor was destroyed, as they became a massive killing machine all focused on Danny.

"Hold it! Hold it, folks!" Danny knew he had lost the battle, but his life was still important to him. "I've just heard from the Captain," he yelled. "He isn't dead! He has no evidence about the kids at all. Now settle down and listen to me, damn it! He says to let the people in. Our guys need help searching. He wants everybody to look for secret panels upstairs and in the attic, too. Big place. The kids may be up there. No one has checked there! We need some folks to check here on the ground floor, too. See about secret passages and hiding places. They have the cellar covered okay. If you will walk slowly into the house, no one will get hurt. No point in getting anyone hurt."

As people passed him in the doorway Dan stopped a few he knew well for their various talents including gossip. He said quietly, "Lots of old valuable stuff in here. Be careful. They might become bargains before the night is out. Fire Department wouldn't mind a reasonable donation if you know what I mean."

Dan turned to the group of firemen standing outside and told them his ideas. They stood just inside the doorway in two lines chatting with curious folks and organizing themselves while the searchers made suggestions about items that had been reported to them. The lives of the children sat at the front of their minds. Valuable souvenirs and cash sat deeply in their souls.

* * *

Sylvia and Neil were seated on the front seat of the jeep. Marge was kneeling on a thick blanket on the floor behind them with her elbows propped up over the driver's seat. She observed the crowd bursting through the front door. "Something's happening."

"Island insanity is happening," Neil replied slowly.

"Do you think we should go in?"

"No. If they find the kids, they'll let us know. I suspect this is just frustration from having no news, and wanting to finally get inside to steal the place blind. There have been too many rumors about this place all their lives. Let's just stay here and wait. Folks can get hurt in a situation like this. I just hope the guys can control them."

* * *

A little earlier Shadik and Claudia remained in the driveway of the town shed as Dale had been opening the large doors. They were joined by the thin boy from next door. He stood outside and watched Dale crawl up into the cab.

"Hey, Rick, how's it goin'?"

"You goin' up to Dr. Banville's?

"Yup, we are."

"He's my customer and I worked with Tad and Lance up there. Maybe I can help. Can I go with you?"

"Sure, ask your mom."

"She's babysitting on Elm Street. It's okay for me to go. I just didn't want to walk up there because I hurt my leg."

"Hop on."

"Get near the barn if you can. I can show you some stuff."

"No problem!"

Five minutes later they found they were unable to get through the mass of cars parked on Island Avenue. They pulled off and went up Water Street to approach the house from the other end of Upper Island Avenue across the bluff. It turned into a very dark ride, but not at all frightening. In fact, every time they went over a bump Rick began laughing. Shadik was seated next to him in the bucket and he roared with laughter, too.

Now, as they approached Banville's land, they realized how cut off they still were. Cars and trucks filled the entire road along the fence.

Claudia leaned closer to Dale and asked over the roar, "Do you think we'll ever get close to the house?"

"Yes, we can. The fence along this end doesn't go all the way to the cliff. There's a driveway that's become a little overgrown, but we'll have no trouble. No trouble at all."

"What about Nick and Rick?"

"If worse comes to worst I'll just raise him over the bushes."

"Just don't let them fall."

"They're perfectly safe."

Spinning the front-end loader ninety degrees, to the obvious satisfaction of its two bucket occupants, he pulled off the road.

The huge wheels of the town loader plowed through to the old driveway. From high in the bucket Shadik could see the crowd surge toward the house.

"Ridin' in style! Ridin' in style!" yelled Nick. "Watch out you damn vultures!"

"Don't worry, guys. Here comes the cavalry," Rick shouted. They both let out a whoop and yelled, "CCHHAAARRGGE!!"

Dale drove across the front lawn at a pretty good clip, scattering the frenzied islanders who had come to feed on an ancient legend. He parked the loader near the front of the barn according to Rick's suggestion.

Seeing Nick Shadik and Rick riding in the bucket of the loader caused Neil Deiter to laugh for the first time in over a year and it broke the tension in the jeep. Dale gently lowered the bucket, hopped out, and helped Shadik into his wheelchair.

"We better put all Tad's tools into the bucket or everyone will steal them," Rick pointed out. He and Dale went to work in the barn.

Claudia came over and put her hand on Shadik's shoulder. "I don't know when I've had so much fun," he said. "And that boy Rick has a magnificent sense of humor. After we get hitched we'll have to have him and his mother over to supper."

"Is that a proposal from you or is that still a proposal just for your son?"

"Why, Claudia, how could you ever doubt me?" Shadik pulled her down to sit on his lap. They both giggled and watched the crazy islanders going into the fun house.

* * *

As the captain made his way up from the wine cellar into the top cellar, he heard the incredible sound of thunder up above. Slowly going up the stairs into the kitchen he knew there was no stopping what was happening. The place was filled with the islands' finest and not so fine. It appeared that firemen were in the process of organizing the movement of the crowd so that no one got hurt. Normally, he would have been thrilled. It was the first time he had seen such cooperation with his department in all the years he had spent on Feather Island.

Then he watched a little more closely. Furniture, old paintings, and even large carpets were slowly disappearing out the front door along with new owners, and those designated to help them. During a planned interval others entered the house. Wasting no time, they explained to designated firemen what they were looking for having already paid a few dollars outside for information as to what remained. The firemen gave them directions. The kitchen seemed to be off limits except for a fireman who had discovered the empty refrigerator and was swearing under his breath.

"Profitable night, Chuck?" asked the captain over his shoulder.

"Well, Cap, it's like this. That crowd was ready to lynch Banville, kill anyone in their way, and burn down the house. Dan was a little worried for our safety, his safety, and the house. We sort of talked it over and well, no names mentioned, but a brilliant idea came up to prevent a lot of folks from getting hurt or killed, and protecting the building for historical purposes so to speak. Well, a few misunderstandings sort of developed into a profitable idea for the department as things were sort of set up quickly to protect everyone. The boys are all honest with these folks telling them of the consequences of their actions if they are ever found out and all. We're sure they all understand. A lot of tension has been relieved. The people don't seem to mind donating quite well to the department for the protection of our organization during this emergency, and for our keeping so busy during this crisis that we may not notice everything around us."

"Profitable for the department while protecting the public and hard-working firemen?"

"Yeah, pretty much we think. George, what are we up to?" he asked the fireman at the table.

"Nine hundred twenty six dollars and four cents. Dan will probably be back in again soon as the guys give him what they have. Creative idea. Dan should receive a citation, Captain. Folks are going home. Streets are being cleared. Should be a quiet night except possibly for a few parties, but I doubt it. Find the kids?"

"I have to get back downstairs. Close up as soon as you can. Grab Banville if you see him and hold him."

People were still pouring out of the house. Many were carrying objects of some sort. It was hard to tell in the dark exactly what was happening. As he followed them outside the captain watched a much different scene filled with utter confusion. Everyone tried to turn their cars around at the same time and head down the hill which had become an insane parking lot now filled with creative and happy drivers. He shook his head and made his way over to Dale, Shadik, and Rick by the barn when he spotted the loader.

"Shadik! See what you created?" he asked laughing. "I'd swear the whole island has turned into some type of strange greedy nut house. I can't arrest that many people."

"Nothing new, just contagious," Shadik said seriously. "We need to relieve some tension or murder among old enemies and family members'll be next. Did you find the kids?"

"No, but we are working on it. We're pretty sure they're here. We discovered their bikes and ropes. We also found a stairway to the wine cellar. The lieutenant and some of the men are exploring everywhere."

"Rick here found something that might help," Dale said. He motioned him to follow him into the barn. "Don't touch the door! It fell on this youngster as he was working with Tad and Lance. Banville and that old artist Sage hauled it off of him I guess."

The captain examined the door. "It looks like it hasn't been fixed in years. Needs new wheels, readjustment, and a heavier track. Dangerous. You okay, Rick?"

"Yeah, Dr. Banville took care of me. My legs still hurt, but I'm okay. He said air protected me a lot. Come see what we found."

Dale opened two heavy metal doors revealing an elevator. "How the heck could they have put this in?" the captain asked. "We never knew about this? They would have had to dynamite the ledge. There's nothing here to indicate when it was made. No inspection stickers. Does it work?"

"Don't know," said Dale. "Stand back. Might just fall." He walked in and pushed a button. The doors closed and he began to descend. Only a slight hum could be heard. Suddenly it stopped and came back up. The door opened and Dale stood there with a large smile. "Yup. She works. Seems pretty modern. Doesn't look too modern, though. Hop on and we'll see where she goes."

Rick was the first one on. Shadik and the Captain both reached for him. "No, Rick. Sorry, but I can't let you go down there. We don't know what dangers we're facing."

"But…I'm the one who showed you, and my friends may be down there."

"Rick, please go and sit with Mrs. Holmes. When I don't come back right away she's going to be awful worried," Shadik said quietly. "Go and tell her I'm talking some with Dale and the captain. We should be right back if this thing really works. You been a great help, but I need you to do this because Mrs. Holmes is pretty sensitive about me at the moment. Roll me in if you will please, Dale."

"Well, well okay, Mr. Shadik, but be careful. Tad told me you cook good."

"We will together, Rick," Shadik said laughing. "Now run along. Come over for breakfast early tomorrow if any us can wake up."

As the boy left he carefully slid the barn door shut. The three men got on the elevator and headed down into the cliff. Dale wiped a smudge off a small metal plate. "Date here, Captain. Nineteen forty-nine."

"Well," the captain said, "at least something makes sense. The good senator had a lot of parties I'm told. He had the wine and who knows what else delivered by truck and placed into the sub-basement. Built himself a wine cellar somehow. Then he brought it up when he needed it for his political gatherings. I'll join the hunt for the kids again, gentlemen."

"Better'n a damn rest home," Shadik giggled properly. "Let's get these bastards!"

There was only one stop. As the door opened they found themselves in the wine cellar.

"I think Dale and me might just explore this room for clues if you don't mind, Captain. Maybe they even have some dandelion wine here. Ain't had any for years and years. Used to make it. Used to pay the island kids two cents a pound for dandelions. Told them it was to help the environment."

"I remember that!" said Dale. "I made over a buck and felt pretty proud about helping the island. I always wondered how you were going to get rid of them. I figured you'd dump them way out in the ocean. How do you make dandelion wine anyway?" As Shadik began explaining and looking at bottles the captain vanished.

* * *

"Is it Linderman?" Becky whispered.

"I don't think so. Wait a minute. Be quiet. I have to open the door a little more."

"No," said Lance.

Tad opened it enough to see the captain heading toward the stairs. He poked his head out and said quietly, "Captain."

"What? Where are you? That you Tad?"

"Shhh. Here under the stairs."

The captain looked all around the hall. As he saw the boy he broke into a wide smile. Tad placed his finger over his lips and beckoned him into the closet. "Everyone on the island has been looking for you kids. What happened?"

"Not now. Everyone is still in danger. Linderman and a few other guys with automatic rifles are still wandering around. Come with us. We have something you have to see. We'll explain everything after we show you."

"I think you better tell me now."

"No. Come on inside."

"Shhh," said Lance and Becky together. As Tad shut the closet door Lance and Becky lifted the coat and opened the back of the closet.

"What the . . .?"

"Shhh."

The group quietly made their way to the living quarters. The captain was impressed.

"My Lord, Banville's living pretty high on the hog. How the hell…?"

"Be real brave for a minute. Over here, Cap."

"Tad," said Becky. "Lance and I will stay in the living room."

When the captain saw the tables and the drains he was confused. When he saw what was in the freezers he was furious. "Okay, kids we can talk about all this later. I have some people to contact immediately. I want you to go back to the wine cellar. Dale and Shadik are out there. They can take you up in the elevator. Your folks are topside. You have to get out of here. Now!"

"Linderman and three other men captured us. We escaped, but they're around here somewhere. They have automatic weapons."

"You're sure of this, Tad?"

"Very sure, but they didn't use them or threaten us with them. They just tied us up."

"Let's get you out of here."

"Great!"

"Quietly."

The group slid back into the closet and closed it carefully. The captain opened the door a crack and saw Dale holding a few bottles. He hissed at him. Dale turned. "What the hell are you . . .?"

The captain put his finger over his lips and beckoned him to the closet. "Dale, take a look around and see if there is anyone else in the wine cellar. I want you to take the kids up in the elevator and get them safely to the station as secretly as you can. Take Shadik with you right now! Lock the kids in the back room at the station and protect them. I'll go up with you and tell their parents in the meantime. They are blocked in by other cars right now. Get out of here. Linderman and his men are still around here somewhere with automatic weapons."

"Holy . . . you got it, Cap. Come on kids." They raced for the elevator. The captain told Shadik and pushed him over there. He was smiling and carrying two large ancient bottles of dandelion wine. Dale grabbed a couple of other bottles along the way. Each of the kids grabbed one also having no idea what they had taken.

As they rode up Shadik asked, "What do you have, Dale?"

"Darned if I know, but I think before this is over I can honestly say I earned them."

In the barn the three kids were hustled into the cab of the loader. Shadik went into his special seat. Rick jumped in with him looking forward to another great ride. He waved to his three friends who laughed as quietly as they could and ducked low. Dale took the loader down the east road past Sage's dark house and the pond. Finally, he drove it into the town garage. From there they walked through back yards to the station.

The captain made arrangements for Marge, Sylvia and Neil to travel with two armed firemen. Other armed firemen followed in another vehicle. He then made arrangements to have the Deiter, Callant, and Bridges houses protected. He gave no reasons other than the fact that Linderman and his crew were loose on the island and carrying automatic weapons. He met the lieutenant inside one of the vehicles in the yard and told him what he had just seen in the hidden living quarters.

"Tell no one at this point. Keep an armed group here you can trust not to go crazy. If you see Linderman, or his men, or Banville arrest them if possible. When I get back to the station I'll notify Lassiter and the State Police by landline. This is going to be an all-nighter. Keep our men away from the wine cellar."

The captain waited a few more minutes before he went down the hill. Following the last few cars and two pickup trucks and their valuable furniture he pulled into his parking place. Ordering the placement of armed guards outside he gave them specific instructions about what he expected of them.

"Others will be coming here. Don't shoot everyone you see. Please don't panic. Don't shoot anyone if you can help it. Any strangers should be checked carefully. Don't send them inside. Let me know and I will send someone out to meet them. Take their weapons if they have any unless they are Lassiter or state cops.

* * *

In the back room of the station the three teenagers sat quietly exhausted waiting for the state police detectives to question them. Tad leaned gently into Becky's shoulder. She leaned back. "Nobody holds us anymore," Becky whispered.

Tad put his arm around her back. Nobody did hold them much anymore, he thought. Then he remembered Mom holding him the other night or was it last night? Lance leaned into Tad's other shoulder. In spite of the dark in the back room where it was necessary to place them, they didn't panic or cry. They knew their parents were in the station itself with a million questions, and filled with pride and fear. Their brief talk with them, and their hugs had brought forth tears, laughing, and the warning they expected: "Wait until you get home!"

"Tad, what do you think this is all about?" Becky sniffed.

"I wish I knew. I can't figure it all out. Dr. Banville said he was working on a project. If that was true, then I guess we found it, but I don't understand it. Linderman may be one of them. But why?"

"Maybe. Maybe not," Lance yawned. "Why would he pretend to be a writer and try to find out all he could about Banville? He may be a cop, but a cop wouldn't hijack the ferry."

Becky said, "If he is one of the men working for Banville, maybe he was asking questions about him just to see what the islanders had already figured out about him. But why would he murder Dan Stark?"

"We don't really know he did. All we do know is that he had the bodies. They may have become buddies or Dan was working for him."

"Maybe because Dan had Banville's electronic bug," Lance said. "But Sage said Linderman had been in his house when he got there before all this happened."

"What bug? Who's Sage? What house?"

"Oh, boy."

"It's a long story," Tad said.

"So tell me, Tad. We don't exactly have anything else to do."

"We can't, really. We promised to keep it a secret. It's complicated."

"That's okay. I understand. If you had told me to keep a secret, I would. Forever. Cross my heart and hope to—"

"Don't say that," Lance interrupted. "Just don't say that. It could still come true soon enough. Maybe we should tell her, Tad. I mean, the promise was just between you and me. If we both decide to tell someone else, then it will be okay. We're all in this together now. It only seems fair that Becky should know what we know. We did get her into this mess in a roundabout sort of way."

"I suppose so," Tad replied, "but you've got to swear not to tell or we can get into a lot of trouble. We lied to the police about the bodies a little."

"I swear. I really do."

The boys told Becky all they knew about Banville and Sage and Linderman. They told their ideas about the deaths of Mr. Finney and Mr. Thompson, and of finding Dan Stark and his two friends at Sage's. They brought her right up to date on why Tad wanted the job working for Banville.

"So you see what could happen to us? I even kind of lied on television where the whole island and the world saw me. You can't tell about what I just told you, Becky. Not ever."

"I won't. I guess we've found out some of the things you wanted to know."

"I'm sorry we had to get you into it, Becky. We never thought anything like this would happen."

"It isn't your fault, Tad. I decided to go inside the house. That was my decision."

"Maybe we shouldn't talk so much," Lance said. "Lots of people are out there. There could be a bug in here."

"Too late then, and I'm glad, and very tired," Tad sighed.

* * *

As the hours went by the three of them were questioned separately by the local and state police and told all they knew except about Sage. It was close to two in the morning when Tad was surprised by the entrance of Carl Linderman and the Captain.

"Tad, you know this gentleman?"

"Yes, he's Carl Linderman. Did you catch him?"

"Tad, this may be difficult for you, especially as tired as you are. Agent Linderman has proven to all of us that he is a federal officer. We have checked that out through our own sources. He has some questions he needs to ask you. Tell him everything. I took him up to the house and showed him the freezers. The FBI crime lab is up there now dealing with the situation. Are you okay with this?"

"I... I... well, yeah, it does make a lot more sense than anything else I guess."

"I won't keep you long, Tad. I need to tie up a few things."

"Okay, I guess. Did you talk to Lance, too?"

"No. I will later, if necessary. I think you and I can finish this quickly, and you can get home to bed. Now, one more time, tell me what you know about Banville."

"Not much."

Over the next few minutes Tad poured out the little he knew. Then he said, "Why did you kill Stark and the two others, and put them in Mr. Sage's little house, and hijack the ferry, and is Mr. Sage okay? I'm really, really tired. Please tell me."

"I know. You deserve to know those things I guess, and I trust that until we release a statement you will keep what I tell you to yourself." Tad nodded. "Stark and his crew were scum, but we had no intention of killing them. My team wanted the electronic bug to see if it would help us in any way. When we entered the shack they were drunk. They attacked rapidly with knives and they were put down. It was that simple. We had no intention of hijacking the ferry. We just needed to deliver the bodies to the proper authorities without disclosing who we were yet. You changed our minds. At that time we couldn't expose who we were. News travels too fast around here, and Banville was of course sensitive to everything and everybody. Our theatrics were necessary and no one was killed. You were the only casualty except for a rather large wet woman."

"And Judy!"

Linderman was very quiet. "Tad, just between us please, it is my hope to be able to talk with her very soon. I like her very much. We have quite an age difference, but perhaps we can become friends again. Who knows?"

"Did Banville kill her father and Mr. Finney?"

"No. As near as we can tell it was a horrible coincidence."

"And what about Banville? Why did he have those kids?"

"We have been after him and his team for quite awhile, not just here. He has jumped from place to place. He is a brilliant man who kidnapped children who were deathly ill. He was insane of course, but he was apparently convinced that he could save them using methods that were not allowed. He has traveled through jobs at many hospitals using many disguises. Finally, he developed a rather large group around the country who began to kidnap them. As near as we can figure this crew and the children were brought in by boat all at one time at night. We don't know how yet. It is a horrible crime if you can imagine having your deathly ill child stolen from you, especially when the possibility of hope existed. We assume that the bodies you saw were just some of his own failures to be experimented with later."

"Sick! He was so sick!"

"He is still so sick, Tad. We are still after him."

"One last question."

"Shoot!"

"Why did you put the bodies in Sage's cottage?"

Linderman looked at the boy and said, "That one is very difficult for me personally, Tad. You seemed to be very close to Sage. He is leaving the island by the way. His work is finished."

Tad looked at Linderman and then said slowly, "I . . . I guess I needed someone to, well, kind of love. My dad's been away so long. I guess Mr. Sage filled something in me, or I dreamed he might. I don't know. I know it sounds strange. I liked him a lot and he never did anything to me. . .I mean, you know."

Linderman said nothing. He bent down, picked up a briefcase, and opened it. Reaching in he said, "There are parts of this business that are really difficult, Tad. Very difficult, even for a hard-nosed professional grown-up. Hurting you is one of them I will carry for a long time."

"You haven't hurt me except when you slugged me at Banville's."

"That, too. We had just entered after you kids left and we weren't sure who else was in the house. I needed you quiet and I reacted foolishly. My team followed suit with your friends. However, I am about to hurt you again, I suspect. I'm sorry, but you have to know the truth." He reached into his case and pulling out a bearded, skin-tight mask, he pulled it on over his head.

Tad said nothing. He leaped up and hugged him. "War is hell, Tad. Not just the killing, but the other types of pain that you cause. I'm so very sorry for this. You mean a lot to me, and I promise that I will continue to see you and write to you. Right now I have to leave, and go catch a well-meaning, very, very sick man. Try to forgive me over time."

"I…I love you."

"Yeah…I guess me too. I lost a son who would be about your age now."

Tad released him from his hug as if he had been stung. "How?"

"To a bad guy, Tad. To a really bad guy because of who I am and who I work for. That's why I love and hate this damn business. See you sometime." He stood, pulled off the disguise, and wiped his eyes with his handkerchief in the doorway and waved.

"Yeah. See you sometime. I . . . I've got to get some sleep."

"I'll tell your Mom, if I can wake her up."

"Is it okay if I tell Lance about Mr. Sage?"

"Let's keep this between us for awhile. I'll let you know later. You can tell him that you heard that his paintings were finished and he needed some peace and quiet."

"Yeah, that will be okay I guess, even for a deaf mute."

"I'll make sure your Dad gets home soon and safely. That's a promise!"

CHAPTER SIXTEEN

MIDDLE OF JULY

During the first three weeks in July, Feather Island made its usual transition from a sleepy little village of working folks and retirees to a bustling summer community of about three thousand. However, this year there were more day tourists than usual — a lot more. The island had received remarkable publicity through all the media, and was the source of amazing stories on the new Feather Island web sites. It didn't matter that most of them were a little more elaborate than the facts.

Those who had been there on that most amazing night of all Feather Island nights wrote of their adventures. They had the souvenirs to prove it, and each had a story of the evil Dr. Banville, although none of them actually knew what he had been doing there in the first place. That part had rarely been told. It was one of the Feather Island secrets that would take ten years to escape.

A new antique co-op had opened near the beach and was so successful it closed by the middle of August. The Art Association put on display old photographs and paintings inexplicably donated by the new, Old Richards Place Restoration Society which had recently been given title to the property. An old island attorney became an instant hero for setting it up.

More ferry boats than normal were placed into the schedule. After some expensive state dredging between Feather Island and Keelscrape Island sightseeing boats circled the island with a running commentary of the jacking of one of their ferries, the remarkable nationwide search for the elusive Doctor Banville, and the latest facts and figures on everything compiled by the "authorities", who may have picked them up in the grocery store or The Dusty Gull Cafe.

The story about the Banville house and its strange, infamous occupant, who went uptown and was never seen again, was a good mystery in itself. A nationwide all points bulletin had still turned up nothing. However, his biography, rumors about his horrible experiments, and what would be done to him when he was finally caught, were turned into a special on television and spread over the Internet.

Three new bed and breakfast establishments opened up behind white picket fences below the Banville house. However, most of the curious left the island at the end of the day. The summer people who stayed remained content with the "quiet life" they had sought all year. The beach was full. The stores were full. The price of tuna fish, peanut butter, and toilet paper tripled even with the new "honorary owner" of the grocery store, Billy Madison. The islanders once again enjoyed with disgust and excitement the visiting summer cattle.

Lance seemed to be enjoying the bay on this day more than anyone as he rowed a new friend to the new southern end of the island. Her family had rented a cottage on the beach. Since Lance had spotted her, his whole world seemed to be upside down, and he even had a problem concentrating on his lobster traps.

"See that large house at the top of the bluff?" Lance asked, pointing.

Kristen nodded, enjoying the gentle rocking of the waves caused by a docking ferry. Lance's company and the warm sun on those portions of her body not covered by her bikini made the day perfect.

"That's where the road makes a sharp curve to go across the bluff. That mansion sets back off the road surrounded by a brand new high fence. It was the scene of the greatest adventure the island ever had. There was a treasure that was supposed to be hidden somewhere in the cliff that smugglers had left there hundreds of years ago, and dungeons, too. We never found those, but what we did find was more amazing. Perhaps you read about it in the *Boston Globe*?"

Kristin shook her head.

Pulling hard on the oars, Lance turned toward the rocky shore at the base of the cliff. "Well, let me tell you about it. It started when Becky and I were looking for Tad."

A scowl passed over Kristin's face.

"No, no you don't understand. You see, Tad and I had taken a job with Dr. Banville to care for the grounds. Just like the job we have now for the Restoration Society."

* * *

Between bouts of fighting to control the four-inch hose at the ancient dump, the young teenagers of the island had gathered the barrels and scraps of wood they needed. In June they had somehow brought them to the pond, not an easy task. The result was a ten by ten, well-made raft supported by eight oil barrels, complete with ladder. It sat in twenty feet of water about thirty feet from shore. Someone had written in paint on the sides of the raft: "The King: Tad Callant, Lance Deiter, and Becky Bridges Private Raft."

Now all alone at the pond, Tad and Becky dove deeply from their raft. As Tad kicked for the surface he had enjoyed the feel of the cold water near the bottom. Becky was right beside him hip to hip. He enjoyed that also. As they burst through the surface, Tad said, "It's getting late."

"I know," Becky replied. "I've got to leave soon, too."

"Do you really have to? This has been a great afternoon being alone with you."

"I've got to go uptown. Mom's taking me shopping for a new bathing suit."

"Yours is great."

"Oh, Tad, it's old. I got it in May. Besides, it's last year's style. Did you see the suit Kristin has?"

"Who could miss it?"

"That's exactly what I mean."

"You going to get one like hers?"

"I might."

"You'd look even better in it."

Becky smiled and pulled herself onto the raft. Tad followed slowly. His upper left leg cramped tightly and as he sat he massaged it, all the while studying Becky.

"You okay?"

"Yeah, it just cramps now and then. The cold water down deep, probably. I need to keep reminding it how it should work."

"I'll massage it for you."

"We better put our suits back on first. Somebody might get the right idea."

She smiled and said, "My mother would kill me if she could see me with you like this now. But Tad, it's just so beautiful as long as we're careful."

Tad smiled, slid his on also, and lay down on his back to let the sun dry him, and hoping he could find out safely if Brian had his mind elsewhere. Becky's hands were firm, soothing, and exploratory as they massaged his left thigh. Closing his eyes, he allowed his body to react any way it wanted to, and he allowed his mind to drift back to the magnificent living room in the cliff. It was easier to do with Becky here during the day. Unfortunately, his vision of that room was always followed by visions of the packages in the freezer, and the two kids staring up at him begging him to do something about it.

The nightmares were fewer now that his father had returned home. He didn't jump at every night sound he heard. He wondered about Linderman and where he was now. He often thought of him and of Mr. Sage. They, in their way, helped him to grow up a little, to understand adult life a little more, and he didn't mind loving them even though he would never tell anyone that.

Tad was hoping for the day when he and his father could talk about their future together as a family. It had to come soon, because his father was headed back to work in a week. Tad felt that too much time had been spent on worrying about him. At least Dad was having fun with the kids. And he had gone out in the boat they had been able to rent for the summer with Dad's help. Dad knew quite a bit about how to deal with their lobster pots and their catches. They laughed a lot. Best of all were the long walks Dad and Mom had taken alone. Maybe it would make a difference for everyone when Dad was gone. He dozed for a few minutes, thinking. Then he opened his eyes and looked at Becky.

"That feels so great. And it's so peaceful here," he said. "This is the way life should always be. I don't ever want to leave. I love being here alone with you."

"I do, too. I love massaging you, Tad Callant. I think about it a lot, and I know we have to be careful."

Tad laughed. "Whoa! If you don't stop what you're doing right now, I'm definitely going to have to dive in or be embarrassed."

"I better stop for another reason, too."   She snapped her hands down nearer to his knees.

"So you can go uptown?"

"That too, but Mickey just pulled up to the top of the hill."

"Damn, what's he want? He'll get all the wrong ideas, or all the right ideas I don't want him to have. And we haven't even done anything really wrong yet. Well, not really."

"Tad!"

"What?" Tad shut his eyes again.

"What's she doing to you?"

"My leg cramped bad, and she's massaging it like you have to sometimes."

"Oh, okay. You have to go help look for Lance. Mom said. They just took his dad up on the fireboat, and this time it doesn't look good. His mother wants him home."

Tad sat up and looked at Becky. She shook her head and said, "Here we go again."

"He'll be all right. He was expecting it this time. They all were. In fact, they even spent a long time talking about it together."

"That must have been hard."

"Yeah, a lot of tears. A lot of tears, and a lot more to come I guess. But it's okay now. It's as okay as it can ever be." Afraid for very obvious reasons, to stand in front of his younger brother, he rolled over into the water and swam to shore, whispering to himself, "Just like the crocuses. Just like the goofy crocuses."